PUFFIN BOOK

YOUNG SAMURAI

THE RING OF WATER

Praise for the Young Samurai series:

'A fantastic adventure that floors the reader on page one and keeps them there until the end. The pace is furious and the martial arts detail authentic' – Eoin Colfer, author of the bestselling Artemis Fowl series

'Fierce fiction . . . captivating for young readers'
– *Daily Telegraph*

'Addictive' – *Evening Standard*

'More and more absorbing . . . vivid and enjoyable'
– *The Times*

'Bradford comes out swinging in this fast-paced adventure . . . and produces an adventure novel to rank among the genre's best. This book earns the literary equivalent of a black belt'
– *Publishers Weekly*

'The most exciting fight sequences imaginable on paper!'
– *Booklist*

School Library Association's Riveting Read 2009
Shortlisted for Red House Children's Book Award 2009
Longlisted for the Carnegie Medal 2009

Chris Bradford likes to fly through the air. He has thrown himself over Victoria Falls on a bungee cord, out of an aeroplane in New Zealand and off a French mountain on a paraglider, but he has always managed to land safely – something he learnt from his martial arts . . .

Chris joined a judo club aged seven where his love of throwing people over his shoulder, punching the air and bowing lots started. Since those early years, he has trained in karate, kickboxing, samurai swordsmanship and has earned his black belt in *taijutsu*, the secret fighting art of the ninja.

Before writing the Young Samurai series, Chris was a professional musician and songwriter. He's even performed for HRH Queen Elizabeth II (but he suspects she found his band a bit noisy).

Chris lives in a village on the South Downs with his wife, Sarah, and two cats called Tigger and Rhubarb.

To discover more about Chris go to *www.youngsamurai.com*

Books by Chris Bradford

The Young Samurai series (in reading order)
THE WAY OF THE WARRIOR
THE WAY OF THE SWORD
THE WAY OF THE DRAGON
THE RING OF EARTH
THE RING OF WATER

For World Book Day 2010
THE WAY OF FIRE

For the Pocket Money Puffin series
VIRTUAL KOMBAT

YOUNG SAMURAI

THE RING OF WATER

CHRIS BRADFORD

PUFFIN

Disclaimer: *Young Samurai: The Ring of Water* is a work of fiction, and while based on real historical figures, events and locations, the book does not profess to be accurate in this regard. *Young Samurai: The Ring of Water* is more an echo of the times than a re-enactment of history.

Warning: Do not attempt any of the techniques described within this book without the supervision of a qualified martial arts instructor. These can be highly dangerous moves and result in fatal injuries. The author and publisher take no responsibility for any injuries resulting from attempting these techniques.

PUFFIN BOOKS

Published by the Penguin Group
Penguin Books Ltd, 80 Strand, London WC2R 0RL, England
Penguin Group (USA) Inc., 375 Hudson Street, New York, New York 10014, USA
Penguin Group (Canada), 90 Eglinton Avenue East, Suite 700, Toronto, Ontario, Canada M4P 2Y3
(a division of Pearson Penguin Canada Inc.)
Penguin Ireland, 25 St Stephen's Green, Dublin 2, Ireland (a division of Penguin Books Ltd)
Penguin Group (Australia), 250 Camberwell Road, Camberwell, Victoria 3124, Australia
(a division of Pearson Australia Group Pty Ltd)
Penguin Books India Pvt Ltd, 11 Community Centre, Panchsheel Park, New Delhi – 110 017, India
Penguin Group (NZ), 67 Apollo Drive, Rosedale, Auckland 0632, New Zealand
(a division of Pearson New Zealand Ltd)
Penguin Books (South Africa) (Pty) Ltd, 24 Sturdee Avenue, Rosebank, Johannesburg 2196, South Africa

Penguin Books Ltd, Registered Offices: 80 Strand, London WC2R 0RL, England

puffinbooks.com

First published 2011
003

Text copyright © Chris Bradford, 2011
Cover illustration copyright © Paul Young, 2011
Map copyright © Robert Nelmes, 2008
All rights reserved

The moral right of the author and illustrators has been asserted

Set in Bembo 11.5 /15.5pt by Palimpsest Book Production Limited, Falkirk, Stirlingshire
Printed in Great Britain by Clays Ltd, St Ives plc

British Library Cataloguing in Publication Data
A CIP catalogue record for this book is available from the British Library

ISBN: 978-0-141-33254-3

www.greenpenguin.co.uk

Penguin Books is committed to a sustainable future for our business, our readers and our planet. This book is made from Forest Stewardship Council™ certified paper.

ALWAYS LEARNING   **PEARSON**

In memory of Nan and Grandad,
always watching over me

CONTENTS

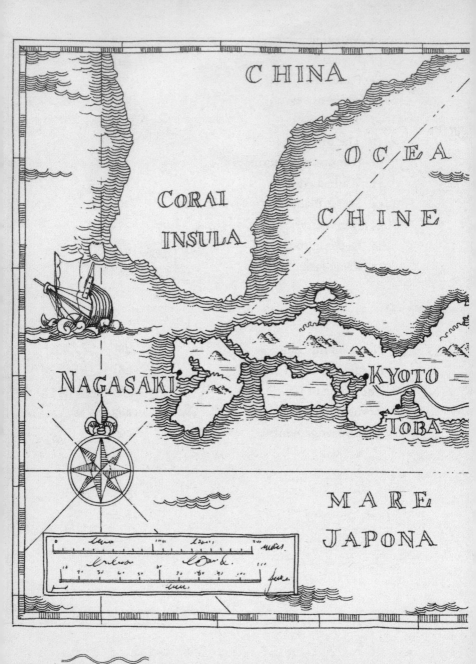

TOKAIDO ROAD

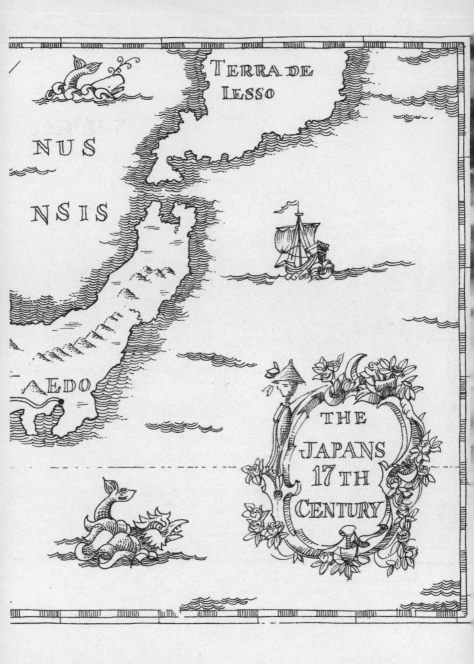

THE LETTER

Japan, 1614

My dearest Jess,

I hope this letter reaches you one day. You must believe I've been lost at sea all these years. But you'll be glad to know that I am alive and in good health.

Father and I reached the Japans in August 1611, but I am sad to tell you he was killed in an attack upon our ship, the Alexandria. I alone survived.

For these past three years, I've been living in the care of a Japanese warrior, Masamoto Takeshi, at his samurai school in Kyoto. He has been very kind to me, but life has not been easy.

An assassin, a ninja known as Dragon Eye, was hired to steal our father's rutter (you no doubt remember how important this navigational logbook was to our father?). The ninja was successful in his mission. However, with the help of my samurai friends, I've managed to get it back.

This same ninja was the one who murdered our father. And while it may not bring you much comfort, I can assure you the assassin is now dead. Justice has been delivered. But the ninja's death doesn't bring back our father – I miss him so much and could do with his guidance and protection at this time.

Japan has been split by civil war and foreigners like myself are no longer welcome. I am a fugitive. On the run for my life. I now journey south through this strange and exotic land to the port of Nagasaki in the hope that I may find a ship bound for England.

The Tokaido Road upon which I travel, however, is fraught with danger and I have many enemies on my trail. But do not fear for my safety. Masamoto has trained me as a samurai warrior and I will fight to return home to you.

One day I do hope I can tell you about my adventures in person . . .

Until then, dear sister, may God keep you safe.

Your brother, Jack

P.S. Since first writing this letter at the end of spring, I've been kidnapped by ninja. But I discovered that they were not the enemy I thought they were. In fact, they saved my life and taught me about the Five Rings: the five great elements of the universe – Earth, Water, Fire, Wind and Sky. I now know ninjutsu skills that go beyond anything I learnt as a samurai. But, because of the circumstances of our father's death, I still struggle to fully embrace the Way of the Ninja . . .

1

THE AMULET

Japan, autumn 1614

For one terrifying moment Jack remembered nothing.

He had no idea where he was, what had happened to him, what he was supposed to be doing. He didn't even know *who* he was. Desperately, like a drowning man, he clung on to any memory he had.

My name is Jack Fletcher . . . from London, England . . . I'm fifteen . . . I have a little sister, Jess . . . I'm a rigging monkey on-board a trading ship, the Alexandria *. . . No! I'm a samurai. I trained at a warrior school in Kyoto . . . the* Niten Ichi Ryū *. . . BUT I'm a ninja too . . . That can't be right – the ninja Dragon Eye killed my father!*

Jack's head throbbed and he felt himself blacking out again. He tried to fight the sinking sensation, but didn't have the strength to resist. His fragmented mind was slipping away, dragged back into unconsciousness.

An incessant *drip . . . drip . . . drip* of water brought him round. Through the dense fog clouding his mind, Jack became aware of rain. Heavy rain, pummelling the wet earth and drowning out all other sounds. Forcing his eyes open, Jack discovered he was lying on a rough bed of straw. Water was seeping through a thatched roof and falling on to his face.

The drip was infuriating. But Jack's body ached so much he struggled to shift himself out of the way. Turning his head to one side, he groaned with pain and came face to face with a cow. Chewing morosely on some cud, the animal stared back at him, clearly begrudging the fact that she had to share her lodgings. As far as Jack could tell, the cow was the only other occupant of the small stable.

Painfully easing himself up on one elbow, the room swimming before his eyes, Jack felt a wave of nausea wash over him. He retched on to the straw-strewn floor, green bile spewing from his mouth. The cow was even less impressed by this undignified display and moved away.

Beside the improvised straw bed, someone had left him a jug of water. Jack sat up and gratefully had a drink, washing his mouth out before taking a large gulp. Swallowing proved difficult. His throat was raw, the acidic contents of his stomach having burnt their way out. He took another sip, more carefully this time, and the pain eased a little.

Jack realized he was a mess. His lower lip was split, his left eye swollen. Dark bruises covered his arms and legs, while his ribs felt sore, though on inspection thankfully not broken.

How did I get like this?

He was dressed in a dirty ragged kimono that certainly wasn't his. The last time he could recall he was wearing the blue robes of a *komusō*, a Monk of Emptiness, as part of a ninja disguise allowing him to pass freely through Japan. He'd been making his way to the port of Nagasaki in the south, hoping to find a ship bound for England and home to his little sister, Jess.

Panic overwhelmed him. *Where are all my belongings?*

Jack's eyes darted around the stable in search of his swords and pack. But, apart from the cow, a pile of straw and a few rusty farm tools, they were nowhere to be seen.

Calm down, he told himself. *Someone has been kind enough to leave me water. That someone may also have my possessions.*

With a trembling hand, Jack took another swig from the jug, hoping the drink would clear his head. But try as he might he had no memory of the last few days. Jack knew he'd left the ninja village in the mountains and was sure he'd managed to reach the borders of Iga Province unopposed. But beyond that he had no recollection.

Outside, through the open doorway, Jack noticed the rain was letting up. He assumed it was morning, although the sky was so dark with thunderclouds it could easily have been the evening. He had a choice – he could wait for whoever had given him the water to appear, or he could take action and find his possessions himself.

As Jack sat there, summoning up the energy to stand, he vaguely became aware of something clasped in his left hand. Opening his fingers, he found a green silk pouch, embroidered in golden thread with the emblem of a wreath and three *kanji* characters: 東大寺. Inside the little bag was what felt like a rectangular piece of wood. Jack recognized the object, but for a moment its name eluded him . . .

An omamori. *That's it! A Buddhist amulet.*

Sensei Yamada, his Zen philosophy master at the *Niten Ichi*

Ryū, had given him one before he'd set off on his journey. It was meant to grant him protection.

But this wasn't his *omamori*. His amulet had a red silk bag. So whose was this?

2

ARREST

Jack staggered out of the stable. Swaying with the exertion, his legs gave away beneath him and he collapsed into the mud. For a while he just let the cool rainwater wash over his face until he felt revived enough to try again.

The stable backed on to a simple wooden building, one storey high, with a thatched roof and bamboo walls. There was a single doorway at its rear and Jack made this his next goal. Pulling himself to his feet, he stumbled and half fell towards the entrance. With a final lurch across the yard, he reached the *shoji* door, hanging on to its frame with relief.

Why am I so weak? Jack wondered as he recovered his breath.

Sliding open the door, he stepped inside a tiny kitchen. A pot of fish-noodle soup simmered away over a fire. Ahead was another doorway in which hung a white cotton curtain, split vertically down its centre. Peeking through the gap, Jack saw he was in a roadside tea house. Straw mats were laid upon a raised floor and immediately before him was a counter stocked with green tea and rice wine. There were a few low wooden tables, but otherwise the establishment was unfurnished and basic. One wall was open to the elements, protected solely by a large curtain. The wind rippled in waves along the sodden cloth.

In the far corner Jack spotted an elderly man in an apron, presumably the owner. Short with spindly legs and thinning hair, the man was haranguing a customer who looked rather the worse for wear. In a plain black kimono marked only with the *mon* emblem of a white camellia flower, the customer had a ragged beard, wayward dark hair and bloodshot eyes. On the floor next to him were a wide-brimmed straw hat and two battleworn swords – a *katana* and a shorter-bladed *wakizashi*. Though they weren't Jack's, he knew that the pairing of swords, a *daishō*, signified the customer's status as a samurai.

'You must pay up and go!' the owner was saying in a firm tone. But judging from the way he was wringing his hands he was scared of the warrior. And rightly so – the samurai were the ruling class in Japan, and the old man, as a lowly tea-house owner, could easily have his head cut off for not showing the appropriate respect.

Ignoring him, the samurai took an irritable swig from his cup.

'I'll summon the local *dōshin* officers,' the owner threatened.

The samurai, mumbling something incoherent, slammed a coin on to the table.

'I'm afraid . . . that's not enough,' said the owner, his voice wavering as his bravado almost broke. 'You've had *three* jugs of *saké* since last night!'

Grunting, the samurai fumbled in his kimono sleeves for more money. Another two coins were produced, but he lost his grip on them and the money rolled across the floor. Snatching up the coins, the owner turned back to the samurai. 'Now you must leave.'

The samurai scowled at him. 'I've paid . . . for my drink,' he slurred, clasping a *saké* jug to his chest. 'I intend to finish it . . . all of it.'

The owner appeared unhappy, but the thunderous look in the samurai's eyes dissuaded him from pressing the matter any further. Retreating with a scant bow, the owner hurried away to serve the only other customer in the establishment, a middle-aged man with a moustache.

Jack was wondering how to get the attention of the owner when he heard a shocked gasp. A girl, not much older than fourteen, had appeared beside the counter and was staring at him in wide-eyed alarm. Slim-faced, with dark hair tied into a bun, she held a tray of teacups that shook audibly in her trembling hands. Jack remembered how appalling he must look and tried to reassure her with a smile. But it hurt his face to even do that.

The girl, putting down the tray, soon recovered herself. She beckoned Jack to enter and sit at a nearby table. Jack was reluctant, concerned about revealing his presence to the samurai. But she was insistent and led him to his seat before disappearing into the kitchen. Jack needn't have worried about the samurai. He was so drunk he didn't even look up. The other customer glanced over in surprise, not so much at Jack's dishevelled appearance as at his foreign blond hair and blue eyes. But with typical Japanese discretion, he merely gave a curt bow and continued his conversation with the owner.

The girl returned with a steaming bowl of noodle soup. Despite the nausea he'd experienced earlier, Jack was ravenous and needed the food to recover his strength.

'*Arigatō gozaimasu*,' he said, bowing and thanking the girl.

Her mouth fell open in astonishment. 'You speak Japanese?'

Jack nodded. He had his best friend, Akiko, to be grateful to for that. After being stranded in Japan, he was first taught the language by a Portuguese priest, Father Lucius. But the man died not long after his arrival and Akiko took over his lessons. Jack had spent many hours with her beneath the *sakura* tree in her mother's garden in Toba, learning about the Japanese way of life. And although he'd lost his memory of the last few days there were some things he would never forget – Akiko's kindness was one of them.

Looking at the bowl before him, Jack said, 'I'm sorry. I don't have any money.'

'It doesn't matter,' said the girl, placing a wooden spoon on the table.

'Thank you,' he replied, savouring the soup's mouth-watering aroma.

The girl turned to leave, but Jack stopped her.

'Please . . .' Jack called, so many questions rushing into his head at once, 'did you leave me the jug of water?'

Offering a shy smile, the girl nodded.

'You're very kind. Perhaps you can tell me where I am?'

'Kamo,' she replied, and, seeing the bewildered expression on his face, continued. 'It's a village on the banks of the Kizu River. We're not far from the main town of Kizu itself.'

'Am I still in the Iga mountains?'

'No, they're some two days' walk east. This is Yamashiro Province.'

At least Jack knew he'd made some progress on his journey home. 'Did *you* find me like this?' he asked, indicating his injuries.

'No, my father did,' replied the girl, glancing over at the tea-house owner who now stood behind his counter, observing Jack. The previous customer with the moustache had departed.

'He found you yesterday morning, left for dead beside the river.'

She looked at Jack's swollen eye and split lip with concern.

'I'm OK,' said Jack, putting on a brave face for her benefit. 'Do you know if your father has any of my belongings?'

The girl shook her head apologetically. 'It was just you.'

'Junko!' called her father sternly. 'The soup's boiling over.'

Bowing to Jack, Junko smiled. 'You're lucky to be alive,' she said, before hurrying into the kitchen.

Alive, yes . . . but for how long? thought Jack.

He had nothing. No money to buy food. No clothes of his own. No disguise to elude his pursuers. No friends to help him. No swords to protect himself with. And he couldn't rely on this girl and her father's charity for more than a few days. After that, he'd be on his own.

Jack took some mouthfuls of soup, wincing as his cut lip stung. But the food's nourishing warmth began to revive him. By the time he finished the meal, he was feeling a little better, and much stronger.

With some more rest, he thought, *I might remember what happened to me.*

His most distressing concern was the loss of his father's prized possession, the *rutter*. This logbook was the *only* means of navigating the world's oceans safely and therefore a highly valuable item. His was one of the few accurate *rutter*s in existence, and its importance reached far beyond its use as a navigational instrument. The country in possession of such a logbook could in effect rule the seas by controlling the trade routes between nations. His father, the Pilot of the *Alexandria*, had warned him *never* to let the *rutter* fall into the wrong hands and Jack had spent the last three years protecting the logbook with his life. It had been stolen once and recovered at great cost, his good friend Yamato sacrificing his life to get it back from the villainous ninja Dragon Eye. So, whatever had happened to Jack this time, the logbook was most definitely in the wrong hands. The question was *whose hands*?

The only clue to his predicament was the amulet. He studied its green silk pouch. The wreath logo meant nothing to him and, although Akiko had taught him some *kanji*, his mind was still so addled he didn't recognize any of the symbols.

Junko brought him a second bowl of soup, which he devoured with equal relish. Draining the last of its contents, Jack decided to ask her about the *omamori*. It was most likely Junko's or her father's, a charm they'd given him to encourage healing. But if it wasn't then she might know who the amulet belonged to and this could lead him to his possessions and the *rutter*.

As he went to beckon Junko over, the curtain shielding the tea house from the road was pulled aside and four armed men entered, followed by the moustached customer. They were dressed officially in black *haori* jackets, tight-fitting trousers and dark blue *tabi* socks. Around their heads they wore *hachi-maki*, bandanas reinforced with metal strips. Each man bore a sword on his hip and in his left hand carried a *jutte*, an iron truncheon with a small prong parallel to the main shaft.

Despite their ominous presence, the owner appeared pleased to see them. 'I didn't really think any *dōshin* would come for him. Not in this weather,' he said to his daughter. Then, pointing, the owner declared, 'He's over there.'

'We're not here for *him*,' snorted the *dōshin* leader, looking down his nose at the drunken samurai who now lay sprawled across his table. Nodding in Jack's direction, the *dōshin* announced, 'We've come to arrest the *gaijin*.'

3

RONIN

Before Jack could react, the four *dōshin* surrounded him, their
lethal *jutte* at the ready. Both the owner and Junko looked
startled by this turn of events.

'Come with us, *gaijin*,' ordered the leading officer.

'But he's causing no trouble,' argued Junko.

Her father restrained her. 'Be quiet. He's none of our business now.'

'But you found him.'

Her father nodded sadly. 'Perhaps it would have been better
if I hadn't.'

The *dōshin* leader indicated for Jack to stand. 'In the name
of the Shogun, you're under arrest.'

'What am I charged with?' asked Jack, playing for time.
His samurai instincts had kicked in and he was looking for a
way out. There was only the back door, but it was blocked by
a *dōshin* and he was in no fit state to fight his way to freedom.

'All foreigners and Christians are banished from our land
by order of Shogun Kamakura. Those found remaining are
to face punishment.'

'I'm *trying* to leave,' insisted Jack.

'That may be the case, but we have reason to believe you're Jack Fletcher, the *gaijin* samurai. And you're accused of treason of the highest order.'

'What did he do?' asked Junko, her hand going to her mouth in disbelief.

'This *gaijin* fought against the Shogun in the battle for Osaka Castle,' the *dōshin* leader explained as his officers manhandled Jack out of the tea house. 'And there's a reward for his head.'

Shoved through the entrance curtain, Jack fell from the raised floor to land sprawled in the muddy rainsoaked road. The four *dōshin* grunted their amusement while putting on their wooden *geta* clogs.

Jack realized this might be his one chance of escape and scrambled to his feet. But he'd barely taken three steps when he was struck from behind. The force of the iron truncheon dropped him to his knees, his eyes screwing up against the flare of pain in his shoulder.

'Where do you think you're going?' snarled a *dōshin*, his round, pockmarked face revelling in Jack's agony. He raised the *jutte* again, eager to cause more damage.

But Jack was ready this time. As the truncheon came down, Jack met it with his own hands, twisting the man's wrist into a lock and flinging him over his head. The *dōshin* crash-landed in the quagmire of mud and sludge, writhing like an eel as his fingers became caught between the shaft and prong of his own *jutte* and snapped on impact. Jack turned to face the other *dōshin* as they rushed to capture him.

Try as he might to defend himself, Jack was outnumbered and too weak to hold out.

'This *gaijin* needs to be taught a lesson,' said the *dōshin* leader, catching Jack across the gut with a heavy blow.

Winded, Jack collapsed in the mud as they struck him repeatedly. He protected his head as much as he could, but the blows rained down from every direction. In the whiteout of pain, Jack become numb to the attacks and was only aware of the dull thud as the iron bars struck his arms, back and legs.

'*Dōshin!*' growled a voice.

The beating stopped and Jack glanced up to see the drunken samurai from the tea house swaying unsteadily towards them, a *saké* jug in his left hand. He was now wearing his straw hat against the rain and bore his two swords on his hip.

'This has nothing to do with you, *ronin*!' said the leader.

The *ronin* wagged a finger at the *dōshin* leader. 'There's four of you and . . .' The samurai's bleary eyes tried to focus on Jack. '. . . two of him. That's not fair!'

'You're drunk, *ronin*.'

Disregarding the officer, the samurai kept coming.

'This is my final warning. Be gone!'

Taking a swig from his *saké* jug, the samurai stumbled a couple of steps closer, then belched loudly into the *dōshin* leader's face.

'Have it your own way,' said the leader in disgust and, nodding to his other *dōshin*, ordered, 'Arrest him too. For obstructing the course of justice.'

The nearest *dōshin*, a young man with hollow cheeks, stepped up to bind the samurai's hands with a rope, while the second-in-command officer went to hold them together. The *ronin* offered this one his *saké* jug. 'Here, take this.'

Without thinking, the officer obediently complied. As the

younger *dōshin* attempted to loop the rope round their new prisoner's wrists, the samurai lurched drunkenly to one side, accidentally headbutting the man in the face.

'Sorry,' he mumbled, while continuing to stagger around the dazed *dōshin*, knocking into him several more times before regaining his balance.

The young *dōshin* looked down to discover he was now completely tied up in his own rope.

'How did *that* happen?' exclaimed the *ronin* in surprise.

Realizing they'd been tricked, the *dōshin* leader thrust his *jutte* at the drunken samurai. The *ronin* reeled away at the last moment and the iron tip of the truncheon struck the bound *dōshin* instead. The young man collapsed to the ground, gasping for breath. The officer who held the *saké* jug was bewildered by the unexpected assault and seemed at a loss about what to do with the jug.

'Thank you,' slurred the *ronin*, taking back his drink and solving the man's problem. Lifting it to take a swig, he knocked the officer hard in the jaw with the bottom of the jug. The officer reeled backwards. The samurai then spun to face the *dōshin* leader, his elbow inadvertently catching the stunned officer in the head and knocking him out cold.

Jack couldn't believe what he was seeing. The samurai could barely stand, yet he was defeating the *dōshin* with startling ease.

'You'll pay for this, *ronin*!' snarled the *dōshin* leader, striking for the samurai's head.

By now the *dōshin* with the broken fingers had recovered and drawn his sword. He came at the samurai from behind, while the leader attacked from in front. Jack cried out a warning to the *ronin*, who was apparently passing out from too much *saké*. But at the last second, he somersaulted out of the way. The two *dōshin* were on a collision course with one another and the officer's sword pierced his leader in the gut.

'That's going to hurt!' said the *ronin*, grimacing in sympathy as the *dōshin* leader fell to the ground, clutching his stomach.

The leader, his face pale with shock, glared at the *ronin*. 'Kill him!'

Mortified at wounding his superior, the remaining officer hesitated before screaming an enraged battle cry as he charged at the samurai. During that split second, the *ronin* had picked up the man's *jutte*.

'I believe this is yours?' he said as the *dōshin* cut for his head.

With lightning speed, the samurai blocked the attack with the iron bar of the *jutte* and caught the steel blade between the *jutte*'s shaft and prong. With a sharp twist, the *ronin* snapped the *dōshin*'s sword in two. The officer took one look at his broken *katana* and turned on his heel.

'Don't forget your *jutte*,' called the *ronin*, throwing the weapon at the fleeing officer. It spun through the air, the handle striking the man in the back of the head. The *dōshin* took a couple of faltering steps before collapsing face first into the mud.

'He was supposed to catch it,' said the *ronin*, raising his hands apologetically. He took another long slug of rice wine, then peered down at the *dōshin* leader who was lying flat out on the ground.

'Is he dead?' asked Jack.

'No, just passed out,' replied the *ronin*, staggering away. 'What's your excuse for still being on the floor?'

'I've just been . . .' began Jack, his body aching from the beating. But the *ronin* wasn't listening.

By the time Jack got to his feet, the samurai was already halfway down the road. Jack didn't know whether the warrior wanted him to follow or not. But, glancing at the four barely conscious *dōshin* in the mud, Jack realized he couldn't stay.

Emerging from the tea house, Junko ran up to him. 'You left this,' she said, handing him the *omamori*.

In the confusion of the arrest, Jack had forgotten his only clue. Yet again, he was indebted to her kindness. But now he knew the amulet didn't belong to her. 'Thank you — ' he began.

'Come on!' the *ronin* roared impatiently. 'No time for girls.'

4

ROBBED OF MEMORIES

At no point did the *ronin* wait for Jack, even as the rain turned into a downpour and he diverged from the main road into a forest. Ascending a steep track, Jack struggled to keep pace, given his earlier beating by the *dōshin*. He eventually caught up with the samurai at a secluded Shinto shrine. Constructed in a small clearing at the top of a hill, the shrine consisted of a simple wooden hut, a couple of lichen-covered standing stones and a wooden *torii* gateway marking the entrance. Jack found the warrior relaxing inside the shrine, sipping from his *saké* jug.

Careful to remember the appropriate etiquette for entering a place of worship, Jack walked through the *torii* gateway. He stopped at a stone bowl filled with water and, using the wooden ladle beside it, washed first his left hand and then his right, before rinsing out his mouth and carefully replacing the ladle. Jack didn't know whether the purification was necessary since he was soaked to the skin anyway, but he wasn't taking any chances.

Although he was a Protestant Christian at heart, his Zen master, Sensei Yamada, had advised him to follow Shinto and

Buddhist practices in order to blend in as much as possible. With the Shogun – and now Japan – set against Christians, it was important for Jack not to offend anyone. Moreover, if he could convince locals, like this samurai, he was of their religious persuasion, they might be more willing to help him on his journey.

Jack bowed twice, clapped his hands two times to wake the *kami* spirits and bowed again. He then clasped his hands together in silent prayer.

'You're wasting your time,' grumbled the samurai. 'Shrines are good for shelter, but little else.'

Jack looked up, surprised at the man's lack of faith. The Japanese were a pious race and he hadn't expected such disrespect from a samurai. Jack entered the shrine and sat down, glad to be out of the torrential rain and to rest his aching limbs.

'So who are you?' demanded the warrior. 'You don't look like you're from these parts.'

'My name's Jack Fletcher,' he replied, bowing his head in deference. 'I'm from England, an island like Japan but on the other side of the world. May I ask who you are?'

'Ronin.'

'But I thought that meant "masterless samurai"?'

'Just call me Ronin,' he repeated gruffly, quaffing on his *saké* before offering Jack the jug.

'No, thank you,' replied Jack, having tasted rice wine once before and choked on its potency. He didn't think his stomach could handle it at this moment. 'But I do have to thank you, Ronin, for saving me back there.'

The samurai grunted indifferently. 'They were in my way.'

'But won't those *dōshin* be after *you* now?'

Ronin snorted with laughter. 'Those excuses for samurai! The *new* enforcement officers of the Shogun's *new* Japan. They're just trumped-up low-ranking soldiers. They'll be too ashamed. Besides, you saw for yourself, they attacked one another.'

Thinking back to the fight, Jack realized this was almost true. The only real injury had been inflicted by the second officer and any retaliation by Ronin had looked purely accidental.

'*You*, on the other hand,' said Ronin, pointing an unsteady finger at Jack, 'will be sought after. Tell me, what makes you such a wanted young man?'

'I fought against the Shogun in the war,' replied Jack, recalling that the samurai had passed out by the time the *dōshin* arrived. He hoped Ronin had also missed hearing about the price on his head. Jack didn't fancy his chances if this samurai suddenly decided to turn him in for the reward.

'There were *many* samurai who fought against the Shogun, but he's not looking for them. Why are you so special?'

Jack briefly wondered whose side Ronin had been on, but was afraid to ask. 'Because I'm a foreigner –'

'I can see that,' he said, giving Jack a cursory yet non-judgemental inspection. 'It still doesn't explain why the Shogun wants *you*.'

Jack realized there could be many reasons, but suspected it was ultimately to do with the *rutter*. Shogun Kamakura was one of the few people in Japan who knew of its existence *and* its significance. Before his death, Dragon Eye, having stolen it for the Portuguese priest Father Bobadillo, attempted to reclaim the logbook on behalf of Kamakura, but failed.

Apparently the Shogun hadn't forgotten about the *rutter* since his rise to power. Despite the fact that Ronin had saved his life, Jack knew it would be foolish to trust the samurai and decided not to mention this likely motive.

'I'm samurai too,' revealed Jack.

'A *gaijin* samurai!' Ronin laughed incredulously. 'Who on earth made you a samurai?'

'Masamoto Takeshi. My guardian.'

Ronin stopped laughing.

'He's the head of the *Niten Ichi Ryū* —'

'I know who he is,' Ronin interjected, his left hand coming to rest upon the hilt of his *katana*. Jack tensed, unsure of the samurai's intentions. 'Masamoto-sama's reputation precedes him. Now I'm not surprised the Shogun's after you. Not only are you his enemy's adopted son, you're the embodiment of everything that man hates about foreign intrusion. Did Masamoto-sama teach you the Two Heavens?'

Jack nodded warily.

Ronin's face burst into a grin. 'I'm envious,' he admitted, letting go of his sword and toasting Jack with his *saké* jug. 'I've always wanted to challenge that samurai to a friendly duel. They say his secret two-sword technique is invincible.'

'He's a very honourable and courageous samurai,' Jack replied, relieved at Ronin's admiration of his guardian. 'But the Shogun's banished him to a remote temple on Mount Iawo and I've heard nothing of him since.'

At this, Ronin lost interest in his *saké* and shook his head with disgust. 'Such a waste!'

They both sat in silence, listening to the rain pound upon the wooden roof. Ronin's head lolled and he seemed to fall into a drunken slumber. Meanwhile, Jack fondly recalled Masamoto's lessons as he attempted to master the Two Heavens. Training to become a samurai at the *Niten Ichi Ryū* in Kyoto had been tough and gruelling, but the sense of purpose it had given him and the lifelong friendships he'd forged there had made it all worthwhile. Jack longed to return, but doubted the school was still open following Masamoto's banishment and the devastating war in which many of the sensei had died.

All of a sudden Ronin roused himself. 'So, young samurai, you trained at the *Niten Ichi Ryū*, fought under Satoshi's flag against Kamakura, somehow survived the Battle of Osaka Castle, then what?'

'I escaped with Akiko to the port of Toba, where we stayed with her mother —'

'Who's Akiko?'

'Masamoto's niece . . . and my best friend,' replied Jack, the corners of his mouth turning up at the thought of her. How he missed Akiko being around. If she'd been by his side, he would surely not be in this mess and he'd feel far less alone and vulnerable than he did now. The smile faded into regret at leaving her.

Seeing the forlorn expression on Jack's face, Ronin raised his eyebrows knowingly. 'So why didn't you stay?'

'I couldn't. After the Shogun passed the law banishing all foreigners and Christians, her family were put in great danger. So I've been heading for Nagasaki ever since. I hope to find a ship there, bound for England.'

'So when did you leave Toba?'

'It must have been springtime,' Jack admitted, realizing that it was now autumn.

'And you've *only* reached Kamo!' snorted Ronin in disbelief.

It hadn't been in Jack's plans to make such little progress, but circumstances had delayed him. Having almost been caught by the Shogun's samurai on the Tokaido Road, he'd escaped into the Iga mountains – the domain of the ninja. Here, he'd ended up living in a secret village with his arch-enemies. But in that time his eyes had been opened to the truth about the ninja's way of life. All his preconceptions and prejudices were brought into question as they trained him in the art of *ninjutsu*, introduced him to their moral code of *ninniku* and taught him about the Five Rings. In the process, he'd learnt some vital skills and his old enemies, the ninja, had become his friends. And though he still struggled with the idea, he now considered himself both samurai *and* ninja. But Jack was reluctant to reveal any of this to the samurai.

'I got lost in the mountains,' Jack explained, which was partly true.

Ronin nodded slowly, but didn't look entirely convinced by this answer. 'Easily done. Is that why you're in such a state? Your injuries aren't just from today.'

Jack looked at himself. The red welts from the *dōshin's jutte* were layered over a patchwork of dark blue bruises that criss-crossed his body. His split lip and swollen eye throbbed dully, as did his ribs. So many injuries and no memory of how he got them all. But these were nothing compared to his stomach, which was still sore from the *dōshin* leader's vicious attack.

'I don't know,' Jack replied, shrugging. 'I can't remember anything of the last few days.'

'I wouldn't worry. That often happens to me,' Ronin grunted, raising the jug to his lips.

'But I don't drink *saké*!' replied Jack, laughing despite himself, then wishing he hadn't as his stomach muscles contracted painfully.

'So what's your plan now?' asked Ronin as he settled back against the shrine wall.

'My first step is to try to get back everything I've lost . . .' Jack began. Then, remembering the *omamori* in his hand, he added, 'Or that's been stolen.'

'You've been robbed not only of your memory but your possessions too!' Ronin exclaimed, raising his eyebrows in sympathy. 'You have been ill-fated. What was taken?'

'Everything. My clothes, my money, my food, an *inro* case given to me by *daimyo* Takatomi, which contained a good-luck paper crane from my friend Yori and a precious pearl that was a gift from Akiko . . .'

'Anything else of value?' asked Ronin, his bloodshot eyes suddenly sparkling.

Jack nodded. Careful not to directly refer to the *rutter*, he added, 'My father's . . . diary, some *shuriken* stars I happened to acquire and, of course, my swords.'

'Your swords!' said Ronin in dismay.

'Yes,' Jack admitted, feeling the shame. The sword was the soul of the samurai and therefore considered unforgivable to lose. 'They belonged to Akiko's father and were made by the swordsmith Shizu. They had dark red woven handles and their *saya*s had mother-of-pearl inlays. I'd recognize them anywhere.'

'*Shizu*,' Ronin breathed with admiration, clearly aware of the reputation of the legendary swordsmith. 'This girl must favour you greatly to bestow such an heirloom. And to have them *stolen* must be intolerable!'

Ronin stroked his beard thoughtfully. Putting down his *saké* jug with a decisive thump, he announced, '*I'll* help you, young samurai. I suspect it's the work of bandits.'

'I appreciate your offer, Ronin,' replied Jack, surprised by the man's altruism. 'But I have nothing to pay you with.'

'I don't do things for money!' he snorted. 'Money is for merchants, not samurai. Yet . . .' He shook the nearly empty *saké* jug. 'A man cannot live on air alone. In return for my services, I ask only that I can choose one item from whatever we recover.'

Jack hesitated. What if Ronin decided upon the *rutter*? But that was highly unlikely; the samurai was interested in only one thing and that was getting drunk. Studying the dishevelled intoxicated man, Jack wondered whether Ronin would be more of a hindrance than a help. But Jack needed whatever help he could get, so nodded his agreement.

'Good. It's settled then,' said Ronin, taking a swig of rice wine to seal the deal, before settling back against the wall and closing his eyes. Within seconds, he was snoring loudly.

Some help he's going to be! thought Jack.

THE RIDDLING MONK

Jack knelt before the shrine's altar, hands clasped, eyes tight shut. He prayed, thinking of his parents up in heaven, desperately wishing for the comforting embrace of his mother and the sound counsel of his father. John Fletcher was a man who never wavered, never lost hope, not even in the fiercest of storms.

A smooth sea never made a skilful mariner, he would say.

Now, as the rain battered the little shrine, Jack called upon that same strength of mind. But, try as he might, a sense of despair seeped into his thoughts. What chance did he have of recovering his possessions, let alone of surviving? He still couldn't remember anything. He had no idea who'd attacked him, or why. It could have been a samurai patrol or, as Ronin suspected, a bunch of bandits. Had they known who he was? Or had it been a random assault? Did they even realize the true worth of what they'd stolen? And, most importantly, where were his possessions now?

There were so many unanswered questions. Jack pounded the floor in frustration, willing himself to remember . . . *a face . . . a name . . . a place . . . anything!*

But his mind remained a blank.

Whoever it was, they evidently thought they'd killed him. That gave him an edge at least, since they wouldn't be expecting him to rise from the grave. On the other hand, he was a wanted *gaijin*, a samurai without his swords, a ninja without a disguise. His situation was desperate, summed up in the fact he had to rely upon a washed-up masterless samurai for help. The ordeal before him seemed insurmountable.

Sorry, Jess, thought Jack, reflecting on his responsibility to his sister back in England. Although she'd been left in the care of a neighbour, Mrs Winters, that was over five years ago and the woman was old then. Jack was worried that Jess, now aged ten, could be on her own – or, worse, in a workhouse for orphans.

Jack bowed his head, a tear rolling down his cheek. *May God take care of you, because I fear I might not make it home.*

'Only dead fish swim with the current,' cried a croaky ratchety voice.

Jack spun round in shock. Ronin was still comatose in the corner of the shrine. But, emerging through the silver curtain of rain, a fiery grizzled demon hopped towards him. Jack's heart was in his mouth as the vision drew nearer.

Then he realized it was a man. Bug-eyed, with a shiny bald pate and a wild bush of a beard, he wore a long red robe, a black *obi* and a necklace of blue prayer beads. Jack guessed by this he was a *yamabushi*, a mountain monk. Over one shoulder was slung a sturdy stick from which hung a white cloth knapsack. In his right hand, he clutched a parasol of broad green leaves to keep off the rain.

The mountain monk skipped lightly down the path, leaping puddles like a deranged toad. In a singsong voice, he cried, 'Riddle me this before I die, what gets wet as it dries?'

The monk landed with both feet in a puddle, soaking Jack by the entrance.

'Purified!' he declared. 'Now do you know the answer to my riddle? Be quick, be fast, be nimble!'

Bewildered, Jack shook his head. The bizarre behaviour of the man left him speechless. The Riddling Monk entered the shrine, eyeballing Jack and tutting loudly.

'This answer I'll give for free, but next time you'll pay a fee,' he announced, giving the sleeping Ronin a cursory inspection. 'What gets wet as it dries? A towel, of course!'

The monk danced a jig, then plonked himself down beside Jack.

'You're a strange-looking fish,' he said, plucking a blond hair from Jack's head and examining it.

'Excuse me,' said Jack, gathering his wits, 'but *who* are you?'

'My name is mine, but other people use it so much more than I. Why not ask them?'

He turned to the altar and began babbling some incomprehensible prayers. Jack quickly gathered the monk was mad. Otherwise he seemed relatively harmless, so Jack saw no reason to wake Ronin.

All of a sudden, the monk seized Jack's wrist.

'My, my, my! What an interesting life!' he proclaimed, running a dirty fingernail along the lines of Jack's palm.

Jack tried to pull his hand away, but the monk was remarkably strong.

'Don't you want to be told what the future may hold?' the monk admonished.

Reluctantly, Jack allowed the man to study his hand. Arguing with a lunatic would get him nowhere. The monk's bulging eyes widened even more and there were numerous coos of surprise, sighs of woe and fits of giggles as he read Jack's palm.

'What have you seen?' Jack asked, curious in spite of himself.

The monk looked up, a deadly serious expression on his face. 'You seek more than you have, young samurai,' he answered, his voice grave and low. 'Know this! What you find is lost. What you give is given back. What you fight is defeated. And what you want is sacrificed.'

Jack stared at the monk, utterly bewildered. 'What does any of that mean?'

'What lies behind us and what lies before are tiny matters compared to what lies within us,' he replied, letting go of Jack's wrist. 'Other hand.'

Sighing, Jack offered his left hand in which he held the green silk amulet, hoping for a more lucid answer.

'The Great Buddha's *omamori*!' the monk exclaimed in delight. 'Did you climb through his nose, or just bow down before his toes?'

Though Jack had no idea what the man was talking about, he was thrilled to discover the monk recognized the amulet. 'You know whose this is?'

'That I do! It's the Great Buddha's,' replied the monk, smiling broadly to reveal a toothless mouth.

'Do you know where he is?' Jack demanded.

The monk nodded. 'From here he's neither near nor far.'

Jack tried to keep calm in the face of the monk's infuriating riddles. 'In which direction?'

'If you went backwards, it would be Aran.'

The monk was making no sense to Jack. Desperation getting the better of him, he asked, 'Can you guide me there?'

Jumping to his feet, the monk pirouetted on the spot and raised his parasol of leaves. 'Do not walk behind me, for I may not lead. Do not walk ahead, for I may not follow.'

Jack realized it would be a futile expedition to go with this crazed man. 'At least point me in the right direction.'

The monk laughed. 'Riddle me this, young samurai! What is greater than God, more evil than the Devil? Poor people have it, rich people need it, and if you eat it you'll die. Tell me this and I shall give it to you.'

Jack thought hard. At the *Niten Ichi Ryū*, Sensei Yamada had often set his class *koan* riddles – testing questions to focus on while meditating. Although familiar with the mindset required to answer such conundrums, Jack was never the best at these mental tests. How he wished his friend Yori was with him now. That boy could figure out any *koan*. But Jack's head was too clouded and confused for meditation and no answer came to mind.

'I don't know,' replied Jack in frustration.

'Come, fish, don't give up so easily! Your soul's not beat until you next meet me!'

With that, the Riddling Monk danced off into the pouring rain.

6

THE RING OF WATER

Jack sat staring at the bend in the path where the crazed man had disappeared, questioning whether he'd seen the monk at all. The encounter had been so bizarre as to be unbelievable. Having already lost his memory, Jack convinced himself the monk was no more than a figment of his fevered imagination – a combination of fatigue, stress and lack of food.

The amulet in his hand was real enough, though. And the pain he felt was all too real. Then he noticed the footprints in the mud, heading towards the forest. They weren't his or Ronin's. They could *only* belong to the Riddling Monk. The rain was falling even harder now, rapidly washing away the evidence. But at least Jack knew he wasn't going mad.

Only dead fish swim with the current.

Had the Riddling Monk been speaking to him? This was the sort of enigmatic advice Sensei Yamada usually offered. Surprisingly, in this instance the monk's words made some sense to Jack. If he simply gave up in this desperate situation, he'd be washed away like a dead fish. Alternatively, he could fight the current and overcome the difficulties he faced.

There *was* a glimmer of hope after all. The Riddling Monk

had recognized the *omamori*. It belonged to the Great Buddha, whoever and wherever he was. Jack would ask Ronin when he awoke.

The path leading up to the shrine began to flood in the torrential rain. A trickle grew into a stream and wound its way down the slope into the forest. Jack watched as a large brown leaf was caught in its wash, briefly held back by a pile of stones, before floating round and away.

Like a river flowing down a mountain, whenever you encounter an obstacle, move round it, adapt and continue on.

The leaf had reminded Jack of Soke, the ninja Grandmaster, and his teachings of the Five Rings: the five great elements of the universe – Earth, Water, Fire, Wind and Sky – that formed the basis of a ninja's philosophy to life and to *ninjutsu* itself. Soke had explained the Ring of Water was about adaptability and *nagare*, flow, its core principle demonstrated by the unstoppable nature of a river. Jack realized if he was to survive he'd have to apply the Ring of Water – adapt to his circumstances, go with the flow and overcome the obstacles on his journey.

While Jack didn't want to admit it, *ninjutsu* was more relevant in this dire circumstance than any of his samurai training. He found it ironic that the skills of the ninja, once utilized by Dragon Eye in his attempts to kill Jack, might now be his salvation.

The first step was to begin self-healing. Sitting cross-legged, Jack clasped his hands together, interlocking his fingers while leaving his index finger and thumb both extended, to form the hand sign for *Sha*. He began softly chanting, 'On haya baishiraman taya sowaka . . .'

Deep within, Jack experienced a warm glow that slowly

spread through his body. *Sha* was one of the nine secret hand signs of *kuji-in*, ninja magic. These powers originated from the Ring of Sky, the element representing the unseen energy of the universe, and this was what he was tapping into now.

After a while, Jack ceased the mantra and tentatively touched his split lip and swollen eye. Although there was no discernible change, his aches and pains seemed to have eased. Jack knew he'd have to repeat the process several more times, its accumulative effect speeding up his body's healing.

During his meditation, the rain had slackened and Jack decided to venture into the forest. Soke had also taught him fieldcraft, knowledge garnered from the Ring of Earth, so Jack knew what berries, fruits and nuts he could or couldn't eat and, more importantly, where to find them. Getting to his feet, Jack left the comatose Ronin snoring away, his arms wrapped protectively round the *saké* jug.

Having taken his fill of the nuts and berries he'd managed to forage, Jack placed a handful beside the still-sleeping samurai. Suddenly a blade was held to his throat.

'Who are you?' growled Ronin.

'It's me, Jack!' he replied, startled by the unexpected attack.

Ronin's eyes narrowed as he pressed the blade harder against Jack's neck.

'The *gaijin* samurai!' added Jack in desperation.

'What were you doing?'

'I've brought you some food.'

Ronin glanced down at the small pile of nuts and berries.

'You're a right little squirrel, aren't you?' he said, releasing

Jack and scooping them up. He popped a juicy red berry into his mouth. 'So how do I know you?'

Jack stared in amazement at the samurai. 'You saved me from the *dōshin* at the tea house.'

'Did I?'

'You offered to help get back my belongings.'

'I said that?'

Jack's mouth fell open in disbelief. 'You mean you've forgotten!'

Shooting him a black look, Ronin snarled, 'I may be drunk, but in the morning I'll be sober and you'll still be ugly! Now get out of here!'

Jack bristled at the man's rudeness. 'Some samurai you are!'

Leaping to his feet, Ronin grabbed Jack and slammed him against the shrine wall. 'What did you say?'

'I . . . I thought samurai were meant to be honourable,' spluttered Jack, taken aback by the man's sudden mood swing. 'You promised to help me. Where's your sense of *bushido*?'

'You've no right to ask *that*!' Ronin spat into Jack's face. 'Before you criticize someone, you should walk a mile in their shoes!'

'I would if I had any,' replied Jack.

Ronin looked down at Jack's muddy and blistered feet. He grunted with amusement and his anger dissipated. 'I remember now,' he said, grinning. 'I admired your fighting spirit. You were the underdog, yet you still bit back.'

He let go, patting out the ruckles in Jack's tattered kimono.

'If I said I'd help you, I will. I *am* a man of my word.'

Ronin sat back down, took a swig from the remains of his *saké* and coughed harshly. 'So remind me, what's our plan?'

'We haven't made one yet,' Jack replied, warily sitting opposite the hungover samurai. The man's temperament was
proving as unpredictable as the sea. Deciding against mentioning his encounter with the Riddling Monk, Jack said, 'But
have you heard of the Great Buddha?'

'Of course.'

'Do you know where we could find him?'

'Depends which one you seek,' replied Ronin.

Taken aback to hear this, Jack pulled out the amulet. 'The
one who owns this *omamori*.'

Ronin attempted to focus his eyes on the silk pouch. 'Tō
. . . dai . . . ji.'

Jack stared blankly at the samurai.

'That's what it says here,' Ronin explained, pointing to the
three *kanji* characters. 'Tōdai-ji. It's the name of the Buddhist
temple this amulet comes from.'

'Is it far?'

'Maybe a day or so's walk. It's in Nara.'

Jack now realized the monk *had* told him where to go. *If
you went backwards, it would be Aran . . .* Nara!

'Can you take me there?'

'I'd be honoured to,' Ronin replied, leaning against the wall
and enjoying a long draft of *saké*. 'Once it stops raining.'

7

A TROUBLED PAST

Flashes of lightning lit the sky and rain poured in a continuous waterfall from the heavens as the thunderstorm battered the little shrine. Sheltered inside, Jack stared into the deepening gloom, troubled that he still had no recollection of the past few days. Ronin, sipping the last of his *saké*, drifted into another drunken slumber. A short while after, Jack surrendered to exhaustion too. Lying down, he listened to the rain drum upon the shrine's roof. Accustomed to bad weather from his time on-board the *Alexandria*, Jack slept through the night, only waking when the dawn chorus heralded a new day. The storm had passed and the early morning sun was burning off the mist in the valley below.

Jack sat up and stretched. His body was still stiff and sore, but the night's rest had done him some good. Cupping his hands, he scooped up some fresh water from a puddle and finished off the last of his berries. While he waited for Ronin to wake, he resumed his self-healing meditation. His senses heightened by the trancelike state of *kuji-in*, Jack heard the forest resounding to a million drops of water falling from leaf to leaf as the ninja magic did its work.

'What are you up to?' demanded Ronin gruffly, eyeing Jack's hand sign with suspicion. Ronin looked like a bear that had been roused from hibernation too early. His beard was unkempt, his eyes red and his expression grouchy.

'Just meditating,' replied Jack, unclasping his hands.

Ronin snorted with derision. 'Meditation won't fill an empty stomach.'

He shook his *saké* jug, then upended it. Not a single drop came out and he threw it away in disgust. 'Let's go.'

Lacking footwear, Jack hobbled as fast as he could after the departing Ronin. The samurai forged ahead down the forest path, irritably glancing back as Jack lagged further and further behind. He eventually stopped and waited for him at a crossroads. To pass the time, Ronin cut a long branch from a tree with his *wakizashi*, sheared the twigs off the main stem, rounded the ends and stripped away the bark. On Jack's arrival, he presented him with the whittled stick. 'Here, use this.'

'Thank you,' replied Jack, weighing up the sturdy branch in his hands. It was straight and strong, ideal not only as a walking stick but as a *bō* staff. Having trained in *bōjutsu* under the blind Sensei Kano at the *Niten Ichi Ryū*, Jack felt more confident now he had a weapon at his disposal.

'Just keep up,' muttered Ronin, turning on his heel and heading down the road.

Jack realized if this samurai was going to help him, he needed to get to know the man and befriend him. He considered the best way would be to show respect for Ronin's fighting skills.

Trying to keep pace, Jack began, 'It's obvious you're a highly trained warrior. Yesterday you defeated four armed *dōshin* single-handedly, even after three jars of *saké*! Where did you learn to fight like that?'

Ronin kept walking, not even acknowledging that Jack had asked a question.

'I realize everything *looked* accidental,' Jack persisted, 'but to my trained eye there seemed more to it than pure luck.'

Jack still got no response, Ronin now avoiding eye contact altogether.

He tried one more time. 'As a student of Masamoto-sama's, I'm impressed anyone can fight like that – and win. How did you do it?'

Suddenly Ronin came to a halt. He turned on Jack, his eyes blazing.

'There are two rules for being victorious in martial arts. Rule one is never tell others everything you know.'

Jack waited for Ronin to continue, but the samurai simply walked on and resumed his stoical silence.

'And rule two?' Jack prompted, hurrying after him.

Ronin raised an eyebrow in irritation. Then it dawned on Jack that he wouldn't be telling him, even if there was another rule.

'Very funny,' said Jack, laughing in an attempt to break the tension.

Ronin didn't laugh, so Jack decided to try a different tack. 'Were you at the battle of Osaka Castle?'

Ronin's expression became grave and Jack took that as a 'yes'.

'On whose side?' he enquired hesitantly.

Glancing at him out of the corner of his eye, Ronin replied, 'The only one I trust – my own.'

'But you must have served a *daimyo*,' Jack continued, not willing to give up now he'd started Ronin talking. 'What was his name? Masamoto-sama may have known him.'

'My sword is my *daimyo*,' Ronin shot back. 'Now, less talk and more walk.'

As Ronin quickened his pace, Jack wondered what could have happened to make the man so bitter and guarded. The samurai walked as if a dark shadow clung to his back. Jack had seen men like Ronin on-board the *Alexandria*, who'd turned to the bottle to blot out some horror or regret in their lives. A troubled past appeared to haunt Ronin's every step. The question was, what was he escaping from?

As they turned a corner in the path, the outskirts of a town came into view.

'You'd better wear this,' said Ronin, shoving his wide-brimmed hat on to Jack's head to cover his face. 'We don't want you attracting any trouble.'

8

TANUKI

Ronin led the way, Jack keeping close at his heel and only risking the occasional glance up. The going in town was easier for Jack compared to the muddy and rocky paths they had been travelling. Hard-packed by countless feet, the main road was even and relatively stone-free. The street itself was a mishmash of wooden buildings and bamboo huts that housed various businesses: an inn, a shop selling cloth, a couple of tea houses, a restaurant filled with customers tucking into steaming bowls of *soba*, and several other stores, their wares hidden behind large cloth awnings. Dotted in between were private houses and the occasional Shinto shrine. In the background, Jack could hear a river flowing, its peaceful wash punctuated by the rhythmic *thunk* of a hammer against wood.

'What town is this?' asked Jack.

'Kizu,' Ronin grunted in response.

The townspeople, going about their daily business, gave Ronin a wide berth as soon as they caught sight of his fearsome appearance. No one even looked at Jack – the peasant boy in the ragged kimono and straw hat who obediently followed in his master's wake. This suited Jack just fine.

'Wait here,' ordered Ronin, striding over to a nearby store, above which hung a large ball of cedar branches.

Jack was pleased to see Ronin stepping out of his wooden *geta*s and into the shop. They would need provisions with a good day's trek still ahead and his hunger pangs were already beginning to bite.

As he lingered outside the entrance, his feet too dirty to enter the store, he contemplated how different this custom was from life in England. Shoes and boots caked in mud soiled the floors of every establishment throughout his homeland. Streets were awash with muck and rubbish, houses and shops grimy and rat-infested as a result. Despite Japan disowning him, along with every other foreigner, Jack still admired much of Japanese culture – its cleanliness and sense of order being among its many virtues. Deep down, Jack didn't want to leave. If he'd had a choice, Jack would have stayed in Toba with Akiko and made a life for himself as a samurai. But, with the Shogun after him and the need to return to England for the sake of his sister, that was not to be. Even though he thought of Akiko every day, he'd long since left that dream behind.

Ronin reappeared, clutching his purchase – a large ceramic bottle of *saké*.

'Time to go,' he said.

'What about food?' asked Jack, worried the rice wine would be their only sustenance.

Delving into his kimono sleeve, Ronin counted the coins he had. 'There might be enough.'

They crossed the road to another store, where a sweet smell wafted through the air. The establishment was small, with space for only a few customers inside. Two men sat round a sunken hearth, sipping hot tea and eating white apple-sized dough balls. At the entrance was a tiny counter and beside the door frame stood a wooden statue. Reaching Jack's knee, the carved figure was of a badger-like creature on its hind legs. It had a round distended belly, imploring eyes and a broad grin. On its head, it wore a straw cone-shaped sunhat and in its paws carried a bottle of *saké* and an empty purse. To Jack's mind, the creature looked exceedingly mischievous.

'We'll eat outside,' said Ronin, indicating a rough wooden bench to the right of the statue. 'That way you won't have to remove your hat.'

He banged on the counter and a little man with bright eyes and a shiny forehead popped up from behind and bowed. 'Yes, how may I be of service?'

'Four *manjū*,' ordered Ronin.

'What flavour would you like?' asked the *manjū* vendor, pointing to a board upon which six fillings were listed:

肉 *(meat)*
抹茶 *(green tea)*
茄子 *(aubergine)*
栗子 *(chestnut)*
桃 *(peach)*
餡子 *(red bean)*

Ronin tugged at his beard as he briefly considered the menu. 'Two meat and two bean will do.'

Bowing again, the little man lifted the lid off a square wooden box. A cloud of steam burst forth, dispersing to reveal a dozen or so milky-white buns. He selected two, then took another two from a different box.

'That'll be four *bitasen*, please,' he said, proudly presenting Ronin with two plates of steamed buns.

Ronin produced four copper coins and paid the vendor. They sat down upon the bench and tucked into their meal. Jack took a bite of his first *manjū*, the doughy outside giving way to a meaty filling reminiscent of pork, and he groaned contentedly. It took a great deal of willpower not to wolf down the entire bun in one go. As they ate, Jack eyed the strange wooden creature next to him.

'What's that supposed to be?' asked Jack, nodding at the statue.

'It's a *tanuki*,' Ronin replied, washing down his *manjū* with a mouthful of *saké*. 'It's meant to encourage customers.'

Noticing the samurai's mood mellowing with the consumption of food and wine, Jack continued, 'Is there such an animal?'

Ronin nodded. 'But many believe they're shape-shifters, taking on other forms to play tricks on people.'

'What do they change into?' asked Jack.

'Trees, teapots, monks –'

Thwack! Thwack! Thwack!

The hammering Jack had heard earlier resumed. It was now much closer and Ronin grimaced at the ear-splitting disturbance.

'Teapots?' queried Jack, amused at the idea, though he did now wonder whether the Riddling Monk might have been a meddlesome *tanuki*. They certainly shared the same bulging eyes.

Thwack!

Ronin nodded, his brow furrowing at the noise. 'But they're not all harmless. There's a tale of one *tanuki* who killed a quarrelsome farmer's wife –' *thwack!* – 'and cooked her up as soup –' *thwack!* – 'for her husband to eat –' *thwack!*

The incessant hammering was making Ronin wince with every strike and Jack could see the samurai's temper rising rapidly.

'WHO'S MAKING THAT DREADFUL NOISE?' demanded Ronin.

The *manjū* vendor poked his head out. 'That'll be the cooper next door,' he informed them sheepishly.

Thwack! Thwack! Thwack!

'How many nails does one barrel need?' complained Ronin, rubbing his temples.

'I believe he's making a coffin,' explained the vendor.

'Well, if he doesn't stop that infernal banging, he'll be making one for himself.'

At that moment, the hammering ceased and Ronin let out a slow relieved sigh. But a second later, the cooper resumed his work.

Thwack! Thwack! Thwack!

'Enough's enough!' Ronin exclaimed, snatching up his bottle and storming off.

'Hold on!' shouted Jack, grabbing their two remaining buns and stuffing them inside his tattered kimono. Staff in hand, he dashed after the enraged samurai.

9

ONE DEAD SAMURAI

Jack caught up with Ronin at the back of the cooper's store, a small yard full of timber, half-finished barrels and an open coffin. The sound of hammering had been replaced by a deathly silence and at Ronin's feet lay a blood-splattered corpse, the victim sliced open from neck to waist.

'NO!' exclaimed Jack, rushing up to the samurai.

Ronin shot him a defiant look.

'You can't just kill someone for making a noise –'

To Jack's utter disgust, Ronin laughed heartily at this.

Jack realized he'd made the mistake of teaming up with a ruthless and unpredictable killer. No longer able to meet Ronin's eye, Jack looked in pity at the dead man. He was dressed in a plain blue kimono, now cut into ribbons by a single vicious sword attack. His face was young, perhaps in his early twenties, but his sudden and violent end had stretched it taut into a pale death mask, the man's mouth frozen in an agonized scream. Jack felt sickened to his stomach by Ronin's cold-blooded murder.

'How could you –?'

'My sincere apologies,' said a rasping voice. A withered

man, all skin and bones like the leg of a chicken, tottered out of a hut. He presented Ronin with a small china cup. 'The best in the entire province!'

The samurai knocked back its contents in one go and smacked his lips appreciatively. 'Excellent *saké*, cooper. Apology accepted.'

The cooper grinned, revealing two front teeth that protruded like tombstones in an otherwise empty mouth. Jack stared at Ronin in disbelief and then at the body.

'If that's the cooper, then who's this?' said Jack, pointing to the corpse.

'I've no idea,' Ronin replied, smiling as he handed the cup back to the barrelmaker. 'Some samurai or other.'

'His name is – *was* – Manzo,' revealed the cooper, chuckling darkly to himself. 'It was an entertaining duel – while it lasted.'

'Was it a test of skill or just a brawl?' enquired Ronin.

'As I hear it,' the cooper sniffed, 'the man was bragging about his ability to defeat anyone with his new swords. A samurai on his *musha shugyō* challenged him to prove his boast. The whole town came out yesterday to witness the duel.'

Jack now realized Ronin had been playing him along like a fish on a line. The samurai certainly had a morbid sense of humour. He wasn't the murderer at all. The man had been killed by another samurai on his warrior pilgrimage.

'Unless an idiot dies, he won't be cured,' Ronin muttered, giving the corpse a disdainful look. 'It's the hand that wields the sword, not the sword itself that matters.'

'Never a truer word spoken,' agreed the cooper. 'But *these* were a very fine pair of swords. A *daisho* forged by the legendary Shizu no less!'

Jack's ears pricked up at this. 'What did these swords look like?'

The cooper thought for a moment. 'Mmm . . . black *saya*s with gold, maybe pearl inlay . . . I can't really remember. But I do recall their handles, very distinctive. Dark red.'

'Those are *my* swords!' exclaimed Jack.

The cooper stared at Jack in amused disbelief.

'Not any more,' he snorted, now curious about Ronin's peasant boy who laid claim to such prestigious weapons.

Jack knelt down beside the body to avoid his enquiring gaze.

'Do you recognize him?' asked Ronin.

Jack studied the face – the high eyebrows, the flattened nose, the jutting jaw – but nothing came back to him and he shook his head.

Stroking his beard pensively, Ronin peered down at the man. 'He looks vaguely familiar . . .' Crouching beside Jack, he inspected the man's blue kimono. 'But he hasn't any identifying *kamon*. We can't be certain he's the one responsible –'

'Yes, I can,' Jack interrupted, spotting a star-shaped tear on the man's collar. 'He's wearing one of *my* kimono! I remember snagging it on an overhanging branch and pulling loose the stitching, just like that.' His voice dropped to a whisper that only Ronin could hear. 'I was also given blue kimono without crests, so I couldn't be identified as a member of any family who fought against the Shogun.'

'Such a shame the kimono's slashed and stained with blood,' said Ronin, raising his voice as he noticed the cooper edging closer to eavesdrop. Reaching down, he pulled off the corpse's straw sandals and handed them to Jack. 'But he won't be needing these any more.'

Jack stood up, turning to keep his face hidden from the barrelmaker, and slipped on the dead man's *zori*. A ghostly shiver ran up his spine, but his feet were grateful nonetheless for the comfort and protection.

'Well, you've found your culprit,' declared Ronin, 'and he's certainly got his comeuppance.' The samurai examined the man's wound, running his finger along the diagonal cut in his chest. 'Whoever his opponent was, he's a highly skilled swordsman. This is a perfect *kesagiri* attack.'

The cooper, his brow creased in suspicion, said, 'Who is this boy –'

'Tell me, who paid for the coffin?' demanded Ronin, cutting off the man's question.

'One of his two so-called friends,' the cooper replied, patting his handiwork proudly. 'They left straight after – not even bothering to wait for the funeral. Funny, isn't it? How the person who pays for the coffin never wants it and the one who gets it never knows!'

'Have you any idea which way they went?' asked Jack.

The cooper shook his head. 'I only know where everyone is going . . .' He paused dramatically, then pointed with a long bony finger down at the ground and grinned.

Ronin began throughly searching the body.

'No good looking for spoils,' said the cooper. 'His friends took all that he owned . . . apart from his swords and this old *inro*.'

The cooper patted a small carrying case tied to his *obi*.

'Is that yours?' asked Ronin of Jack.

Jack shook his head. The rectangular box was plain with an ivory toggle carved into a monkey. 'No, mine has a *sakura* tree engraved upon its surface and the *netsuke* is in the shape of a lion's head.'

Ronin turned back to the cooper. 'What happened to the swords?'

'The other samurai claimed them as his prize.'

'Does this samurai have a name?'

'Oh, yes. He made certain *everyone* knew. Eager to spread his reputation, he announced this was the final duel of his *musha shugyō* – all without a single defeat,' replied the cooper as he lowered the finished coffin beside the victim. 'His name is Matagoro Araki.'

'Did *he* say where he was going?' asked Jack, hoping they could follow this samurai's trail at least.

The cooper looked at the bloodied corpse and then at Jack.

'If you seek a similar fate, then you should head to Kyoto.'

10

CROSSROADS

The very thought sent an ice-cold shudder through Jack. It would be suicidal to return to Kyoto. Someone could easily recognize him. Any of his old enemies could be there. In particular, those who'd attended the *Niten Ichi Ryū* with him and had objected to a foreigner learning the secrets of their martial arts – Nobu, Hiroto, Goro and, of course, his arch-rival, Kazuki. Jack had no wish to meet him ever again. Kazuki bore a deep hatred towards all foreigners, one of whom had inadvertently and tragically killed his mother through the spread of a fatal illness many years before. Being the only foreigner at the school, Jack had been the prime victim for his persecution.

But equally he might run into a friend in Kyoto. And this thought gave Jack a small thrill. Perhaps he'd find Saburo or Kiku, who'd both remained behind at the *Niten Ichi Ryū* during the war. Maybe Sensei Kano, having led the escape from Osaka Castle, had returned to the school. Or he might even encounter Emi and her father, *daimyo* Takatomi, residing at Nijo Castle. Jack knew their lives had been spared and that the *daimyo* was now serving under the Shogun.

But the risks were far too high.

Besides, while Akiko's father's swords were important to him, retrieving the *rutter* had to be his priority. The concern was that if the two bandits had the logbook they might not realize its value, especially to the Shogun. They could have thrown the logbook away or, worse, used it as tinder for their campfire.

'Come on, make your mind up!' demanded Ronin impatiently.

The two of them now stood at the crossroads in the centre of town. Being located on the route between Kyoto and Nara, Kizu was a convenient stopover and therefore unusually busy for a rural settlement. A constant flow of foot traffic passed in all directions.

Jack hesitated, still unable to decide.

'Kyoto's north,' stressed Ronin, pointing towards the long wooden bridge that spanned the Kizu River.

So is a great deal of trouble, thought Jack.

Behind him in an easterly direction lay the Iga mountains, beyond which was Toba and the false hope of staying with Akiko. Heading directly south would take them to Nara and the Tōdai-ji Temple. This was where the clue of the *omamori* had been leading them – it could be the destination of Manzo's two friends and hopefully the rest of his belongings. But it was a gamble at most. West down a dirt track would bring them to Osaka and the coast, which he then planned to follow in the long trek south to Nagasaki. However, with nothing to his name, no swords with which to defend himself and a drunken samurai as company, the odds were stacked against him ever making it to Osaka, let alone Nagasaki.

Four directions. Four choices. And none offered Jack any certainty.

'One who chases after two hares won't even catch one,' said Ronin, seeing the dilemma played out on Jack's face.

Jack held up the amulet. 'This clue says go south.'

'Your swords are *north*.'

'But everything else has gone the other way: my pearl, my money, my father's diary –'

'You don't know that for certain. Anyway, what's so special about a diary compared to a samurai's swords?' snorted Ronin.

Jack considered it unwise to explain the significance of the *rutter*. The samurai couldn't yet be trusted with knowledge of its value as a navigational tool and a political instrument – though for Jack it was so much more than this. The *rutter* was his passage home to England, the key to him becoming a ship's pilot, and the means for providing for his sister, Jess. But the logbook was also his *only* remaining link to his father. With it gone, Jack felt as if his father had been taken from him again. He'd do anything to get it back.

'Do you think the men who stole from me were samurai or bandits?' asked Jack, avoiding Ronin's question.

'They could be either,' replied Ronin. 'Manzo obviously thought himself a swordsman, but he acted like a bandit. Without a lord to serve, some samurai are turning to crime to survive. There are many more on the road now the war's over.'

'Well, we won't know until we find them. The cooper said the duel was yesterday, so they can't have gone too far.'

'*This* way,' argued Ronin, indicating the bridge north, 'we have a name, a destination and a definite lead.' He pointed south. '*That* way we have nothing. A guess, a hunch at most. We don't even know what these two men look like, or if the *omamori* has anything to do with them.'

Jack had to concede this point. 'But what happens when we find this Matagoro Araki? He won't just hand over my swords.'

'Why not? He's a samurai concerned with his reputation,' replied Ronin. 'He'll want to protect his good name, not have it smeared with rumours he's bearing the stolen swords of a distinguished samurai family. Besides, he can only use one *daisho* at a time!'

Jack shook his head doubtfully. 'Kyoto's too much of a risk.'

'You say you're samurai! But a samurai is *nothing* without his swords,' said Ronin, grasping the hilt of his *katana* emphatically. 'Besides, you'll stand a far better chance of getting back your other possessions if you have your rightful weapons in hand.'

Only dead fish swim with the current. The problem was Jack didn't know which way the current was flowing, and he realized he could end up dead if he chose the wrong way.

'Looks like the decision's been made for you,' said Ronin, nodding south in the direction of Nara.

Marching up the road was a patrol of *dōshin*, scattering anyone in their path.

'Best not wait around,' said Ronin, walking briskly in the opposite direction and towards Kyoto.

Jack hurried after him. The heavy rains of the previous day were now washing down from the mountains and the Kizu River was a powerful torrent. Weaving in between the other travellers, they reached the opposite bank and kept up their brisk pace until they entered the forest.

'Do you think the *dōshin* spotted us?' asked Jack, looking back over his shoulder. The road was busy and he couldn't see for certain if anyone was wearing the distinctive *hachimaki* of an officer.

'Can't be too sure,' Ronin replied. 'But we shouldn't stop to find out.'

The day drew on and the further they got from Kizu, the fewer people they met. By the time dusk fell, not a single soul was in sight. At this, Ronin veered off deep into the forest, finally coming to a halt in a small clearing.

'We'll camp here for the night,' he said, settling against a fallen log.

Jack sat beside him, as the samurai uncorked his bottle and took three large gulps. He wondered if Ronin got drunk every night, or if he was just drowning a recent sorrow. Jack decided it wasn't his place to ask. Removing the two *manjū* he'd saved, he passed one to Ronin.

'You have it,' said Ronin, waving the steamed bun away.

Jack didn't argue, but decided to save Ronin's for the following morning. Taking a bite of his, Jack was surprised at the sugary taste of the red-bean *manjū*. While it wasn't as filling as the meat one, Jack relished it nonetheless and the sweet dough ball was gone all too soon.

As he finished his paltry meal, Jack felt a prickling sensation run down the back of his neck. During his *ninjutsu* training, the Grandmaster had taught him not to ignore such signs. Pretending to make himself more comfortable against the log, Jack took the opportunity to subtly look round. There was no one there, but he thought he caught a slight movement among the bushes.

Turning to Ronin, Jack whispered gravely, 'Someone's watching us.'

11

SHADOW IN THE NIGHT

The forest was pitch-black, the trees blocking out any moon-light. Only the clearing was open to the stars and that made them sitting ducks. Jack and Ronin scanned the undergrowth for further movement, but whoever might be watching was well hidden.

'Are you certain?' breathed Ronin, his hand reaching for his sword.

Nodding gently, Jack clutched his *bō* in readiness to fight. He felt eyes upon him. Someone was definitely out there. *Dōshin?* But they didn't seem the type to sneak up on people. More likely they'd charge in and overwhelm with numbers. Could it be bandits? It would be just his luck to be ambushed a second time. Or *ninja?* For once, Jack hoped it was.

The ninja were no longer his enemy. Soke had shown him a secret hand sign – the Dragon Seal – that could be used as a signal of friendship. There was no guarantee it would work, however. What ninja would believe a foreigner was one of them?

Besides, Ronin was still a target. And he wouldn't be so welcoming to an assassin. Without doubt, there would be a fight.

Ronin stood up.

'Where are you going?' hissed Jack.

'Call of nature,' he replied loudly, raising an eyebrow to indicate it was a ruse.

The samurai disappeared into the darkness, noisily making his way through the undergrowth. Left alone, Jack kept up his vigilance and surveyed the forest for movement. He knew the ninja were able to disguise their presence by assuming the shape of rocks, blending into tree trunks and hiding within long grass. The forest could conceal any number of assassins, and Jack began seeing them in every bulge and fleeting shadow.

All of a sudden, Ronin became silent.

Jack turned in his direction. '*Ronin*,' he whispered. '*Are you all right?*'

There was no response. Jack tightened his grip on the *bō*. Perhaps the samurai had simply stopped walking and was out of earshot. On the other hand, he could have been seized, possibly even killed. The ninja were experts in silent assassination. And if Ronin was dead Jack would be next.

The silence stretched on; even the forest seemed to have stopped breathing.

Judging by their stealth, Jack was now convinced it was a ninja ambush. Clasping both hands together, middle fingers entwined, thumbs and little finger extended in a V-shape, he formed the Dragon Seal and turned slowly in a circle.

Jack waited for a reponse.

Nothing.

'*Ronin!*' he whispered more urgently.

A branch snapped behind him. Jack whirled round, staff held high to strike. The steel blade of a battleworn *katana*

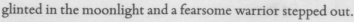

glinted in the moonlight and a fearsome warrior stepped out.

'Didn't find anyone,' Ronin grunted.

Jack lowered his staff. 'But I *know* I sensed a presence.'

'*You* should stay on the alert then,' replied Ronin, sheathing his sword and lying down on the ground.

'What are you going to do?' Jack asked.

Ronin didn't bother replying. He just folded his arms behind his head and closed his eyes, leaving Jack to guard their camp alone.

Jack still had the unnerving feeling of being watched. But after sweeping the bushes he'd found no one and put the sensation down to anxiety at the thought of returning to Kyoto.

Tired as he was, Jack forced himself to perform another self-healing meditation. His swollen eye was already going down and the bruises were fading fast, but it would still be a few more days before he was back to full health. He quietly murmured the words of the *Sha* mantra to ensure he didn't disturb Ronin.

At some point, Jack leant back against the fallen log and drifted in and out of sleep.

A soft furred creature emerged from a bush, its bright inquisitive eyes twinkling in the starlight. Its snout twitched, sniffing him out. Jack let the animal approach.

You're a *tanuki*, thought Jack.

Suddenly a swirling tornado of leaves enveloped the tanuki, *rising to the height of a man. A second later, as if the wind had died, the leaves fell to the ground, revealing a bushy-bearded man in a blood-red robe.*

'*Riddle me this, young samurai! What is greater than God, more evil than the Devil? Poor people have it, rich people need it, and if you eat it you'll die. Tell me this and I shall give it to you.*'

Jack thought he knew the answer, but his mouth wouldn't open. His lips were sealed as tight as a tomb.

The Riddling Monk began to shrink before his eyes, the voice falling away like a pebble down a well. 'What you find is lost . . . What you give is given back . . . What you fight is defeated . . . What you want is sacrificed.'

The monk's robes consumed him until he was no more than a cloth heap. A tanuki crawled out and sauntered off into the forest, leaves crackling like fresh snow beneath its paws . . .

Halfway between sleep and waking, Jack sensed a shadow pass before his eyes. He caught a whiff of pine needles and saw a hand reach for Ronin's swords. In that instant, Jack became alert. Without hesitating, he leapt upon the shadow crouching beside Ronin. Executing a punishing shoulder throw, he pinned the shadow to the ground, pressing his staff hard across its throat. Ronin was immediately by his side, a *tantō* knife in his hand ready to kill the intruder.

'No . . . Stop!' spluttered a terrified voice.

Jack stared into the dark eyes of a waif-like girl. She had a bob of knotted black hair that framed a slim impish face with ruddy lips and a petite nose.

'What sort of ninja are you?' he said, noticing her clothing was tatty and only black because of ingrained dirt.

'What sort of samurai are *you*?' she retorted, her eyes wide with alarm at the sight of her blond-haired, blue-eyed attacker.

Jack released the pressure on the girl's throat, but still didn't let her up. 'One who protects his friends from murderers like you.'

'I'm no murderer!'

'So what were you doing?'

'I . . . I . . . just wanted to look at his *inro*,' she protested, pointing to the small battered wooden carrying case on the samurai's hip.

'A petty thief!' spat Ronin in disgust, his bloodshot eyes glaring at her.

'No, I'm not!' responded the girl indignantly.

'What are you then?' demanded Ronin.

She considered for a moment, then answered, 'A highly skilful thief.'

'Not that skilful,' Ronin snorted. 'You were caught.'

'Well, I evaded *you* in the bushes!' she said, a haughty look in her eyes. 'You passed right by me behind the pine tree. I could've taken your *inro* then!'

Ronin stood up, waving Jack aside. 'We'd better check what you *do* have.'

Grabbing the girl by the ankles, Ronin held her upside down and roughly shook her.

'Let go!' she cried, struggling in vain.

Three ornate brass hairpins dropped to the ground, followed by an ivory fan, a tortoiseshell comb, a bag of coins and a small blunt knife.

'Not bad takings,' muttered Ronin, dropping the girl and picking up the bag. He emptied its contents into his hand. 'What's this? Your lucky charm?'

A little paper crane sat among the coins in Ronin's palm.

'Don't tell me. Thieves now practise the art of *origami*!'

Jack stared at the bird. 'Let me see that.'

Ronin handed him the crane and Jack lifted its wing. Beneath it, inscribed in tiny *kanji* characters, was the word: *Senbazuru.*

Jack knew this meant 'One Thousand Cranes' according to the legend that said any person who folds a thousand such *origami* birds is granted a wish. His friend Yori had made *this* paper crane and had wished for Jack's safe journey home.

'Did you steal this from me?' said Jack to the girl, who'd sat up and was moodily brushing off leaves.

She glanced up, a flash of defiance in her eyes. 'No.'

'Then where did you get it?' Jack demanded, grabbing her arm for her full attention.

'Some samurai,' she replied, shrugging him off. 'But he doesn't care; he's dead now.'

'What else did you steal?'

The girl became tight-lipped.

'Answer him!' snarled Ronin.

'Nothing . . .' she murmured, shrinking from the samurai.

Ronin advanced on her, knife in hand.

'Some money . . . and a black pearl from his friends,' she added quickly.

'A *black* pearl!' breathed Ronin, stopping in his tracks.

'Where is it?' asked Jack, his eyes darting from the coins in Ronin's hand to the spoils on the ground.

She offered him a smug smile. 'I sold it.'

12

THE THIEF

'That hurts!' whined the girl thief as Ronin bound her to the fallen log.

'Stop complaining!' said Ronin, tying up her hands with the *sageo* cord from his *saya*. 'Or I'll be forced to gag you.'

The girl stuck her tongue out at him, but kept quiet. Having secured her, Ronin withdrew his knife and rested its razor-sharp edge upon her cheek.

'Now you *will* tell us who's got the pearl, or . . .' He left the rest unsaid.

She glared back at Ronin, her eyes daring him to do it.

'Ronin!' Jack interrupted, worried the samurai might carry out his threat. 'Let me try first.'

'Be my guest,' he replied, offering the knife.

Jack politely refused, considering a more friendly approach might loosen the girl's tongue. He knelt down beside the thief.

'What's your name?' asked Jack, smiling.

'Hana.'

'I'm Jack.' He inclined his head respectfully, but was stopped mid-bow by her reply.

'I know. The *dōshin* were talking about you. Some big reward for your head.'

At this Jack felt Ronin's eyes suddenly upon him.

'Don't know why anyone would pay a whole *koban* for your head?' Hana smirked, eyeing up Jack. 'That amount of gold could keep me in rice for three years!'

Jack glanced at Ronin. *Had this knowledge changed everything?* Surely such a reward was tempting for even the most honourable samurai – and Jack was yet to be convinced of Ronin's virtue. The man could literally drown himself in *saké* with all that money. But the samurai's expression remained inscrutable.

'Tell me, who did you sell the pearl to?' demanded Ronin.

'What's it to you?'

'That pearl belongs to Jack.'

'Prove it!'

'I was given the pearl by my best friend, Akiko,' Jack explained. He remembered the moment with perfect clarity. Last year in Toba on a glorious summer's day. How Akiko had swum deep like a mermaid, surfacing with an oval-shaped shell in one hand. He'd prised it open to reveal a black pearl, the colour of Akiko's eyes. He'd treasured her gift ever since. 'She dived into a bay near Toba and found it.'

'Such a sweet story,' said Hana, pretending to blink away tears. 'I almost believe you.'

'*Please* tell me who's got it.'

Hana pursed her lips as if weighing up the truth in his story. 'If you ask nicely, I might . . .'

Jack took a deep breath. It was like getting blood out of a stone. Bowing before Hana, he said, 'I'd be indebted to you if you'd tell me who has the pearl. We'll let you go if you do.'

'A merchant,' she replied, smiling coyly at him, pleased with her victory.

'Which merchant?' Jack persisted.

'The one who sells fancy hairpins and kimono in Kizu.'

'Do you know his name?'

Hana shook her head.

'*If* you sold it to this merchant,' said Ronin, 'where's the money gone?'

'You've got it all!' she said, exasperated. 'Now I've done what you asked. Let me go.'

Ronin snorted in disbelief. 'That was a *black* pearl you sold. Very rare. It's worth at least a hundred times what you have here.'

Hana's eyes widened with genuine shock. 'B-b-but the merchant said black pearls were worthless.'

Ronin laughed coldly. 'You've been robbed!'

'Wish I'd stolen more of his precious hairpins now,' muttered Hana, seething at being swindled.

Jack contemplated what to do next. His predicament was becoming more complex by the day. He'd been robbed by at least three men, possibly samurai, but one of them was now dead and the other two had disappeared. His swords had been won in a duel and were on their way to Kyoto, while the pearl had been sold to a merchant in the very town they'd just been forced to leave. Where his other posessions were was anyone's guess. He still had the clue of the *omamori*, but no memory of how he'd got it or what had happened to him.

'You said you stole the pearl from the dead man's friends. Would you recognize them?' asked Jack.

'Probably.'

Jack turned to Ronin, who beckoned him away from the bound Hana.

'What do you want to do?' asked Ronin quietly.

'If she's telling the truth, there's a good chance we could get back my pearl and identify my attackers.'

'Well, we can't take the girl to Kyoto. She'd be too much trouble,' he replied, stroking his beard thoughtfully. 'And it is a valuable pearl. Perhaps worth half a *koban*.'

'That pearl means more to me than money,' said Jack. 'It was a gift from Akiko.'

'All the more reason to return to Kizu.'

'But what about my swords?' asked Jack, despite being secretly relieved at the prospect of no longer going to Kyoto.

'A samurai is *nothing* without someone to fight for,' replied Ronin, a roguish grin on his face. 'Once we've got back your precious pearl, we can resume our journey to Kyoto. Now we'd best get some sleep.'

Ronin gathered the stolen items together, slipping the knife into his *obi* and the rest inside his kimono sleeve, before settling down against the log. Jack found a place near a tree, so he could keep one eye on Hana and the other on Ronin, just in case the idea of the reward became too enticing for the samurai. He tried to make himself comfortable on the forest floor.

'Hey! You promised to let me go!' protested Hana, struggling against her bonds.

'We will,' replied Ronin. 'After you've got Jack's pearl back.'

13

THE MERCHANT

'Don't make me do this,' pleaded Hana.

The three of them stood beside the merchant's premises in Kizu, hidden from passers-by down a side alley.

'Perhaps we should turn you over to the *dōshin* instead?' suggested Ronin.

Hana scowled at him. 'The merchant won't just *give* me the pearl. Besides, he must suspect I stole his hairpins.'

'Convince him otherwise,' said Ronin, passing her the money she'd obtained in exchange for the pearl.

'Good luck!' Jack whispered, realizing they were *all* taking a risk by returning to Kizu. A *dōshin* patrol could appear at any moment.

'I'll need more than luck,' replied Hana coolly.

As she turned to go, Ronin seized her by the arm. 'Don't even *think* of running. We'll be watching you. And if you don't come back with the pearl . . .' Ronin drew a grim line across his neck with his forefinger.

'What an encouraging thought!' replied Hana, shooting him a sarcastic smile as she stepped out into the street.

Ronin waited by the entrance to the alley, ready to cut off

any escape attempt, while Jack peeked through a tiny gap in the wooden wall of the shop to follow Hana's progress.

The merchant was clearly proud of his store. The floor was spotless, the wooden surfaces polished to a bright gleam. Arranged in neat piles were swathes of cloth and exquisite kimono, offering an irresistible rainbow of colour to any browsing shopper. The merchant sat upon the raised floor, inspecting his stock of glittering hair ornaments – brass pins and silver clasps, painted combs of tortoiseshell and lacquered wood, silk flowers and shimmering ornate chains, all displayed upon a large black square of cloth.

Jack saw Hana enter, slip off her sandals and approach the merchant. He was a balding man with narrow eyes, thin lips and a sharp ridge of a nose. Everything about him suggested he was a shrewd merchant and a hard bargainer. Suddenly aware of his new customer, the merchant's face softened and he offered his most welcoming smile. But it instantly vanished upon seeing Hana.

'*You!*'

'Pleased to meet you again,' she replied, bowing and smiling sweetly.

'Where are my hairpins?' he demanded, pointing angrily to empty spaces in his display.

'I'm sorry. I've no idea what you're talking about. Perhaps you lost them?'

The merchant snorted with contempt. 'You stole them. I'm missing *three* and a comb since yesterday.'

'Why on earth would I steal hairpins? I don't have the hair for it,' remarked Hana, tugging at her black matted bob. 'Besides, if I was a thief, would I *really* return to your store?'

The merchant glared at Hana. She continued to smile innocently back, as if butter wouldn't melt in her mouth. He didn't appear wholly convinced by her act, but a seed of doubt had been sown. 'So what *do* you want?'

Hana cleared her throat. 'The black pearl I sold you belongs to –' she glanced uncomfortably to where she knew Jack was watching – 'my master. It was given to him as a love-token and he would like it back, please.' She held out the coins to the merchant and waited expectantly.

Not even glancing at the money, the merchant stared blankly at her. 'What pearl?'

'The one I sold you yesterday.'

'I don't recall any such transaction.'

Dismissing her with a wave of his hand, he busied himself with rearranging his stock of hair ornaments.

Jack turned to Ronin. 'Perhaps Hana's lied to us?'

But Ronin was no longer paying attention. His eyes were drawn to a young lady gliding down the main thoroughfare. Even Jack's concentration was broken by the vision. The beautiful woman was dressed in a striking red silk kimono, embroidered with white chrysanthemum blossom. Her long black hair was tied up and adorned with a glimmering golden butterfly. This was embellished with silk flowers that cascaded down either side of her angelic face. As she walked, a soft tinkling could be heard accompanying her every step – the tiny silver chains dangling in her hair chiming her approach.

The attractive lady entered the shop, spotted Hana and wrinkled her nose in disgust at the girl's dishevelled appearance. Immediately the merchant was by the woman's side, bowing and scraping as he led her to a seat.

'Who's *she*?' questioned the lady.

'A nobody,' replied the merchant, shooing Hana out of the door.

Hana bristled at this and stood her ground. The lady, no longer paying Hana any attention, began to preen before a small looking glass. She adjusted a large gold pin in her hair so that it sat beside the butterfly for the greatest effect.

'I can't express my joy enough at your new gift,' said the lady to the merchant. 'My friends were *so* envious. They'd never seen a black pearl before.'

Hana gasped in outrage when she spotted the gem now mounted on the end of the lady's hairpin. 'Isn't *that* the pearl I sold you?' Hana demanded of the merchant.

Jack squinted through the gap. It might just be a coincidence, but he thought it highly unlikely that there were *two* identical black pearls in this town.

'Oh, *that* pearl,' acknowledged the merchant begrudgingly. 'It's not for sale.'

'But my master wants it back,' insisted Hana.

'The pearl now belongs to my wife.'

'*His wife!*' Ronin muttered, shaking his head in disbelief. 'She's half his age. He *must* be rich . . .'

'What's the problem?' demanded the merchant's young wife.

'Nothing, dear,' replied the merchant, trying to steer Hana out of the store.

'But I *must* return it to its rightful owner!' cried Hana, looking nervously in the direction Ronin was concealed.

'*I'm* its rightful owner,' snapped the young wife. 'There's only one of these in the whole province and it's *mine*.'

71

'*Please* . . . my life depends upon it.'

The lady laughed shrilly at Hana's plea. 'Your life's not worth the dirt on my sandals – let alone *my* pearl. Now get out before my husband calls the *dōshin*.'

The merchant went to throw Hana into the street.

'I *beg* you! It belongs to a samurai,' said Hana, struggling in his grip.

The merchant pulled her close until they were face to face. His narrow eyes had widened in concern at the revelation. 'Which samurai?' he hissed, hoping his wife hadn't heard the exchange.

'The . . . *gaijin* samurai.'

The merchant laughed. 'Nice try. Even if it were true, that *gaijin* traitor would be long gone by now . . . or else dead.'

With that, he kicked Hana out of the store.

'And don't come back!' said the merchant, wiping his hands of her. He turned to his wife, who was now glowering at him.

'I thought you said you *handpicked* this pearl yourself, Isamu!' she scolded.

'I did! I did!' he insisted, fussing around her. 'The girl's lying. She's a thief . . . a nobody! Now, my darling butterfly, have you seen this beautiful gilded comb? It only arrived today . . .'

While the merchant tried to placate his wife with gifts, Hana dusted herself off and rejoined Jack and Ronin in the alley.

'I tried my best,' she said defiantly to Ronin. 'Now either cut my throat or let me go!'

'Well, your best wasn't good enough,' Ronin replied, his fingers grasping the hilt of his sword.

Fearing for Hana's life, Jack stepped forward to protect her, but Ronin had already grabbed her wrist and forced her against the alley wall.

'You're a *highly skilful* thief,' reminded Ronin, prising the coins from Hana's trembling hand and grinning at the panic in her eyes. 'You'll just have to steal the pearl back. Won't you?'

14

BREAKING AND ENTERING

The streets of Kizu were virtually deserted, an autumnal chill to the night air. The merchant's house, a two-storey building with an ornate balcony to its rear, was situated within a walled garden on the outskirts of town.

'Are you sure we should be doing this?' whispered Jack, peering through the impressive wooden gates.

'It's not stealing if it's stolen from you in the first place,' Ronin replied.

Jack couldn't argue with that, but it didn't allay his fears.

'Besides,' Ronin added, '*she's* the only one breaking the law.'

Hana stood sullenly next to Ronin. They had spent the afternoon discussing the best way to retrieve the pearl. A daylight robbery was considered too dangerous. There'd be witnesses, the possibility of a violent and unwanted confrontation, and a good chance of being caught by *dōshin*. A night-time burglary, on the other hand, should give them enough time to make their escape before the pearl's disappearance was discovered.

Jack beckoned Ronin to one side. 'Now Hana knows the

pearl's true value, what's to stop her running off with it?'

'Good point. Go with her.'

'Me?'

'It's *your* pearl,' remarked Ronin, between swigs of *saké*.

Jack wondered whether it was worth taking such a risk, but he dearly wanted Akiko's gift back. The pearl symbolized their undying bond — *forever bound to one another*. And its imminent recovery gave him hope that he would eventually find *all* his possessions — most importantly, the *rutter*.

'I'll need the money for the pearl then,' said Jack.

'We need it for food and . . . ' Ronin shook the half-empty *saké* jug.

'I know, but as samurai we must follow the code of *bushido* and be honest. This money belongs to the merchant, even if he is a swindler.'

Acknowledging this fact with a grunt, Ronin handed him the coins and strode over to the treeline.

'I'll keep watch from here,' he said, crouching in the shadows with his dwindling supply of *saké*. 'Off you go!'

Hana looked at Jack. 'He's good at giving orders. Does your friend *ever* lift a finger?'

Jack wouldn't have described Ronin exactly as a friend, but he remembered how the samurai had saved his life at the tea house. 'Sometimes.'

Leading the way, Hana headed to the lowest section of garden wall.

'You'd better not make a sound,' she cautioned.

'Don't worry, I won't,' replied Jack, offering his hands to boost Hana over.

Little did Hana know that Jack had trained in *shinobi aruki*, the ninja art of stealth-walking. He silently slipped over the wall and landed nimbly beside Hana in the moonlit garden. A small tea house was set beside a pond amid well-tended shrubs and bushes. A pebbled pathway wound through this sculpted landscape, passing a carved stone lantern before reaching the back entrance to the house.

Avoiding the path – and the noise it would make – they crept towards the main *shoji*. The house was in darkness, but they knew the merchant and his wife were at home, having seen them return earlier that evening. As gently as she could, Hana eased the door open and peeked inside. The room was empty, except for an alcove containing a display of flowers and a hanging scroll of two birds perched upon a branch.

Leaving the door open for a quick escape, they entered a darkened hallway, at the end of which was a wooden staircase. Cautiously, they ascended to the second floor. But as Hana stepped on to the landing, one of the floorboards creaked.

They both froze.

For what seemed an eternity, they listened for the alarm to be raised and the sound of pounding feet. But no one came to investigate. Breathing a sigh of relief, Hana and Jack began to check each of the rooms in turn.

The first two were unoccupied and yielded nothing, but from the room overlooking the garden came the rhythmic sound of snoring. Jack put an eye to the crack between the *shoji* and the frame. The merchant lay on his back, fast asleep. Next to him, on a separate *futon*, was his wife – her head raised upon a box pillow, which supported her neck so her elaborate hairdo wasn't spoiled during the night.

As silent as a shadow, Hana tiptoed into the bedroom and

began to hunt through the drawers of a finely wrought lacquered cabinet. She seemed to be taking an age rifling through its contents. Concerned the merchant or his wife would wake, Jack joined Hana in the search. But Akiko's black pearl was nowhere to be found among the lady's accessories.

Shaking her head, Hana closed the last of the drawers. As she turned to leave, Jack noticed a gleam of silver concealed in her left hand. During the planning, he'd made it clear that they were to retrieve the pearl, and *only* the pearl. He gestured for her to put it back. Grudgingly, Hana returned the stolen jewel to its rightful place. It was then, with a clear view of the merchant's wife, Jack spotted the gold pin still fixed in her hair – the black pearl almost invisible in the darkness.

He motioned his find to Hana. She grimaced at the impossible task ahead. To remove the pin called for nerves of steel and a *very* steady hand.

Jack, however, was prepared for just such a job. He'd once been tasked with stealing a pillow from beneath the sleeping head of the ninja Grandmaster. Through a combination of cunning and skill, Jack had succeeded where many others had failed.

Quietening his mind in preparation for the task, Jack crept silently over to the sleeping woman. Crouching beside her, his breathing matching hers so as not to disturb her, he reached for the pearl. Ever so gently, he pulled . . .

But try as he might, the pin was caught fast in the lady's layers of hair. There appeared to be no way of removing it without waking her. Hana, seeing the problem, moved in to help. Ushering Jack aside, she reached over to undo the lady's artful knot of hair. But a comb she'd secretly stolen slipped from the folds of her kimono and clattered to the floor.

All of a sudden, the lady's eyes opened.

She stared in horror at Jack. A split second later, she let out a piercing scream.

Jack grabbed Hana and they fled from the room on to the balcony, where they jumped to the garden below. Hitting the ground running, they leapt over the wall and disappeared into the darkness.

15

A NEW PLAN

'I told you *not* to steal anything!' said Jack as the two of them caught their breath in a paddy field outside the town.

'It was just a comb,' mumbled Hana apologetically.

Jack fumed. 'I had the pearl in my hand –'

A snap of a branch made them both spin round. They were about to bolt when, weaving slightly, Ronin emerged from the cover of the forest.

'Did you get it?' he asked.

Glaring at Hana, Jack shook his head.

'What went wrong?'

'The lady woke up,' Jack replied through clenched teeth. He omitted Hana's blunder, knowing Ronin wouldn't be so forgiving.

'What are you going to do now?' Hana asked Jack in a timid voice. Her eyes flicked apprehensively to the swords on Ronin's hip.

Shrugging, Jack slumped down on an old tree stump, his head in his hands. It would be almost impossible to retrieve the pearl now. The merchant and his wife would be on their guard and would have alerted the *dōshin* to the break-in.

'We simply need a new plan,' said Ronin, handing Jack's staff and straw hat back to him. Then he settled himself against a tree, took a long draught from his bottle of *saké*, and closed his eyes.

'Sleeping's a *great* plan!' remarked Jack, his tone heavy with sarcasm.

'Never do anything standing that you can do sitting, or anything sitting that you can do lying down. Now let me think.'

Leaving Ronin to his drunken contemplation, Jack stabbed angrily at the ground with the end of his staff. He considered abandoning the quest altogether. Was Akiko's pearl really worth the risks they were taking? However slim his chances, the sensible thing to do would be to head for Nagasaki as fast as he could – instead of wasting time in pursuit of his lost belongings.

Hadn't the Riddling Monk said *What you find is lost* . . . and *What you want is sacrificed*? He'd just have to accept that Akiko's precious pearl, though found, was otherwise lost to him.

Compelled by Jack's obvious dismay, Hana crept over to him. 'I'm really sorry . . .'

'Forget it,' said Jack, his initial anger with her having passed. 'This isn't your problem. You shouldn't have been involved in the first place. Listen, you can go if you want.'

Hana laughed nervously. 'Your friend'll slice me into eight pieces if I do.'

'I won't let him.'

Hana didn't leave, though. She stood staring at Jack. She seemed almost reluctant to go, as if she didn't know *where* to go.

'This Akiko means a lot to you, doesn't she?'

Jack nodded, smiling at the very thought of her. 'Akiko's my best friend. She's been by my side from the first day I arrived in Japan.'

'Why's she not with you now then?'

Jack sighed deeply. Feeling the ache in his heart, he remembered the time he'd left Akiko in Toba to ensure her family's safety, and then how she had said goodbye to him at the ninja village. 'Akiko needs to be with her mother. A daughter's duty,' explained Jack.

Hana nodded her understanding. 'It must be nice to have a mother.'

For the first time, Jack sensed a hollow loneliness behind the girl's spirited nature. 'Where's your family?' he asked.

Hana shook her head. 'What family? I've survived on my own for as long as I can remember.'

Jack suddenly felt compassion for this girl thief. Like him, she was an orphan, but at least he'd been fortunate enough to experience family life. Hana had no one. And despite the traumatic loss of both his mother and father, as far as he knew he still had Jess waiting for him in England.

The memory of his sister broke his melancholy and spurred him to act.

Realistically, he couldn't give up on his quest. Without his swords he was defenceless. Without money he'd starve. And without the *rutter*, he had no future. Although the pearl wasn't essential for his journey, it was for the peace of his heart. Retrieving the gem was the *first* step in recovering not only his possessions, but hopefully his memory too.

A complete blank still remained about what had happened

to him. How had Manzo and his friends overcome him? He was a trained samurai warrior who'd fought in major battles and survived. He possessed the skills of a ninja and was in disguise at the time. Perhaps he'd been ambushed? Or maybe there'd been a whole gang of them? The only way to find out was to follow the clues he had, to get his life back piece by piece.

And the first piece was Akiko's pearl.

He vowed to himself to try one more time to retrieve it, then he'd go to Kyoto to find his swords, before hunting down those who had the *rutter*. Once it was in his possession, he'd resume his journey to Nagasaki.

'I *must* get back the pearl,' said Jack.

'I'll help you,' Hana offered.

'Thank you, but you don't need to,' replied Jack, realizing the girl had enough problems of her own.

'But I want to,' Hana insisted. 'It's my fault you don't have it now. Besides, I want to teach that merchant a lesson. He swindled me . . . and called me a *nobody*!'

Jack saw the defiance in her eyes and, deeper down, the hurt the merchant's cruel dismissal had inflicted.

All of a sudden, Ronin sat up and announced, 'We can make the merchant return your pearl – *willingly*.'

'How?' asked Jack.

'To start with, I need to get a job.'

16

THE GAMBLER

Clouds had gathered and a persistent drizzle fell from the sky as Ronin looked for a suitable place to shelter for the night. They kept to the outskirts of town, but most buildings appeared occupied.

'When will it *ever* stop raining?' complained Hana, hugging herself for warmth.

Suddenly up ahead a door opened and light spilled into the rain-washed street. A man stepped out, looking thoroughly dejected. From behind him raucous shouts of 'Odd!' and 'Even!' punctuated the night air. A moment later, these were replaced by cries of elation mixed with groans of disappointment.

'A gambling den,' Ronin hissed as the three of them ducked into a side alley to avoid being seen.

The man slammed the door shut, then morosely wandered down the road. As he drew near, Hana gasped. 'I recognize him.'

She squinted harder. Dressed in a dark blue kimono, the man's topknot hairstyle indicated he was a samurai, although he wasn't carrying any swords.

'I think he's the man I stole your pearl from,' whispered Hana.

'Are you certain?' asked Jack, feeling a small thrill of hope at their unexpected good fortune.

Hana nodded. 'This isn't a big town. There aren't that many samurai around.'

Ronin strode out of the alley and into the man's path.

'Do I know you?' enquired the man, trying to make out Ronin's face in the darkness.

'No! And you don't want to,' Ronin replied, grabbing the man by the scruff of his kimono and dragging him into the alley. 'But you do know *this* samurai!'

The man's eyes widened in shock when Jack removed his straw hat to reveal his blond hair and foreign face.

'But . . . but . . . we left you for dead,' spluttered the man.

'Not dead enough,' said Jack, clenching his fists in anger. He fought to restrain himself, calling upon the discipline Masamoto had ingrained in him. 'Where are my belongings?'

Overcoming his initial shock, the man stared defiantly at Jack and remained tight-lipped.

'Answer him!' ordered Ronin, driving his forearm across the man's throat and pinning him to the wall.

'I don't know . . . what you're talking about.'

'We can do this the easy way or . . .' Ronin pressed harder and the man choked. 'Now where's the money you stole?'

The man gulped nervously. 'I gambled it.'

'*All* of it!' exclaimed Jack.

'I had a run of bad luck,' snapped the man, as if that excused him. No longer able to meet their eyes, he mumbled, 'I even lost my *swords*.'

Ronin stared at the man in astonishment. 'You *bet* your swords! What sort of samurai gambles his soul away?'

'But it was a *sure* win,' he protested. 'The dice must have been loaded!'

'Well, it just isn't your night, is it?' said Ronin. 'You're about to lose the kimono off your back too.'

Ronin beckoned Jack closer. On inspection, the kimono had no identifying *kamon* and was of the same blue cloth as the one Akiko's mother had given him. Jack nodded in agreement. Releasing the chokehold, Ronin ordered the man to hand over Jack's clothes.

'But I don't have anything else to wear! I'll catch my death!'

'You never gave Jack that courtesy,' said Ronin, unsheathing his sword as an additional incentive.

Hurriedly, the man stripped down to his loincloth and stood shivering in the rain.

'We know the fate of Jack's swords,' said Ronin, resting the tip of his *katana* over the man's heart. 'If you don't want to end up like your friend Manzo, then tell us where the rest of his belongings are.'

'I-I . . . don't have them,' stammered the man.

'That's plain to see,' said Hana, giggling at the samurai's scrawny torso.

'Then who does?' demanded Ronin.

'Botan!' he confessed, spitting the name angrily. '*He* blamed me for losing the pearl. Thought I'd gambled it. But I reckon he stole it for himself.'

Jack and Ronin glanced at Hana, who was trying to suppress a grin.

'Where's this Botan now?' pressed Jack, the *rutter* foremost in his mind.

'How should I know? We parted company after Manzo's

death. He could be *anywhere* by now.'

In the blink of an eye, Ronin flicked the razor-sharp *kissaki* up to the samurai's throat, drawing a bead of blood. 'You can do better than that.'

'M-m-most likely Nara,' blurted the man. 'That's where he's from.'

Ronin withdrew his sword. 'You've been most helpful. Now for your reward –'

'Wait!' interrupted Jack, seeing the intent in Ronin's actions. 'I need to find out about my father's diary and what they did to me.'

The man laughed coldly at this revelation. 'Of course . . . you can't remember!' His eyes flicked to Ronin, a smirk on his face. 'I *know* you –'

'Don't change the subject. TELL HIM!' roared Ronin, his face like thunder.

The man's bravado crumpled under Ronin's ferocity. But just as he was about to reply, Hana hissed, '*Dōshin!*'

The light from several lanterns could be seen coming up the street, accompanied by the sound of marching feet. A patrol was checking each and every alley.

'Looks like your luck's back in,' growled Ronin, sheathing his sword with annoyance. 'But if you say one word to the *dōshin* you'll lose far more than your clothes.'

Leaving the gambler in his loincloth, the three of them hurried away down the alley.

'See you again, Ronin!' called the gambler, daring a parting shot now he was safe.

Ronin stopped in his tracks and glared at the man. 'Pray you never do.'

Cutting through Kizu's backstreets, they emerged into paddy fields. Ronin spotted an old rice store and they ducked inside.

'Do we have to stay *here*?' protested Hana, holding her nose.

Ronin nodded. 'It'll do for the night.'

'But it smells like some animal's died. It stinks.'

'So do you,' snarled Ronin, peering through the door to check the *dōshin* weren't following. 'We'll need to keep watch. I'll go first.'

Jack found a dry spot in the corner of the storehouse and folded his blue kimono into a makeshift pillow. 'Hana, you can sleep here. It doesn't smell quite so bad.'

Mumbling her thanks, Hana curled up, exhaustion overwhelming her as soon as she closed her eyes. Jack cleared a space for his own bed, but he wasn't ready yet. Their encounter with the gambler had given him fresh hope they'd find the *rutter*. Rubbing the green silk *omamori* for luck, he now knew the amulet *had* been leading them in the right direction. They also knew who to look for – Botan.

As Jack settled down to sleep, a thought occurred to him. 'Ronin, how did the gambler know your name?'

The samurai turned on Jack, his dark eyes blazing. 'What's it to you?'

Jack recognized the haunted look in Ronin's face. 'It just seemed rather odd –'

'Listen, I've met many samurai in my time and made a few enemies along the way. I don't always remember the reasons.' He swigged on his *saké*. 'Now get some rest. You'll need it for tomorrow.'

17

THE BODYGUARD

'I've got the job,' announced Ronin the next morning, triumphantly returning to the storehouse. 'He's even paid today's wages in advance.'

Ronin produced a cloth sack, opening it up to reveal several steaming *manjū*. While Hana and Jack greedily tucked into their breakfast, Ronin uncorked a fresh bottle of *saké* and went over the final details of his plan.

'Best save the two redbean *manjū* for later,' Ronin advised. 'Now, the merchant closes his shop at the Hour of the Rooster, and I've learnt he and his wife like to walk along the riverside on their way home. There's a wooded path that runs from it to their house, so that's where you two will lie in wait.'

'Are you certain this'll work?' asked Jack.

Ronin stood, neatened his kimono and adjusted his swords. 'There's only one way to find out.'

'Can you see them yet?' asked Hana as they hid in a ditch beside the path.

'No,' replied Jack, beginning to wonder if the merchant and his wife had taken a different route home.

'Do you think something's gone wrong?'

'I hope not,' said Jack. The sun was close to setting and there was still no sign of them . . . or Ronin. Their plan would be a lot more risky the darker it became.

'Perhaps Ronin's drunk.'

Jack didn't answer, not wanting to consider that possibility.

The longer they waited, the more impatient Hana became.

'Do you trust this samurai?' she asked, digging at the earth with her blunt knife, Ronin having returned it. 'I mean, you've only known him a few days –'

'They're coming!' said Jack, glad the conversation had been interrupted by events. Hana's concerns were mirrored in his own heart. Ronin was unpredictable and his past history murky, but the samurai was the only option Jack had.

At last, the merchant and his young wife could be seen making their way along the riverbank towards home. As they turned up the woodland path, Jack and Hana jumped out, Jack wielding his staff, Hana her knife.

'I've come to claim what is rightfully mine,' declared Jack.

The merchant's eyes widened in disbelief. 'The *gaijin* samurai! So *you* were the intruder!'

The wife's hand instinctively went to her hair. 'You can't have it. This pearl's mine!'

'It was a gift to *me* before it was stolen,' explained Jack. 'Now I respectfully ask for its return.'

The merchant laughed. 'What does a foreigner know about respect?'

'More than a merchant!' said Hana. 'You lied to me about its value.'

'Business is business. Besides, you don't deserve respect – you're an outcast, a nobody.'

Fuming at the repeated insult, Hana took a step towards the merchant.

'Have you met my bodyguard?' said the merchant, arrogantly clicking his fingers.

From behind the couple, Ronin appeared. Jack and Hana stared in shock, but he displayed no flicker of recognition – just a cold murderous stare.

'Kill them!' ordered the merchant.

Hana took one look at this Ronin, no longer a drunken washed-up samurai but a fearsome warrior, and ran. But Jack stood his ground. 'I'm not here to fight. I just want my pearl back.'

'That's not a choice you have,' said Ronin, drawing his sword.

Like a bolt of lightning, Ronin attacked, his *katana* slicing for Jack's head. Barely having time to duck, Jack felt the deadly steel skim past. He thrust his staff in retaliation, but the samurai evaded the strike and cut down across Jack's chest. Jack leapt away, the blade whistling past his face.

Whatever they'd planned, Ronin was fighting for *real*.

Perhaps the merchant's job offer had been more than persuasive. Or maybe the temptation of the reward for his head had finally turned Ronin against him. Whatever, Jack was now fighting for his life . . .

He blocked the samurai's thrust for his heart and whipped the end of his staff round at Ronin's head. Jack had the advantage of the *bō*'s length, but Ronin proved the more skilful warrior. Dodging Jack's assault, he brought the hilt of his sword down upon Jack's fingers. Crying out in pain, Jack lost his grip on the *bō* before reeling from an elbow strike to the jaw.

Stunned, Jack was left defenceless as Ronin drove his blade straight through his side. He crumpled to his knees. Jack felt no pain, but an ominous patch of dark red instantly stained his ragged kimono.

'*He's bleeding! He's bleeding!*' the young wife squealed, in a mixture of horror and delight.

Jack, too shocked to fight back, clutched at his wound in a futile attempt to stem the flow.

'Behead him!' she screeched, her beautiful face contorted with murderous glee.

'Only *real* samurai deserve such a death,' replied Ronin.

Jack collapsed to the earth, letting out a last gutteral moan.

'Is he dead?' asked the merchant, peering over his wife's shoulder.

Ronin prodded the body with his toe and got no reaction. 'Yes,' he replied, flicking Jack's blood from his blade before resheathing it.

'Then what are we waiting for? Dinner's ready,' said his wife imperiously.

'Perhaps we should take care of the body first?' suggested Ronin as his employer followed his heartless wife.

'We can do that later,' tutted the merchant. 'Just get him off the path. The crows can pick at his remains.'

Ronin rolled Jack's lifeless body into the ditch. Then he strode after his new master.

18

ONRYŌ

Jack lay at the bottom of the ditch, no longer breathing, his eyes rolled back with only the whites showing. The point where Ronin's sword had penetrated him was an oozing red mass. Hana's concerned face appeared out of the encroaching darkness and she knelt beside Jack's lifeless form.

'Jack!' she gasped in shock, pressing her hand against his sodden wound. 'You're not dead . . . are you?'

The corpse's head lolled towards her, then grinned. 'For a moment I thought I was.'

Hana breathed a sigh of relief. 'You looked *really* dead.'

'I've had some practice,' replied Jack, sitting up and rubbing his jaw where Ronin had struck him. Hana took this as a joke, but Jack was actually referring to his *ninjutsu* training, which included feigning death as one of its hidden arts.

Hana, her fingers thick with Jack's 'blood', began to lick them appreciatively. 'Such a waste of red-bean *manjū*.'

Peeling his clothes away from the fake wound, Jack removed the remains of the steamed buns and checked Ronin's sword thrust had not pierced his flesh as well.

'That was some fight,' said Hana.

'It had to look convincing,' replied Jack, getting to his feet. 'But I didn't expect Ronin to attack with *such* ferocity. Now where's the rice flour he bought?'

Hana produced a small cloth bag and began to douse Jack's hair and face with it until he was deathly white.

'How do I look?' asked Jack.

'Like you're ready for baking!' smirked Hana.

Jack shook his head with dismay. 'I thought so. This is stupid. Who's going to believe I'm a ghost?'

Stifling her amusement, Hana turned serious. 'They will. Everyone fears an *onryō*.'

'Let's hope so,' said Jack as they made their way to the merchant's house. 'Otherwise we're *all* in serious trouble.'

Ronin's plan relied upon the superstitious beliefs of the merchant and his wife. An *onryō* was a vengeful ghost. And Ronin had explained that anybody who died unjustly or by violence could become an *onryō* if they weren't enshrined after their death. These angry spirits haunted the living and caused great misfortune. The only way to exorcise an *onryō* was to satisfy its reason for revenge and bestow upon its remains a proper burial.

Hana and Jack waited in the treeline until all the lights had been doused.

'Almost time to go,' whispered Hana, sprinkling Jack's hands with the last of the flour. 'Good luck!'

'I'll need more than luck,' he replied, echoing Hana's own words. He'd been crazy to let Ronin talk him into such a ludicrous plan. The man had been drunk at the time. But what excuse did Jack have – apart from sheer desperation?

A candle flickered three times from an upstairs window. It

was too late to pull out now. Ronin had given the signal.

In the pale light of the moon, they ran across the road and scaled the wall. As they passed through the garden, Jack caught sight of his own reflection in the pond and almost leapt out of his skin. His face was stark and flaking like old parchment. The bean paste had dried to a dark berry-red, all the more vivid against his flour-whitened kimono, which was hanging off him more ragged and ripped than ever.

For the first time, Jack felt a glimmer of hope.

This disguise might just work.

Hana urged him on. Climbing up to the balcony, Jack felt a breeze and the telltale drops of rain. Storm clouds were rolling in. They'd have to be quick. Once in position, he nodded to Hana.

With theatrical flamboyance, Hana flung open the *shoji* to the bedroom and Jack howled at the moon. Startled cries greeted him as the merchant and his wife sat bolt upright on their *futons*. Shock turned to terror when they set eyes upon the phantom of the *gaijin* samurai.

'*Return! Return! Return!*' rasped the ghostly Jack, letting his voice rise and fall like the wind.

The merchant was the first to recover. 'W-w-what do you want?'

Jack stretched out one limp hand, pointing to his wife's head. '*The pearl! The pearl! The pearl!*'

The wife scrabbled away from the evil spirit, her screams awaking the rest of the household. On cue, the door from the hallway burst open and Ronin appeared, sword in hand.

'But . . . I killed you!' he exclaimed, his face the picture of abject horror.

'*Vengeance! Vengeance! VENGEANCE!*'

At that moment, the sky flared with forked lightning. It couldn't have been planned better. Silhouetted against the storm, Jack took on a demonic appearance. An almighty thunderclap shook the house to its foundations and the heavens opened.

But the effect would be short-lived.

Jack felt the rice flour washing off his face and the red-bean paste running from his clothes. He began to panic as the ghostly illusion disintegrated before everyone's eyes. But the wife screamed –

'*His face is melting!*'

Seizing upon her delusion, Jack howled, '*So will yours! Return the pearl!*'

The lady wailed at the prospect of losing her beauty in such a hideous manner.

Jack decided he'd done enough. Before his disguise completely vanished in the rain, he signalled to Hana. She slammed the door shut and they both clambered on to the roof. A moment later, the *shoji* flew open again and Ronin charged out.

'The *onryō* . . . he's gone!' exclaimed Ronin, his voice horror-stricken. 'But it'll be back . . . they *always* come back!'

19

BAND OF THREE

The black pearl sat in Jack's hand, an old friend returned.

'The merchant's wife literally *begged* me to take it away,' explained Ronin with a roguish smile on his face. He sat down beside Jack in the middle of the storehouse and helped himself to some cold rice he'd bought for breakfast.

'I can't believe they fell for it,' said Jack, unable to take his eyes off Akiko's pearl for fear it was a dream.

'Did you see their faces!' Hana exclaimed, pulling an expression of extreme terror and imitating the wife's voice. '*He's melting!*'

Convulsed with laughter, Hana rolled around, clutching her stomach. Jack, however, felt a little guilty. But he reminded himself that no one had been hurt, no theft had occurred and the pearl was back in his possession. It had been an elaborate plan, but one that ensured they weren't pursued by *dōshin*. There was certainly more to Ronin than met the eye.

'Thank you, Ronin, I'm indebted to you,' he said, carefully pinning the precious gem to the inside of his kimono.

The samurai bowed his head in acknowledgement. Finishing his rice, he washed it down with a large gulp of *saké*, then looked out of the door at the lightening sky. 'The rain's easing. We should get going.'

'But won't the merchant suspect something if you don't return?' asked Jack.

'I told him to hire a priest for protection. Samurai don't fight spirits!' replied Ronin, rising to his feet. 'But, as my last duty, I agreed to return the pearl and bury your body.'

He snorted with amusement and picked up his bottle of *saké*. 'Ready?'

Nodding, Jack disposed of his old torn clothes beneath a rotting pile of straw. Dressed in his smart blue kimono, he felt more like his former self. A sense of optimism filled his heart and he was eager to go after the *rutter*.

'So, on to Kyoto!' said Ronin, raising his bottle in salute.

'*Kyoto?* Botan's headed for Nara,' said Jack.

'And your swords are in Kyoto.'

'But –'

'We agreed. A samurai is *nothing* without his swords.'

'But Botan's got everything else, including the *inro* and my father's diary.'

'What's *so* important about this diary?' enquired Ronin.

Careful with his answer, Jack explained, 'My father was murdered by ninja. The diary's the only remaining possession of his that I have.'

Ronin fixed Jack with a curiously intense stare, his usual harshness giving way to something approaching compassion.

'A sentimental motive, but I understand,' he said, laying a hand proudly on his swords. '*These* were my father's.' He uncorked his bottle and drank deeply. For a moment, Jack thought he wouldn't stop. 'But if it's the Botan I've heard of, he's a ruthless warrior and despises foreigners. You'll *need* your swords when you encounter him.'

Jack considered Ronin's advice. The samurai was probably right. Kyoto and Nara were equally dangerous, but he'd stand a better chance with his swords in his hands.

'Kyoto it is,' agreed Jack, taking up his staff and putting on Ronin's straw hat.

With no other belongings to pack, there was little reason for delay.

'See you around, thief!' said Ronin, barely glancing at Hana.

He was halfway through the door when Hana, a hopeful expression on her face, asked hesitantly, 'W-what about me? Can't I come too?'

Ronin gruffly shook his head. 'No.'

'I only –'

'I said NO!'

Her face fell, crushed by Ronin's outright rejection. Glancing at Hana, now crouched in the corner, forlorn and lost, Jack realized she not only wanted their company, she *needed* it.

Jack pulled Ronin to one side. 'Why can't she come?'

'The girl's a liability. She's a thief, dishonest and untrustworthy.'

'But Hana *did* help us,' argued Jack.

'And she's served her purpose. Besides, she's another mouth to feed and we don't have the money to spare.'

'You never know, her skills could come in useful for recovering my swords.'

Ronin looked far from convinced, but Jack had made a valid

point. 'All right,' he relented. 'But one false move and she meets the sharp end of my sword.'

Jack turned to Hana, but she'd already jumped to her feet and was by his side.

'I've always wanted to go to the capital city,' she beamed. 'Do you think we'll see the Emperor?'

Leaving Kizu, they kept to the backstreets but through an alley caught sight of the merchant's store. The building was now strewn with lucky charms, *ofuda* talismans and protective amulets from the local Shinto shrine. Inside, the merchant was desperately trying to placate his wife, showering her with new jewellery and kimono. But she was having none of it, questioning where each piece came from and to whom it had belonged *before* her – all the time wafting incense above her head.

Jack couldn't help but smile at their antics. Perhaps in future they'd be more respectful to strangers and the merchant more honest in his dealings.

Keeping their heads down, the band of three took the road north to Kyoto. The river was swollen from the night's storm, threatening to burst its banks. As they crossed, Jack noticed the pillared bridge creaking under the strain of the current and prayed it wasn't about to give way. He didn't fancy staying in Kizu another day.

As they made their way north, Hana chatted cheerfully away about nothing and everything. Ronin walked several paces ahead, preferring the company of his *saké* bottle. Jack, however, was happy to listen to her ramblings. It kept his mind off the prospect of arriving in Kyoto. He couldn't deny he was excited at returning to the place that had been his home for the past three years, but he feared what he'd find there.

They wound through the forest, following the main track, stopping briefly for a sparse lunch of cold rice. By late afternoon, they were the only travellers on the road. Hana, still as vocal as ever, enthused, 'This is like being part of a *kōshakushi*'s story. I once saw one of those storytellers giving a street performance in Kizu. He recited from the *Taiheiki* and *Heiki Monogatari* and told tales of legendary battles and brave samurai and —'

She stopped, cocking her head to listen to a strange noise. Jack heard it too — a kind of strangled crooning. They looked at one another, then up ahead to Ronin. To their utter astonishment, he'd begun singing to himself — if his tuneless wailing could be called singing. Throughout the day, Jack had noticed the samurai's manner gradually lightening the more he drank. Ronin had insisted on buying another two bottles for the journey, along with their food supplies. Having got through the first, he was apparently on to the second and was now weaving slightly as he walked.

'Is he *dancing*?' asked Hana incredulously.

Jack couldn't believe what he was seeing either, yet it appeared Ronin was performing a jig, kicking out his feet and waving his arms. Catching Hana's eye, Jack could no longer keep a straight face. They both started sniggering at the bizarre spectacle, Ronin oblivious to their amusement.

'What a merry yet strange band of travellers!'

A dark figure stepped out in front of them. He was broad as an ox, his hair tied back into a single plait and with a nose as wide and flared as a pig's. In one hand, he nonchalantly swung a large wooden club.

'A drunken samurai, a giggling girl and a *gaijin*!'

Ronin swayed where he stood, appearing a little surprised by the man's sudden appearance.

A rustle of bushes signalled the emergence of five more men. The first, also carrying a club, was short and squat like a tree stump. The one nearest Jack was bald with muscular arms and held an axe. Beside him was a younger man, armed with a staff. The fourth possessed a vicious barbed spear. The fifth, thin as a rake, crept up from behind. He snarled at Hana, revealing a large gap where a tooth had been knocked out, and raised a bloodstained knife.

As the bandits surrounded them, Hana edged closer to Jack.

'We're as good as dead,' she whispered.

20

DRUNKEN FIST

Without taking his eye off the bandits, Jack smiled reassuringly at Hana. 'Don't worry. We've got Ronin on our side.'

Hana stared at Jack as if he was crazy. 'But he's *drunk*!'

'Exactly,' replied Jack, his staff poised for the moment Ronin made his move.

'If you wish to pass, you must pay a toll,' declared the bandit leader.

Ronin hiccupped. 'How mushh?'

'*Everything* you've got.'

'Oh, good!' replied Ronin cheerfully. 'We've got nothing . . . that means we can pass.'

Waving Jack and Hana on, Ronin started walking. But the leader put a hand to Ronin's chest.

'I don't think so, samurai. We'll have that bottle for starters.'

'Thisss?' slurred Ronin, giving the bottle a shake. 'But it's empty.'

To prove his point, he drained the last of its contents into his mouth.

'I can see you've got another bottle! Hand it over –'

At that moment, Ronin pretended to choke and spat the

rice wine into the bandit's face. The man shrieked as the alcohol burnt his eyes. Ronin drunkenly lurched forward, headbutting him in the nose and breaking it. The leader staggered away, blood gushing down his face.

'*Get them!*' he yelled.

Immediately, the squat bandit attacked Ronin with his club. Swaying to one side, Ronin's arms whirled as if trying to catch his balance. He easily evaded the vicious swipe and in the process smashed the ceramic bottle over the bandit's head. The man was unconscious before he even hit the ground.

Jack leapt into action. Spinning his *bō*, he cracked the nearest bandit across the knuckles. The man grunted with pain and was forced to let go of his weapon. The axe cut the tip off his little toe as it dropped on to his foot. Hopping in agony, the bandit made an easy target as Jack whipped his staff round, caught the man's legs and flipped him over. A quick jab to the gut ensured he wouldn't be getting up any time soon.

Jack heard a scream from behind and saw Hana being snatched by the gap-toothed bandit.

'Duck!' he shouted, thrusting the end of the staff at Hana's head.

Hana obeyed and the *bō* struck her assailant in the chest. Wheezing from the blow, the bandit released her and threw his knife at Jack in retaliation. The blade headed straight for Jack's throat. Only split-second timing and his samurai training saved him. He instinctively deflected the knife with the *bō*'s shaft.

Furious, the bandit charged at Jack, who flicked the staff's tip up beneath the man's jaw. There was a nasty crunch and several more teeth flew out. Then Jack brought his staff whipping round and sent the toothless bandit hurtling into a tree, knocking him senseless.

He now turned to face the fourth robber armed with a staff.

Meanwhile, Ronin was battling with both the leader and the spear-wielding bandit. Hana watched open-mouthed as Ronin toppled, tumbled and turned between his assailants. But at no point could either of them land a strike on the drunken samurai.

The bandit with the spear tried to drive his weapon into the rolling Ronin, and promptly got the tip wedged into the earth. Springing to his feet, Ronin stomped on the shaft, snapping it in two. A drunken fist to the throat brought the fight to a swift end.

Disorientated from all his multiple twists and turns, Ronin's legs went from beneath him and he collapsed to the ground.

'Now I've got you!' snarled the furious leader, raising his club to smash the samurai to pieces.

Suddenly Ronin rebounded to his feet, threw out a leg and struck him in the face a second time. The bandit was stopped mid-swing and toppled like a felled tree.

'Never *ever* take my *saké*!' said Ronin. He peered down at the bandit's battered features. 'And I really didn't think you could get *any* uglier!'

The vanquished leader could only manage a feeble groan in response.

Ronin glanced over to where Jack was still locked in combat with the final bandit.

'Come on! We haven't got all night,' he complained impatiently.

He leant against a tree to watch the fight, but didn't have

long to wait before Jack disarmed his opponent. One glance at his fallen comrades was enough to convince the bandit to run while he still had the chance.

'Leave them to lick their wounds,' said Ronin, tottering off down the road.

Jack and Hana followed close behind, Hana speechless for the first time since they'd started walking that day.

Eventually they stopped by a river and found a suitable and safe spot upstream to camp for the night. Jack built a fire and they gathered by its warmth, while tucking into chestnut-flavoured *manjū* and sharing a straw container of rice.

'You were amazing!' said Hana, admiring Ronin with spell-bound eyes.

'What?' he grunted, through a mouthful of *manjū*.

Hana rolled around on the ground, imitating his drunken fighting. She tried to spring to her feet, but only got halfway before landing heavily on her rear. Jack burst out laughing.

Ronin tutted in irritation. 'That's *not* how you do it! Drunken Fist is a *highly* skilful martial art.'

'Oh, it can't be that hard. You just need to get drunk,' she said, picking up Ronin's last bottle of *saké*.

'Give that here!' he growled, snatching the rice wine from her grasp. 'You don't need *saké* for Drunken Fist. You need training.'

'Why don't you teach us then?' suggested Hana.

'I'm no sensei.'

'Well, I'm no student,' retorted Hana. 'Never been taught in my life. That will make you the best teacher I've ever had.'

Ronin didn't answer, just took another slug of rice wine.

'So where did you learn Drunken Fist?' asked Jack, having

suspected Ronin's moves were part of a formal fighting style.

'From a Shaolin priest, a warrior monk on a pilgrimage from China. His name was Han Zhongli.' Ronin smiled at the memory. 'I watched him defeat twenty men single-handedly. After that, I asked to become his student.' He stared into the fire, lost in his reverie.

'And?' prompted Hana.

Ronin got to his feet, bottle in hand.

'Drunken Fist relies on deception,' he explained, staggering slightly. 'You mimic a drunkard with his cups.' He held one hand out as if grasping a cup. 'You move around, soft but strong.'

Ronin swayed, rocking and rolling on the balls of his feet.

'When I reach for another drink, it's actually a strike.' He flung out his hand, stopping just short of Hana's nose. 'Or a grab technique.' He clamped down upon Hana's shoulder and she squealed as his fingers bit in. 'You aim for pressure points, or else take the opponent's balance.'

Despite his initial reluctance, Ronin was clearly warming to his role as sensei. Hana watched intently, while Jack made mental notes of everything Ronin was imparting.

'The principle tactic is to feign defence while trying to attack. To appear to aim in one direction, while moving in another.'

Staggering to his right, Ronin executed a devastating side-kick with his opposite leg.

'I use all these movements to confuse my opponent, so I always look off-balance.' Ronin tottered on one foot. 'But I always stay in control, maintaining my centre of balance –'

Suddenly Ronin flailed his arms and fell to the ground,

bringing the lesson to an abrupt end. The ungainly finish caused Hana to burst into a fit of giggles. Jack knew Ronin wouldn't take kindly to this and, glaring at Hana, hurried over to help the drunken samurai to his feet.

'You thought I fell,' challenged Ronin as Jack came near.

In the blink of an eye, Ronin twisted on his back, spiralling upwards. His foot would have caught Jack in the jaw, if Jack hadn't dodged the surprise attack. But a second later, Jack was struck in the chest with a palm strike and he was sent flying. He landed on top of Hana, both of them stunned by the unexpected assault.

'*That* is Drunken Fist,' proclaimed Ronin proudly. 'Just when your opponent thinks you're most vulnerable . . . you strike!'

21

UMESHU

'Why not use the bridge?' asked Hana as they resumed their journey the next day.

'You won't learn anything from a bridge,' replied Ronin, leaping from the bank and on to a rock poking out of the water.

He landed on one foot, arms outstretched, the *saké* bottle in one hand, his swords in the other. Jack and Hana watched as he swayed slightly above the rippling waters.

'Balance can make or break a martial artist.'

He jumped to the next stepping stone, smaller than the first and more slippery. But he had no problem keeping his footing. Just as he'd fought in a drunken lopsided manner, so Ronin leapt from rock to rock, flexing like a reed to counterbalance himself, until he reached the opposite bank.

He raised his bottle in a toast to them and took a swig.

Hana looked at Jack. 'If *he* can cross it, I definitely can.'

Taking a running leap, she reached the first stone.

'Easy!' she cried, tottering slightly on her tiny island.

Drawing in a deep breath, she readied herself for the next jump. As she landed, her foot slipped and she lost her balance.

Arms cartwheeling in the air, Hana looked like a frenzied sparrow as she tried to right herself. But it was no use. She toppled head first into the river.

Ronin guffawed loudly at Hana's misfortune as she came up spluttering and gasping.

'*I can't swim! I can't swim!*' she yelled, splashing frantically in the water.

Jack kicked off his sandals and was about to jump in after her, when Ronin said, 'STAND UP! It's not deep.'

Finding her feet, Hana stopped panicking and looked a little sheepish. The water only came up to her waist and she waded the rest of the way.

Ronin turned to Jack. 'Your turn, samurai boy!'

Jack, who'd experienced many such tests during his training at the *Niten Ichi Ryū*, wasn't troubled by the crossing. He even had the advantage of his *bō* to maintain balance. Tucking his sandals into his *obi*, he jumped effortlessly from stone to stone, his bare feet gripping their slimy surface just as they had the yardarm of the *Alexandria* when he'd been a rigging monkey.

'Impressive,' Ronin grunted as Jack reached the last of the stepping stones. 'Here, catch this.'

Ronin tossed his bottle at Jack. With little time to react, Jack let go of his staff and clutched at the flying bottle. It hit him squarely in the chest.

'Don't drop it!'

Jack managed to keep hold but, with his balance gone, he splash-landed in the river. Floating there, bedraggled and with the bottle in his lap, Jack now became the focus of Ronin's mirth, Hana joining in the laughter too.

Ronin offered his hand. Appreciating the samurai's gesture,

Jack reached up to be helped out of the chilly mountain waters.

'The *saké*!' said Ronin, ignoring Jack's outstretched arm.

He should have known. He passed the samurai back his precious bottle.

'You can't let a simple distraction like that take your balance,' observed Ronin as Jack dragged himself out of the river.

Despite all his training both as a samurai and a ninja, Jack realized there would always be more to learn. He wouldn't be caught out like that again.

Ronin passed a cursory eye over the two of them, standing beside him like drowned rats. 'Don't worry, you'll dry off by the time we reach Kyoto!'

They welcomed the warmth of the mid-afternoon sun as they left the forested mountain slopes of Yamashiro Province and entered the plains of Kyoto Prefecture. Following the main road, they passed by an immense field lined with row upon row of small bush-like trees, none much taller than Jack himself.

'We've reached Aodani!' said Ronin in delight. 'This place is famous for its flowering plum-tree groves. There are some ten thousand trees here. In spring, the blossom must be truly magnificent.'

'I didn't take you for an admirer of blossom-viewing,' said Jack, looking archly at the effusive samurai.

'I love *hanami*!' interjected Hana. 'All the flowers are so pretty . . .' A mischievous smile formed on her lips. 'And no one seems to notice if one or two things go missing.'

Ronin laughed. 'I much prefer harvest when the plum fruits

are used to make *umeshu*. Aodani plum wine is reputedly the best in the whole of Japan!'

He quickened his pace when a village came into view. 'Let's see if it's true.'

Jack and Hana followed in his wake. The village was small but well-to-do. Several thatched houses with verandas lined the road. There was a store selling provisions and a tea house. Two men sat outside near a palanquin, their eyes closed. They were evidently recovering their strength from bearing their master, a large round ball of a man, who was inside enjoying a pot of *sencha* and tucking into several sweet red-bean *wagashi*.

'We're in luck!' announced Ronin, taking a seat. 'They have a fresh barrel.'

'We should really keep going,' said Jack, eyeing the other customers warily from beneath his hat.

'Just one drink,' insisted Ronin. 'Then we'll go.'

Reluctantly, Jack agreed. What harm could it do? And moving on now might arouse more suspicion than staying.

The tea-house owner served Ronin a cup of honey-golden liquid. Breathing in its fragrant aroma, Ronin knocked back the drink in one. He smacked his lips appreciatively. 'Mmm, sweet *and* smooth. Certainly the finest I've ever tasted.'

The tea-house owner bowed at the compliment, then poured him another.

'*But you said just one!*' whispered Jack.

Ignoring him, Ronin asked the owner, 'Do you have any *umeboshi*?'

The man nodded and returned a moment later with some wrinkled red fruit in a bowl.

'You can leave the bottle,' said Ronin as the owner went to serve his other customers.

'Ronin, you promised –'

'Try this!' said Ronin, waving away Jack's protests and passing him one of the small dried fruits. 'It's a pickled plum.'

Hana took one too. Sighing in frustration, Jack relented and bit into his. He immediately gagged. The *umeboshi*'s sour salty taste was revolting.

'Eat up!' said Ronin, greatly amused by the disgusted look on Jack's face. 'They're good for combating tiredness in battle.'

Hana chewed hers enthusiastically. 'And if you have one every morning it'll ward off misfortune.'

'I'm not surprised,' said Jack, grimacing. 'Nothing could be worse than one of these!'

Ronin helped himself to more plum wine, steadily making his way through the bottle, while Jack became increasingly impatient to leave.

'We *need* to go,' insisted Jack. 'You said Kyoto's still some way off. We won't get there until after dark at this rate.'

'My lassst one,' promised Ronin, slurring slightly from the effects of the alcohol.

As one of the customers stood up to leave, Ronin leant forward and whispered in Jack's ear. 'Did you say your *inro* had a *sakura* tree engraving on it?'

Jack nodded. 'And a lion's head *netsuke*.'

'Well then, that man's got your case.'

22

INRO

Paying the tea-house owner, the three of them hurried outside in pursuit of the man. Dressed in a fine silk kimono of deep green, but bearing no swords, he looked to be a successful merchant on his way to Kyoto.

Jack only caught a glimpse of the *inro* as the man stepped into his palanquin. Yet the carrying case did appear to be remarkably similar. The *inro* that *daimyo* Takatomi had given him, as a gift for foiling an assassination attempt by the ninja Dragon Eye, was unique – crafted from thickly lacquered wood, it had been decorated in gold and silver leaf, with a *sakura* tree engraved upon its surface, its blossom picked out in ivory; while the lion's head *netsuke* was expertly carved out of the same material.

'You could be right,' said Jack as the two porters lifted the enclosed seat from the ground and set off in the direction of Kizu.

'Then let's go after him!' said Hana.

'It's only a box,' replied Jack, reluctant to retrace his steps yet again.

'But what if the man's involved?' said Ronin. 'Or knows who attacked you?'

Ronin had a point. They *had* to follow. The *inro* could very well lead them to the *rutter*.

The palanquin had already turned the corner and was fast disappearing among the trees. Without a moment to lose, they raced after their quarry, Jack and Hana in front with the inebriated Ronin trailing behind. The two porters were clearly very fit as it took the three of them a while to catch up with the palanquin – only to find it standing empty in a small clearing, the porters taking a rest next to a stream.

'Where's the merchant?' whispered Hana as the three of them hid behind a clump of trees.

'I'll stay here . . . while you look for him,' said Ronin, sipping from his *saké* bottle and recovering his breath.

Circling the clearing, Jack and Hana discovered the merchant squatting in the undergrowth and waved Ronin over. The merchant cried out in surprise as they surrounded him.

'Show us your *inro*,' demanded Ronin.

Staring aghast at his three assailants, the merchant exclaimed, 'Can't a man answer the call of nature without being robbed?'

Hana could hardly suppress her giggles at finding the man in such a compromising position.

'We're not here to rob you,' Jack explained quickly. 'We just . . . want to look at the *inro*.'

With trembling hands, the merchant passed Jack the carrying case. Although the *netsuke* was a beautifully carved lion's head, the *inro* was decorated with a cedar, not a *sakura* tree.

'My apologies, this isn't mine,' said Jack, returning it guiltily.

'Of course it's not,' fumed the merchant. 'I bought this only yesterday in Kyoto!'

114

The three of them backed awkwardly away, leaving the merchant to finish his business. Once on the road, Jack felt his frustration explode.

'I can't believe you led us on that wild goose chase!'

'But you said the *inro* looked like yours,' replied Ronin tetchily.

'I didn't get a clear view and now we're halfway back to Kizu again!'

Furious, Jack kicked a branch from his path and pointed accusingly at Ronin.

'If *you* hadn't drunk so much plum wine, we wouldn't have wasted an entire afternoon and got sidetracked by that merchant. It's all your fault!'

'Don't point your finger at *me*,' snarled Ronin, swaying on his feet as he took a swig of *saké*. 'Remember, there's always *three* pointing back at you! I wasn't the one who was robbed in the first place.'

'What's your problem?' snapped Jack. 'Why are you always drinking?'

'In order to suffer fools like you!' shot back Ronin.

'Stop! Stop!' exclaimed Hana, stepping between them. 'This isn't helping us get to Kyoto.'

Jack and Ronin glared at each other, neither willing to back down.

'It's no one's fault here. The only people to blame are those who attacked Jack.'

Recognizing the sense in Hana's words, Jack now felt deeply ashamed of his outburst and bowed his head in remorse.

'I'm sorry, Ronin. I should be thankful for all the help you've given me. It's just that I seem to be getting nowhere.

We may have the pearl, but what chance do I have of ever recovering my other possessions? It's hopeless.'

Ronin took another swig from his bottle and smiled encouragingly at Jack.

'It's never hopeless,' he said, gripping Jack's shoulder. 'Tomorrow's a new day and I promise we'll find your swords.'

23

KYOTO

Jack's breath caught in his throat at the first sighting of the Heart of Japan. The home of the Emperor, of Nijo Castle, of the *Niten Ichi Ryū*, and of many experiences . . . good and bad.

He recalled how awestruck he'd been upon his first arrival at the capital city three years before and was no less impressed by its size and scale this time. Approaching from the southern plain, Kyoto lay at the heart of an immense horseshoe of forested mountains. To the north-east, Jack could see Mount Hiei rising up towards the clouds. Perched upon its slopes was the ruined temple complex of Enryakuji, destroyed forty years ago by the samurai General Nobunaga. But Jack knew that a lantern, the 'Eternal Light', continued to burn in a crumbling shrine, for he had trained in one of its courtyards under the guidance of his blind *bōjutsu* master, Sensei Kano. And, like that flame, his memories now reignited.

He remembered how he and Akiko had sat on that very mountain, her head resting upon his shoulder as they watched the first sunrise of the New Year.

Drawing closer to the city's boundary, Jack spotted the towering pagoda of Kiyomizudera, its spire poking above the tree canopy near where the Sound of Feathers waterfall thundered down the mountainside. That had been where he and Yamato had fought over the Jade Sword and subsequently forged the beginnings of a friendship. A wave of sadness always consumed him when he thought of Yamato, his loyal and brave friend who was now dead, having sacrificed his life to save Akiko and Jack from the ruthless ninja Dragon Eye.

Crossing a wide wooden bridge into the city, Ronin, now sober, guided them along the grassy treelined banks of the Kizugawa River. Hearing laughter and seeing a family enjoying a picnic together beneath the *sakura* trees, Jack was reminded of Akiko's *hanami* party, the annual flower-viewing celebration in spring.

As they wound through the streets of Kyoto, passing the countless Shinto shrines and Buddhist temples, private villas and miniature gardens, busy shops and crowded inns, Jack recognized more and more places from his past. The golden maple leaves of the Eikando Temple caught his eye; the street vendor selling *okonomiyaki*, the fried pancakes that his friend Saburo had relished; the store displaying papier-mâché masks like the ones they'd all worn for the Gion Matsuri Festival. And down that alley Jack knew was concealed the mysterious Ryoanji, the Temple of the Peaceful Dragon, where a monk with knife-like hands had secretly taught Akiko the Art of the Ninja.

So many memories, so many experiences, but they were just like ghosts now. And the city for all its familiarity felt hostile to Jack.

The throng of the central market made him nervous. Although he could hide in a crowd, there were more people

– more eyes – that might notice him. He kept his head bowed, ensuring Ronin's wide-brimmed hat covered his face.

Ronin forged a path through the streets, congested with shoppers, browsers, samurai and traders. They cut down a side alley before emerging into a small square, quieter and more placid than the others.

'Stay here,' ordered Ronin, stopping beside a tea house on the corner. 'I'll make some enquiries as to Araki's whereabouts.'

He ordered a pot of *sencha* for Jack and Hana, paid the serving girl and headed off down the street in search of the samurai who now had Jack's swords.

'How long do you think he'll be?' asked Hana, pouring the tea for Jack.

'Not long, I hope.'

Jack felt terribly exposed having come to Kyoto. He now wished he hadn't taken the risk. It was like entering a lion's den. He had to hope that most of Kyoto's citizens were too busy with their own daily lives to notice a traveller in a nondescript blue kimono and straw hat.

Hana gazed around in awe. 'I never imagined Kyoto to be like this!'

As Jack sipped his tea, she gave him a running description of everything she saw – the white-faced geisha girl, the strutting samurai, the lion-dog statue outside the local temple, the hawker selling wooden spinning tops.

After a while, the proprietor of the tea house came over. 'More *sencha*?'

Hana looked to Jack, who shook his head.

'No, thank you,' she replied.

'You're not from these parts, are you?' observed the man.

Hana smiled sweetly. 'We're on a pilgrimage with our master,' she said, repeating their pre-planned answer.

'Of course,' said the proprietor, glancing with interest at Jack but making no attempt to enquire further. 'A friendly word of warning, travellers don't go unnoticed in this city. And *some* are not so welcome as they once were.'

Jack daren't look up.

'You two appear to be of *particular* interest.'

'What do you mean?' asked Hana.

'To the *metsuke* on the other side of the street.'

Hana gave him a blank stare. The proprietor leant in close, as if to clear their table.

'A watcher. One of the Shogun's spies.'

24

METSUKE

'What does the *metsuke* look like?' Jack asked Hana, once the proprietor left to attend to his other customers.

Hana was sharp-witted enough as a thief not to look directly at their observer. Instead she pretended to admire her surroundings, while casting a casual glance across the street. At first she didn't see anyone. Then she noticed a figure lingering outside the entrance to the temple. He appeared to have little interest in praying. Nor was he in any rush to go elsewhere.

'Young,' replied Hana. 'Thin as a chopstick, with eyes that look a little too close together. He's wearing a black kimono and a pair of samurai swords. The odd thing is he can't be much older than you.'

Jack felt a chill run through his body. Hana's description was worryingly familiar.

'Where is he now?' asked Jack.

'Over by the lion-dog statue.'

Jack warily peeked from beneath the brim of his hat. A steady flow of traffic crossed the square, but no one wore a black kimono. '*Where?*'

'In front of the —' Hana looked around. 'He's gone!'

'We should leave too,' said Jack, reaching for his staff.

'Why? It's got to be a good thing. He obviously doesn't think we're a threat.'

'Perhaps,' replied Jack, thinking they should head towards Nijo Castle. 'But it could also mean trouble.'

'But we can't leave before Ronin gets back. How will he know where to find us?'

Jack pondered this a moment. They hadn't arranged an alternative meeting point. Nor did they know in which direction the *metsuke* had gone. They could run straight into him. And if Jack's hunch was right they'd need the protection of Ronin's swords.

'All right, we'll stay a little longer.'

The passing minutes were excruciating. Even though it wasn't a particularly warm day, Jack began to perspire. He felt as if everyone was watching him. They *all* knew he was a *gaijin*. They could tell by his manner, *smell* his foreignness.

Jack thought about leaving a message with the proprietor, but there was no guarantee they could trust him.

'Let's move to the temple,' said Jack, the uneasy feeling growing in the pit of his stomach. 'We can keep an eye on the tea house from there.'

'Wait!' said Hana, pointing down the road. 'I see Ronin.'

But Jack didn't look round. His eyes were fixed on the four figures clad in black kimono, headed directly for them from the opposite direction. Leading the pack, a red sun *kamon* emblazoned on his left lapel, was the person he'd feared most to encounter in Kyoto.

Kazuki.

The last time Jack had seen his old school rival was on the Tenno-ji battlefield, Akiko having shot an arrow through his sword hand. But this traitor – the student responsible for the downfall of the *Niten Ichi Ryū* – appeared to have recovered from his injuries, looking stronger than ever. With a shaved head, fierce dark eyes and a grimace of hate that marred an otherwise handsome face, he cut a formidable figure as he strode across the square towards them.

He was accompanied by the surviving members of his Scorpion Gang. Nobu, even larger than Jack remembered, was barrelling people out of the way like an irate sumo wrestler; Goro, muscular and broad, a born warrior, marched behind, his hand clamped upon the hilt of his sword; and by Kazuki's side was Hiroto, the person Jack had suspected to be the *metsuke*.

Jack felt his chest tighten at the sight of them. The Scorpion Gang had been the bane of his life at the *Niten Ichi Ryū*. Even as individuals they'd bullied him from the moment of his arrival. But the formation of the Scorpion Gang had given a focus for their persecution of him. It had been organized under the leadership of Kazuki, in honour of *daimyo* Kamakura's campaign to rid Japan of foreigners. All members were tattooed with the emblem of a black scorpion and swore an oath of allegiance – 'Death to all *gaijin*!'

Jack tightened his grip upon his improvised staff. Though he stood little chance against the entire gang, he wouldn't give in without a fight.

25

By Order of the Shogun

'We have to get you out of here!' cried Hana, grabbing his arm.

'Too late,' he replied, their opportunity to run long gone.

The Scorpion Gang was converging on them fast. As they crossed the square, a man suddenly stumbled into their path. His arms reeling, the drunkard knocked into the hawker, scattering his wooden spinning tops everywhere and halting the gang in their tracks. The resulting chaos brought the entire square to a standstill. Barely keeping his feet, Ronin then lurched into Kazuki and grabbed hold in order to steady himself. Kazuki furiously shook him off, sending his bottle of *saké* sloshing into Nobu's face. Goro and Hiroto rushed to disentangle their leader from the inebriated samurai's embrace, but kept falling over the spinning tops.

'Sooo sssssorry,' slurred Ronin, more rice wine flying as he reeled away into the crowd.

All of a sudden the proprietor was by their side. 'This way,' he whispered, leading them inside the tea house.

With no choice but to trust the man, Jack and Hana followed him through the kitchen and into the back alley.

'Please tell the *ronin*, we'll meet him south of Nijo Castle,' instructed Jack hurriedly. 'And thank you for your help.'

'A fellow Christian cannot see another lamb suffer,' whispered the proprietor.

Jack was taken aback by the man's confession. Not only were foreigners being persecuted in the Shogun's new Japan, but Japanese Christians too, many being sought out and burnt at the stake for their beliefs. This man had taken a great risk in aiding them.

Checking no one was watching, the proprietor made the sign of the cross. 'May God be with you.'

'And you too,' replied Jack.

'Come on!' urged Hana.

Criss-crossing their way through Kyoto, Jack led Hana towards the castle, its tall majestic keep visible above the city's rooftops. Deep down, Jack harboured hopes he'd find *daimyo* Takatomi and his daughter Emi still residing there and be able to seek refuge. But as they approached its outer fortifications, Jack realized what a grave mistake he'd made.

Guarding the main gate and patrolling the high walls along the moat were the castle's sentries – none of whom bore *daimyo* Takatomi's *kamon* of a white crane. All were emblazoned with the red sun crest of Kazuki's father, Oda Satoshi. For his family's service in the war, the Shogun had evidently rewarded him with the governance and prestige of Kyoto Province.

Jack cursed his error of judgement. Nijo Castle had seemed the easiest and safest place to meet, but this was also where Kazuki would return.

'We'd best keep moving,' said Jack to Hana, explaining their predicament.

With no real destination in mind, he kept his head down and allowed his instincts to guide them. Rounding the corner, they made their way along a wide boulevard and were crossing to the opposite side of the street when Jack stopped.

'Where now?' asked Hana.

Jack looked up to get his bearings and felt his knees almost give way at the sight before him. An entranceway of dark cypress wood and white earthen walls greeted him. Carved above the gate was a large wooden crest of a phoenix, its flaming wings broken but defiant.

'*We're here*,' breathed Jack, emotion choking him and his eyes welling with tears.

Without thinking, he'd led them straight to the *Niten Ichi Ryū*.

'Are you all right?' asked Hana.

Jack swallowed and nodded mutely. With hesitant steps, he approached the outer gate. The wood was battered and weatherworn and in places splintered. His fingers traced a set of *kanji* characters carved into a large wooden board hammered across the entrance:

将軍の命令により閉鎖

'What does it say?' asked Hana in a hushed tone.

'Ummm . . .' Jack racked his brains, trying to remember all the *kanji* Akiko had taught him. 'Closed. By order of the Shogun.'

He pressed an eye to one of the cracks. On the other side lay his school, just as he remembered it, with the grey pebbled courtyard that was the hub of the *Niten Ichi Ryū*, and the awe-inspiring *Butokuden*, the celebrated training hall for *kenjutsu* and *taijutsu*. To his right, up a flight of stone steps, he could make out Sensei Yamada's *Butsuden*, the Buddha Hall where he'd taken Zen meditation classes and inside which hung an immense temple bell, the size of a mountain boulder.

Behind the Buddha Hall, Jack could just make out the pale russet tiles that formed the roof of the *Chō-no-ma*, the Hall of Butterflies, so named for the exquisite panels of painted butterflies and *sakura* trees that lined its lush interior. On the far side was Masamoto's residence and personal *dojo*, the *Hō-oh-no-ma*, where the priviledged few were taught the secret art of the Two Heavens. Next to it was the Southern Zen Garden and over to his left the *Shishi-no-ma*, the Hall of Lions where the young samurai slept . . .

Jack blinked in amazement. It was all there, just waiting for his return.

But then he began to see the truth. In his excitement, his mind had been playing tricks on him. The courtyard was unraked and strewn with debris, leaves littering all four corners. The garden was overgrown, filled with weeds, a standing stone toppled on its side. The doors to the Buddha Hall were hanging off their hinges. Beside the *Butokuden*, like an unfinished grave, lay the charred foundations of the Hall of the Hawk – the first building Kazuki had set fire to. And beyond that, the Hall of Lions, only one wall left standing, was no more than a crumbling burnt-out wreck.

There was no movement. No students. No sensei. No life.

Surely the place hasn't been entirely *abandoned*, prayed Jack.

'The proprietor said the south side of the castle. This is east!' pointed out a rather breathless and irate Ronin.

127

Jack spun round, both surprised and relieved. 'You weren't arrested . . .'

'I merely pretended to be drunk. And *that* isn't a crime . . . yet.' The samurai stared at him with eyes that were stone-cold sober and Jack knew his earlier intoxication had all been an act. Ronin looked back over his shoulder. 'We should go. That troublesome troop of young samurai are headed this way.'

The three of them ducked down the first side street they came to, and Ronin led them in silence across the city, only slowing when they reached a narrow canal in a quiet residential district. They followed it north, walking at a leisurely pace so as not to arouse suspicion.

'Now, who were they?' demanded Ronin.

'The leader's Kazuki,' replied Jack, the name leaving a bad taste in his mouth. 'An old school rival. A traitor.'

'He's *very* dangerous. I saw it in his eyes. What about the rest?'

'They're all part of his Scorpion Gang. Their sole purpose is to hunt down *gaijin* like me and kill them.'

'The skinny one's a *metsuke*,' added Hana helpfully.

'That explains it,' said Ronin. 'They suspected you were a foreigner but, as I staggered off, they were arguing over whether it was actually *you* or not.'

'We must leave Kyoto now,' said Jack, feeling the city closing in on him like a noose. 'If Kazuki thinks I'm here, he'll tear the place apart looking for me.'

'This is a big city,' reassured Ronin. 'And I have good news – we won't need to stay much longer. I've found Matagoro Araki.'

'Where?'

'We're headed there right now,' replied Ronin. 'In keeping with what you seek from him, he's at the renowned sword school – the *Yagyu Ryū*.'

26

YAGYU RYŪ

Jack felt as if he was jumping from one fire into another. He had a history with the *Yagyu Ryū* and the last place in Kyoto he wanted to go was the samurai school founded by the Shogun himself. Especially one he'd so publicly disgraced two years before by defeating their students in a *Taryu-Jiai*, an inter-school martial arts contest.

'Araki's the eldest son of the Matagoro clan. He's revered and feared in equal measure,' explained Ronin, oblivious to Jack's alarm. 'But, from what I can gather, he values his integrity and is essentially honourable. I'm confident we can persuade him to return your swords.'

'That might be more difficult than you imagine,' interrupted Jack. He retold the events that led up to the *Taryu-Jiai* and of his part in the *Niten Ichi Ryū*'s controversial victory over their rival school.

Ronin grunted with amusement. 'You're right, the *Yagyu Ryū* will *never* forgive you for that! But it's a bit late to turn back now,' he said, approaching a large wooden gate set into a walled enclosure. 'We're here.'

'But what's to stop Araki turning me over to the Shogun?'

'Nothing. Just keep your hat on, your head bowed and let me do the talking.'

Ronin reached for a rope attached to a bronze bell hanging above the door and pulled. 'Hana, stay here. Keep an eye out for the Scorpion Gang. If you see anything suspicious, ring the bell three times and run. We'll meet you back at the *Niten Ichi Ryū*.'

Nodding obediently, Hana hid from view in a nearby alley.

As the bell's chime faded away, the sound of shuffling feet could be heard on the other side of the door. A slat opened and two brown-flecked eyes peered out. 'Yes?'

Ronin bowed. 'We have come to seek an audience with Matagoro Araki.'

'Does he know you?'

'No, but he may have heard of my father, Obata Torayasu.'

'Wait!' The slat snapped shut.

Several long moments passed and Jack began to worry that word of his arrival in Kyoto had already spread, that the *Yagyu Ryū* were preparing their reprisal and about to greet him, swords drawn.

Then the shuffling feet returned, followed by a click of the latch, and the gate swung open. A wily old man impatiently beckoned them inside.

'Leave your swords,' he rasped, pointing to a rack in the entrance hall.

Ronin glared at the man. 'This is a sword school, isn't it? Surely you don't expect me to walk around without mine.'

The old man looked Ronin up and down, and clearly decided the argument wasn't worth the hassle. 'Please yourself. It was for your own safety. Those carrying weapons can be challenged to a duel at any time by anyone. No refusal allowed. School rules.'

Ronin didn't even blink at this veiled threat. The old man, glowering at the samurai's brazenness, ushered them along a corridor, not even bothering to ask Jack to remove his hat. Through a latticed window, Jack glimpsed lines of young samurai in a courtyard, training with their *bokken*. As their wooden swords rose and fell in unison, cries of *kiai* echoing off the walls, he felt a wave of nostalgia for the glory days of the *Niten Ichi Ryū*.

The old man led them into a reception room, carpeted with fawn-coloured *tatami* mats and a polished cedar dais at one end. Hanging from a wall was a calligraphy scroll, each *kanji* brushstroke looking like the slash of a blade.

'Wait here,' instructed the old man, closing the door behind him.

Left alone, Jack began to raise his head. 'Do y–'

'*Head down and be quiet!*' whispered Ronin. '*They'll be watching us.*'

Ronin respectfully gestured for Jack to kneel before the dais, then joined him by his side. They waited together in silence.

After a while, a *shoji* in the far wall slid open and a man entered. Jack risked a quick peek. Young, fit and confident to the point of arrogance, the samurai knelt down on the dais, flicking the folds of his *hakama* to one side in sharp precise movements. The top of his head was shaved and his hair tied into a tight topknot as befitted a samurai of his status. He wore a crisp green and black kimono with specks of iridescent purple like a peacock's tail feather. His face was handsome yet severe, his dark eyebrows being too dominant and the corners of his mouth permanently downturned.

Araki glanced at Ronin, then eyed the hat-wearing Jack with suspicion.

'Welcome to the *Yagyu Ryū* – the New Shadow School – and home to the official swordmasters of the Shogun.'

'We appreciate you taking the time to see us,' said Ronin, bowing his head. Jack followed suit.

Araki returned the greeting, his eyes never leaving them.

'I was sorry to learn of your father's fate,' replied Araki, without any hint of true remorse. 'I'd heard *you* had died too.'

The steely expression on Ronin's face barely flickered. For a moment, Jack wondered whether Obata Torayasu *was* his father or merely a ruse to get an audience with Araki.

'Don't believe every rumour you hear,' replied Ronin.

Araki and Ronin held one another's gaze, as if a silent battle of wills was taking place. The tension in the room grew and Jack realized one false move on either his or Ronin's part could result in their downfall.

'Have you travelled far?' said Araki, finally breaking the silence.

Ronin nodded. 'Your reputation has spread the length and breadth of Japan.'

Araki smiled at this news. 'So you're here for a . . . duel?'

'Much as I'd be honoured by such a privilege, I'm here on behalf of my master,' he explained, inclining his head in deference to Jack.

'Your *master*?' queried Araki, somewhat surprised at Jack's status considering his appearance. 'Can't he speak for himself?'

'I'm afraid not. Allow me to explain. An unfortunate incident resulted in his swords being stolen.'

Araki raised an eyebrow, but said nothing.

'In respect of this, he's taken a vow of silence and keeps his head bowed in order to separate himself from the world, until the day his swords are back in his possession. As you'll appreciate, for a samurai they're his soul.'

Araki pursed his lips and nodded in approval of such a symbolic sacrifice.

'And how may I be of service?'

'We've been led to believe you have his swords.'

Araki's expression grew thunderous. 'Are you implying *I* stole them?'

'Of course not!' replied Ronin, his tone conciliatory. 'They've come into your possession by virtue of your esteemed duelling skills.'

The flattery went some way to pacifying Araki's indignation. 'I've acquired many *trophies* in my time,' he bragged. 'But who's to say any belong to your master?'

'My master's swords are unique. They're a family heirloom. Black *saya*s inlaid with mother-of-pearl, unusual dark-red woven handles and upon the blade is inscribed the name of its swordmaker, *Shizu*.'

An undeniable flicker of recognition passed across Araki's face.

'Do you recall them?' pressed Ronin.

'Perhaps,' he replied carefully. 'Your description sounds familiar.'

'Then we humbly request their return to the rightful owner.'

'That won't be possible.'

Jack, who'd been mutely following the progress of the conversation, felt his heart sink at the news. But it was now that Ronin made his play.

'I'm sure you don't wish it to be known that you use *stolen* swords?'

Araki laughed without humour. 'Spoken like a true samurai. A fine attack upon my sense of honour.' He paused, evaluating the threat posed by Ronin and his enigmatic master. 'You've judged me well. But you must appreciate that I can't be known for giving out *daishō* to every samurai who's been careless enough to lose theirs.'

'They were *stolen*,' repeated Ronin, his tone firm and even. 'We can prove they're my master's. Just examine the tang of the blade, there's –'

'They *may* very well have belonged to your master,' Araki interrupted, raising his hand to Ronin. 'Your description is precise and your word as Obata's son is more than enough. But I won those swords fair and square in a duel. By all rights, they belong to me now.'

'That doesn't change the fact they were taken unlawfully by your opponent.'

Once again Araki and Ronin fell into a staring match, waiting to see who would break first.

'I'll return them,' declared Araki, much to Jack's astonishment.

Ronin remained deadpan, aware the samurai had yet to finish.

'On one condition. That your master defeats me in a duel.'

Jack's elation was instantly quashed, replaced with a cold dread.

'Surely no one need die over these swords,' countered Ronin.

'First blood will be enough,' Araki conceded. 'However, your master must *prove* he's worth such magnificent swords. My last opponent was a great disappointment, despite the promise of his weaponry. So anything less than an *impressive* display of swordsmanship *will* result in sudden death.'

'Agreed,' said Ronin without hesitation, much to Jack's growing dismay. 'When and where?'

'The Sound of Feathers waterfall, tomorrow at dawn.'

Jack's consternation increased. Not only did he have to contend with the forthcoming duel, but they'd have to evade detection by Kazuki and his network of *metsuke* for another day.

Above the sounds of the students training, a bell rang out three times.

'We'll look forward to it,' said Ronin, getting to his feet and bowing respectfully. Jack did the same, doing his best to remain calm, despite the threat presented by Hana's warning.

The old man reappeared to guide them out.

'Oh, by the way,' said Araki, a smirk on his face, 'does your master need to *borrow* some swords?'

'No,' replied Ronin coolly. 'He'll use mine.'

27

BACK TO SCHOOL

'The *metsuke* were *huge*! And very hairy!' exclaimed Hana as they hurriedly put distance between themselves and the *Yagyu Ryū*. 'They wore black kimono with red sun *kamon* like the others. That's how I spotted them.'

'Our luck was in. We got out just in time,' said Ronin in amazement.

'Did these watchers look like overgrown apes?' asked Jack. Hana laughed. 'Yes!'

'They're Kazuki's cousins from Hokkaido – Raiden and his brother Toru – both students of the *Yagyu Ryū*.'

'Then it may have been a coincidence. They could have simply turned up for training,' said Ronin, leading them across a bridge spanning the canal. 'But with so many *metsuke* around, we need to find a place to lie low.'

'Why not Jack's old school?' suggested Hana.

'Because it's right next to Nijo Castle!' said Jack, shaking his head at her naivety.

'Exactly,' replied Hana. 'That's the last place they'll look.'

'Good thinking,' agreed Ronin, much to Jack's surprise that

the samurai had even listened to Hana. 'Where better to hide than under the enemy's nose?'

Outvoted, Jack allowed himself to be led across the city and back to the *Niten Ichi Ryū*. If he was honest with himself, Hana's idea wasn't a bad one. It was just that he was reluctant to return, preferring to keep alive his memories of the place as he'd known it.

'We can't go through the main gates,' said Ronin as they neared their destination. 'It's too exposed.'

'There's a side gate that the students used,' stated Jack.

The three of them cut through a network of alleys and reached the smaller entrance unopposed. Even at this gate a sign had been posted, declaring *Closed by order of the Shogun*. When the street was clear, they approached and Ronin tried the handle.

'It's locked!' He backed up to shoulder-barge it open.

'Let me try first,' said Hana, stepping into his path. 'It'll be obvious someone's broken in if you do that.'

She pulled out a knife, tucked discreetly into the back of her *obi*. The blade gleamed, its edge honed razor-sharp.

'Where did you get that?' demanded Ronin.

'Off the gap-toothed bandit.'

'You *stole* it?'

'No,' objected Hana, her mouth dropping open as if that was the last thing she'd ever do. 'He threw it away. Anyway, I left my old one for him.'

Slipping the tip of the knife into the lock, she carefully twisted and jiggled the blade until there was a sharp click. The gate swung open. Hana turned to them, a smug grin on her face.

Ronin grunted with almost a hint of admiration.

'Good work!' said Jack, pleased Hana had proved her usefulness to Ronin twice in quick succession.

They hurried inside and shut the gate behind them. Their feet crunched loudly as they crossed the deserted pebbled courtyard. Jack felt as if they'd entered a cemetery, the derelict buildings no more than tombs to the martial arts that were once taught here.

'I can see this was an impressive school,' commented Ronin, heading for the *Butokuden*. 'Such a waste!'

They entered the great hall, its rounded pillars of cypress wood still propping up the immense panelled ceiling, with its criss-cross of beams like the skeleton of a beached whale. Shafts of late afternoon sun pierced the vast interior, catching dust motes in the stale air and illuminating the ransacked Weapons Wall. Stripped of all its equipment during the height of battle over the school, just a broken *wakizashi* and a worn *bokken* now remained discarded upon the floor.

Walking over to the ceremonial alcove, their footsteps echoed off the bare walls. Ronin picked up the wooden sword and casually tested its weight. He sighed. 'To have trained in a place like *this* must have been a great honour.'

Jack nodded in agreement. Yet his experiences hadn't been *all* good. Sensei Kyuzo, the dwarf-sized yet lethal *taijutsu* master, had spent many a lesson demonstrating excruciatingly painful combat techniques upon him for the benefit of the rest of the class. And, as a punishment once, he'd forced Jack to spend the entire night cleaning every single woodblock of the *dojo* floor. But Jack would willingly suffer all that again to see the *Niten Ichi Ryū* back to its former glory.

They left the *Butokuden* and made for the *Chō-no-ma*.

'It's beautiful!' gasped Hana, running her fingers over the exquisite silk-screen paintings of butterflies and *sakura* trees that lined the dining hall.

Some of the tables were still set for dinner as if waiting for the students and their sensei to appear. Jack almost expected Masamoto to stride through the door, proclaiming his return. But then he caught sight of a dried bloodstain upon one of the tabletops. This was where Saburo had lain to have his arrow wound tended to and bandaged. That night had been the beginning of the end.

Jack wondered what had become of his friend, and of Kiku who'd stayed behind as his nurse. Were they still alive? If so, were they hiding like him? Or had they escaped the Shogun's purge of his enemies?

While Jack contemplated his friends' fate, Ronin found the kitchen and returned a few moments later with some dishes, three pairs of *hashi* and a cooking bowl.

'Time to eat. You'll need your strength for the duel tomorrow.'

Ronin led them outside and ordered Hana to collect some wood from the ruins of the Hall of the Hawk. Then he found a suitable spot in the Southern Zen Garden to make a fire, in the lee of an immense standing stone to shield the light and beneath a tree to disperse the smoke, so that their presence within the *Niten Ichi Ryū* wouldn't be detected. As the rice cooked, Hana cut up some vegetables and Jack gutted a fish that Ronin had bought earlier with their dwindling money supply.

By the time dinner was ready, however, Jack had lost his

appetite. He'd been unable to shake off his sadness at coming back to the school and he was worried about the impending duel. Returning to the *Niten Ichi Ryū* had reminded him that he'd not practised his swordwork, let alone the Two Heavens technique, since regaining consciousness several days before.

'I need a walk,' he said, smiling apologetically when Hana offered him his share.

'And I need a drink,' replied Ronin, lifting a bottle of *saké* to his lips.

'But you must eat, Jack . . .' said Hana.

Ronin silently shook his head at Hana, warning her to let Jack go.

Jack wandered through the abandoned school. With early evening settling in, the *Niten Ichi Ryū* merely appeared to be asleep, not dead. Climbing the stone steps in front of him, he found himself outside the *Butsuden*, the wide wooden doors hanging off like broken wings. He stepped inside its shadowy interior.

'Hello?' he called.

Only the echo of his voice responded. *What more had he expected?*

Solitary and stoic, the great bronze Buddha sat unworshipped in the darkened recesses of the hall. Above, like a heavenly crown, hung the immense temple bell. The Buddha seemed to glow in the afterlight of the fading sun and Jack felt himself drawn to him. Before he even realized it, he'd crossed the room and was kneeling at the statue's feet.

Bringing his hands together, he prayed. For Saburo. For Kiku. For Masamoto. For the memory of Yamato. For the friendship of Akiko. And . . . for his sister, Jess, in England.

Once again he found himself facing the possibility of death by the sword and his only thoughts were for his friends and the welfare of his remaining family. No matter what it took, he *had* to survive. How he wished for Sensei Yamada's guidance now. The Zen master always had an answer, even if it wasn't always obvious.

All of a sudden there was a noise and a bird in the rafters took flight, its wings flapping in a wild panic.

Jack spun round. 'Who's there?'

Distant laughter.

He turned the other way, his eyes darting around the gloomy hall. He caught a flash of red reflecting off the bronze Buddha. He felt his throat go dry with fear.

Surely not?

His senses on high alert, Jack heard every creak and groan of the derelict building. Shadows seemed to spring to life.

Riddle me this, young samurai! What is greater than God, more evil than the Devil? Poor people have it, rich people need it, and if you eat it you'll die. Tell me this and I shall give it to you.

'How should I know?' hissed Jack, his voice thin and lost in the emptiness of the hall as the Riddling Monk's words plagued his mind. Like an incessant irritating tune, he couldn't get the riddle out of his head.

Getting to his feet, Jack edged round the bronze Buddha, his hands out in front ready to fend off any attack.

Know this! What you find is lost. What you give is given back. What you fight is defeated . . . What you fight is defeated . . . What you fight is defeated . . .

Turning the corner, Jack came face to face with a fire-red monster. Fearsome, with a wild moustache and a single black eye, it towered over him. In his panicked state, his brain barely registered that the monster was merely an oversized Daruma Doll. And the unexpected shock of seeing it in the darkness sent Jack fleeing from the temple.

He flung himself through the doors and outside, his heart beating rapidly in his chest. He knew he'd let his imagination run away with him, but it didn't make the terror any less real. He was certain he'd felt the Riddling Monk's presence and a shiver ran through him.

Stopping to get his breath back on the steps, Jack heard Hana scream . . .

28

PLUM FLOWER POLES

Jack burst into the garden as Hana's cry of pain turned to laughter – the same laughter he'd heard from the Buddha Hall. Ronin sat cross-legged upon the garden's veranda, his chin resting upon the hilt of the *bokken* he'd picked up. Hana was lying on the floor amid a small forest of poles.

'You must be relaxed and free-flowing –' instructed Ronin.

'How can I? I'm always falling off!' said Hana, rubbing her rear.

Ronin scowled at her. 'Don't interrupt! If you want to learn, keep your mouth shut.'

Hana nodded obediently and sealed her lips.

'A rigid body is easily knocked off centre,' he explained. 'A flexible fighter, one relaxed as if drunk, can easily dodge, recoil and strike from any angle. To master the art of balance you need to find your centre.'

Hana spotted Jack. 'I've saved you some food,' she said, pointing to a dish piled high with rice and fish. Then she saw the worried expression on Jack's face. 'Are you all right?' she asked.

'I thought you were in trouble.'

Hana laughed again. 'I am! Ronin's teaching me.'

'And I have an inept student!' huffed Ronin, taking a swig of *saké* and turning to Jack. 'I hope you prove better.'

'What are they?' asked Jack, eyeing the peculiar arrangement of wooden stumps. At least a dozen of them stood in a spiral pattern, driven into the earth at different heights.

'They're plum flower poles,' explained Hana eagerly. 'Ronin built them to help improve my balance.'

She leapt on to the first stump, then stepped up to the next level.

'The higher you go, the more they wobble.' Her arms wavered as she climbed. 'And the harder it is to –' She fell, this time managing to stay upright. 'It isn't easy!'

Ronin tutted. 'Keep your centre!'

He irritably strode over and mounted the plum flower poles with ease. Halfway up, he leant back until his body formed an arc. To all appearances, he was completely off-balance and about to topple over.

Ronin pointed to his stomach. 'See, when I move, my centre is always above my point of balance –' indicating his feet – 'That way I always stay in control.'

Jumping from one stump to another, he reached the topmost pole and stood on one leg, arms primed in a fighting guard.

'Be nimble like a cat.'

He leapt off to land lightly beside Jack. 'Now you try. Remember, put the weight on the balls of your feet.'

Jack tested the lowest pole with one foot. It hardly moved and he had little problem standing on it. As he climbed higher, he compensated for the growing sway of the poles with his body, while his feet instinctively sought the best placement. He discovered the plum flowers were just like being atop the main mast of the *Alexandria*.

'You've done this before!' said Ronin.

'I *was* a sailor –'

Without warning, Ronin threw his bottle at Jack. But Jack was ready this time and caught it confidently, not even wavering.

'Good, you're learning,' said Ronin as Jack stepped down to return his prized *saké*. Picking up his swords from the veranda, Ronin offered them to Jack. 'You need to practise with my *daishō* for tomorrow.'

Jack bowed, holding out both hands to receive Ronin's swords with respect.

'I appreciate the honour, but why didn't you take up Araki's offer?'

'Not a chance,' snorted Ronin, seizing the *bokken*. 'Any sword he lent you would be unbalanced and flawed. Araki may be honourable, but he'll do everything in his power to ensure he wins.'

Sliding the *saya*s into his *obi*, Jack unsheathed the two weapons and weighed them in his hands. They were functional, brutally efficient and well used. Their balance was good and the cutting edges expertly honed, numerous times. While they weren't crafted like the Shizu blades Akiko had given him, he was confident he could defend himself with them.

'You're skilled in the Two Heavens,' said Ronin, taking up a fighting stance, 'and I only have a *bokken*. You should easily beat me.'

With that, he struck at Jack's neck. On instinct alone, Jack blocked the wooden blade and countered using the *wakizashi*. Ronin evaded the attack and came at him with a surprise upward cut. Jack barely moved out of the way in time. He was slow and unsure from lack of practice, while Ronin was an experienced and highly skilled swordsman.

'Is that your best?' challenged Ronin, and the duel really began.

They fought through the garden, the huge standing stones forming a natural arena. As the night drew in, the two fighters flickered orange in the firelight. Hana watched with dread fascination from the veranda.

'Come on, Jack! You can beat him!' she cried.

A sharp look from Ronin, though, made her quickly change allegiances.

'Take him down, Ronin!'

But Jack was warming to the swords and gradually his Two Heavens moves began to flow once more. *Flint-and-Spark strike. The strike of Running Water. Mountain-to-Sea. Moving the Shadow. The Autumn Leaf strike.* Ronin felt the pressure and retreated towards the plum flower poles. As Jack made a cut for his chest, Ronin jumped on to the first stump. He now had the advantage of height.

'Follow me if you dare!'

Jack drove him further up the poles, and the fight shifted to a mid-air battle. They leapt between the stumps, each seeking to gain the better footing. Ronin, however, was more adept with his balance and Jack's knowledge of the Two Heavens no longer gave him the edge over the samurai.

The duel progressed higher and higher. More of Jack's concentration shifted to simply staying upright. Then he caught Ronin off-guard with a thrust for the stomach and the samurai was forced to make a desperate leap for another plum flower pole. He landed poorly and his free arm whirled in the air as he toppled sideways.

Jack seized the moment to finish the duel. Stepping closer to execute the winning move, he realized too late that he'd been tricked. Ronin instantly regained his balance and swept Jack's lead leg away with his *bokken*. Jack's foot was knocked from the top of the pole and he tumbled to the ground.

Hana wildly applauded the samurai's victory.

Ronin, high upon the plum blossoms, peered down at the vanquished Jack and placed the tip of his *bokken* on Jack's stomach.

'Keep your centre,' he warned. 'And don't be deceived like that tomorrow!'

29

DEATH THREAT

The water thundered over the cliff edge, plunging deep into the lush gorge below. A fine mist was thrown up and the magnificent view of Kyoto in the valley basin was veiled in a silvery sheen. This mystical quality was only deepened by the golden blanket of autumnal leaves that now swathed the mountainsides and appeared lit from within by the rays of the rising sun.

From where Jack stood on the river's bank, he could see down on to the curving roof of the Kiyomizudera pagoda and the rest of the temple complex. Oblivious to the impending duel above, monks in saffron-coloured robes and pilgrims weary from travel stood upon the *butai* – the wooden platform that jutted out into the gorge and allowed visitors access to the legendary curative waters of the Sound of Feathers waterfall.

The last time Jack had been here was to retrieve the Jade Sword. Even now he could see the shrine in which it was housed, upon a small island on the lip of the waterfall, a precarious set of stepping stones running to it from the bank. In his race with Yamato, he'd been the one to get there first. But their bitter argument while hanging off the cliff face had resulted in them both falling into the rock pool below. Only good fortune had saved them from drowning or breaking their necks.

'I now *truly* believe these swords belong to your master,' called Araki, patting the red-handled *daishō* on his hip as he approached along a mountain path. 'To risk his life in such a quest proves it to be so.'

'Are they the ones?' whispered Ronin, Hana standing close by with Jack's staff.

Black *saya*s, mother-of-pearl inlay, red-woven handles. Jack nodded. He'd found his swords!

He now had to fight for them.

A crowd of *Yagyu Ryū* students followed in Araki's wake. It was evident the samurai was held in awe by many of them, and an opportunity to see their hero in action was clearly not to be missed. As Araki took off his outer *haori* jacket, two of the students were immediately by his side to collect it. He stretched, tightened his *obi* round his waist and adjusted the swords on his hip.

'Am I to see the face of my opponent before we begin?' enquired Araki, raising an eyebrow at Ronin.

Before Ronin could reply, there was a shout and the crowd of students parted as the towering bulks of Raiden and Toru forged a path for Kazuki and his Scorpion Gang. They surrounded Jack, Ronin and Hana.

'I want to see his face *too*,' said Kazuki.

Jack hadn't thought his situation could get any worse. But there was no hiding now. Even if captured or killed, he'd stay sword in hand and his head held high.

'Kazuki,' greeted Jack, giving Ronin back his hat and bowing curtly to his old rival. 'How's the hand?'

'The *gaijin* samurai!' exclaimed Araki with a look of delight upon his face.

'It *is* you!' snarled Kazuki, fury and astonishment halting him in his tracks. 'I heard there was to be a duel over a pair of Shizu swords and knew you fought with Masamoto's pair. But the ones on Araki-san aren't Masamoto's!'

'No, they belonged to Akiko's father,' replied Jack. 'She gave me the honour of bearing them.'

'Akiko! She *lives*?' queried Kazuki. 'I thought . . . hoped I'd killed that traitor.'

'She's tougher than you think,' retorted Jack.

Kazuki held up his right hand. Covered in a black glove, the fingers were curled into a permanent and useless claw.

'*This* is her fault,' he spat. 'When I've killed you, I'm going to punish your precious Akiko for her crime. She won't be so pretty when I've finished with her.'

Jack felt his anger start to boil, both at himself for having let slip Akiko's survival and at Kazuki for his malicious threat. He would *never* let Kazuki harm her.

'Is she here with you in Kyoto?' demanded Kazuki.

Jack didn't answer. In spite of his error, Akiko remained safe as long as Kazuki had no idea of her whereabouts.

'Where then?' he demanded, drawing his *katana* with his left hand.

'Kazuki-san,' addressed Araki, stepping between them. 'I appreciate you have debts to settle and traitors to punish, but first I have a duel arranged with this samurai.'

'*Samurai?* He's no samurai!' said Kazuki with utter disgust.

'Oh, but he is,' corrected Araki. 'He's the infamous *gaijin* samurai. A master of the Two Heavens.'

'*I* could do the Two Heavens,' muttered Kazuki tetchily. 'It's nothing special and it didn't help Masamoto in the end, did it?'

'Please respect our arrangement, Kazuki-san,' insisted Araki firmly, ignoring Kazuki's bitter comments. 'This duel is a matter of honour. Of course, if he survives, he's yours. If not, you may have his . . . head.'

Kazuki glared at Araki, then stepped back a pace and sheathed his sword.

'Don't disappoint me by dying too soon, *gaijin*,' said Kazuki. 'But if you do I want you to go to your grave knowing that I *will* find Akiko.'

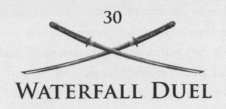

30

WATERFALL DUEL

'What a perfect day for a duel!' said Araki, admiring the sunlight glinting off the waters. 'This will be a fight to remember.'

Jack turned to Ronin and whispered, 'If I lose, I die. If I survive, I die. Not much of a choice, is it?'

'You win a war one battle at a time,' replied Ronin, his hand not leaving the hilt of his *bokken*. 'Focus on this battle first.'

The excited crowd organized itself into a large semi-circle to create a duelling area, its boundary marked by *Yagyu Ryū* students on one side and the waterfall behind.

'*When* you are ready!' said Araki, bowing formally to Jack.

Putting aside his immediate concerns about Kazuki, Jack returned the bow. Araki drew his *katana*, slowly and precisely. The Shizu blade was like quicksilver in the sun.

Faced with a battle against his own swords, Jack felt his resolve momentarily give way. Only now did he truly understand the awesome power of the weapon. Victory seemed etched into the very steel itself and Jack knew his defeat was no more than a single sword thrust away.

Taking a deep breath to calm his nerves, Jack unsheathed

both Ronin's swords. In one flowing motion, he raised his *katana* to the sky and held the shorter *wakizashi* across his chest as a guard. He *only* had to get first blood, he reminded himself. A simple nick or cut would suffice.

Araki seemed in no hurry to attack. He circled slowly and Jack kept in step with him, always maintaining a good sword length's distance between them. Jack knew Araki was assessing his competence by the sureness of his footwork. The samurai then fell back into a side stance, his *katana* held low and the blade hidden behind his body. This made it very difficult for Jack to predict the direction of any impending sword strike.

All of a sudden, Araki stamped his front foot.

Jack jumped back, his swords primed to receive the attack.

But none came.

'Nervous?' laughed Araki, once again circling like a hawk over its prey.

Jack didn't answer. The samurai was playing with him, but he wouldn't give Araki the satisfaction of a response. Instead he waited patiently for the samurai to make his move.

From nowhere, the tip of Araki's sword soared high into the air, catching the sunlight. Jack was momentarily blinded by the glare. Yet he still heard the *swish* of steel as it raced towards him. Calling upon the blind fighting skills he'd learnt from Sensei Kano, Jack judged the sword's trajectory and stopped the blade with the back of his *wakizashi*, before swiftly retreating out of harm's way.

The crowd gave a disappointed groan.

Araki glared at Jack, clearly astonished and incensed his first attack hadn't brought him instant victory.

'Not many survive a Swallow strike,' he commented coldly. '*KIAIIIIII!*'

Araki screamed, whirling in with a vicious slice across Jack's chest. Jack leapt aside, barely deflecting the assault due to its immense force. He attempted a counter-thrust to the gut, but Araki twisted from its path at the last second and darted away.

'And fewer still, Strike Like Thunder,' Araki seethed, wrestling to contain his frustration at yet another failed assault. 'Now what skills do *you* have, *gaijin*?'

Araki lowered his guard to tempt Jack in. Jack realized it was a trap, but he wouldn't get a better opening than this. With lightning speed, he swung his *wakizashi* at the samurai's head. Araki went to block it, exposing his left-hand side, and Jack immediately thrust for the chest with his *katana*. A moment of panic flashed in Araki's eyes at being duped, but he managed to redirect his weapon to clash with Jack's *katana*.

For a second, there was stalemate.

Then Jack drove his blade along the length of Araki's sword, trying to force it aside and strike for the heart . . . just as Masamoto had taught him . . . but Araki's *katana* began to rise and fall like a wave, dissipating the strength of his thrust. His attack failed and Jack had to spin away before he impaled himself on Araki's blade.

Araki grinned. 'Great Wave meets your Flint-and-Spark strike.'

There was a smattering of applause from some of the *Yagyu Ryū* students. Araki was now performing for his followers, trying to appear as if the fight was under his control and he was merely tormenting Jack. But Jack knew otherwise. The samurai was disconcerted by the Two Heavens and threatened by his unanticipated skill as a swordsman.

They fought on. Hana shouted encouragement, while Ronin observed in grave silence. But the crowd was distinctly one-sided, hissing and jeering every time Jack made an attacking move or defended himself successfully. Kazuki stood, arms folded, glowering. Meanwhile, Araki gave a running commentary on all his techniques. The lecturing was annoying, but Jack realized this was the point, to demonstrate his superiority and attempt to put Jack off his guard.

The duel grew in intensity. Jack's heart beat fiercely in his chest and the roar of the waterfall now mixed with the rush of blood in his ears. He was tiring and knew he could make a mistake at any moment. Araki was so precise and his techniques so flawless that Jack struggled to find a way to beat him. He was driven back by a particularly vicious thrust and his foot splashed down into the river.

Of all the elements, a ninja should choose water to be his closest ally . . .

Suddenly Jack recalled the Grandmaster's teachings of the Five Rings and how to use nature to his advantage. He ducked as Araki's blade cut for him.

Not even the strongest may resist . . . It can be a weapon or a defence . . .

Retreating along the water's edge, Jack let Araki come for him. Technically perfect as Araki's sword-work was, Jack realized the samurai was too rigid in his movements.

Jack needed to use his knowledge of the Ring of Water.

Draw your enemy into a river . . . Force them to fight in the water . . .

It was a risky strategy. Jack could be taken by the current just as easily as Araki. He could lose his footing first, stumble in the shallows. But he had trained in water combat with the ninja clan. He knew to keep a low stance. To step high and slow. Araki, on the other hand, lacked flexibility and would struggle in the water without experience of the element.

The duel entered the river and the crowd rushed forward to line the bank.

But Jack had underestimated his opponent. Araki still proved strong in the water. Swords clashed and they edged closer and closer to the waterfall. The current grew in strength and it became harder to keep one's feet. Hana and Ronin watched with increasing concern.

'Plum flower!' cried Hana, pointing to behind Jack.

He glanced round and spotted the stepping stones. Immediately he mounted the nearest. Araki, not wanting Jack to have the advantage of height, clambered on to another. He almost slipped on its slimy surface, but quickly recovered.

Jack jumped to the next one and Araki followed. They fought, tottering upon the uneven stones, the river rushing over the lip of the waterfall next to them. Parrying a thrust from Jack, Araki countered with a surprising diagonal cut. The only way Jack could avoid it was to arch his body away and over the cliff edge. For a moment, he appeared to hang in the balance, the slightest breeze able to send him over the cascade.

Find your centre.

Araki moved in to seal his victory as the crowd began chanting, '*Kill him! Kill him! Kill him!*'

'Time to end this duel,' Araki declared breathlessly and raised his sword. 'This is Heaven Crowns Earth.'

'But we agreed first blood!' gasped Jack, still teetering on the edge.

'That was *before* I knew you were the *gaijin* samurai,' replied Araki, grinning maliciously. 'I'll go down in history for taking your head!'

31

ON A KNIFE'S EDGE

The blade cut down like a guillotine for Jack's neck. In that instant, Jack righted himself and leapt to the next stone. The sword missed and, in his fervour to behead Jack, Araki overswung and toppled forward. Jack drove his sword through Araki's *obi*, stopping him just before he lost all balance.

Araki now teetered on the brink, his eyes wide with fear as he stared into the watery abyss.

'And *that* was Drunken Fist,' said Jack. 'Strike when you appear most vulnerable.'

A small red patch, where Jack had caught Araki in the side, seeped through the samurai's kimono.

'I believe *that's* first blood,' noted Jack.

'Never!' snarled Araki, in spite of his precarious position.

Suddenly there was a sharp ripping sound as Araki's attempts to right himself pulled the fabric of his *obi* against the back of Jack's *katana*. He lurched forward, his fate now resting on a knife's edge.

'Looks like first blood to me,' said Jack calmly, letting the petrified Araki hang over the waterfall. 'But if you're not sure perhaps I should pull the blade out and have a look.'

'No! Yes! I mean . . . Agreed, agreed! First blood! You win!'
cried Araki as the *obi* tore again.

Jack grabbed Araki's collar and pulled him to safety. Fuming
and trembling with outrage, Araki looked intent on continuing the fight. But, bound by the samurai code of *bushido*, he
sheathed his weapon and stepped away on to another stone,
his head bowed in shame.

'My swords?' reminded Jack.

Araki wordlessly pulled them from his tattered *obi* and
surrendered them. As soon as they were in his hands, Jack felt
a new strength within him. Not only did he have Akiko's pearl,
he now possessed his Shizu swords. He was almost complete.
Apart from *daimyo* Takatomi's *inro* case, which was more of
sentimental value than anything else, just the *rutter* remained
essential to his journey.

Hana came skipping over the stepping stones as Araki
trudged back to the riverbank. Ronin was not far behind.
Returning him his *daishō*, Jack then hurriedly secured his own
upon his hip, fastening the *saya*s with the *sageo* cord round his
obi.

'That was unbelievable!' cried Hana, the thrill of Jack's
victory making her forget their perilous predicament for a
moment.

'It isn't over yet,' replied Jack, glancing over her shoulder.

The crowd of *Yagyu Ryū* students had turned into an angry
mob at seeing their hero defeated. Kazuki and his Scorpion
Gang were at the head of it. They stood upon the bank, swords
drawn.

'Seize the *gaijin* and kill the two traitors!' ordered Kazuki.

Raiden stepped on to the first stone, Goro, Hiroto and his

brother, Toru, right behind. Taking one look at the baying mob and the beast that was Raiden, Ronin confessed, 'This looks like one battle we can't win.'

'Why not surrender?' suggested Hana, desperation cracking her voice as Ronin unsheathed his *katana*. .

Ronin didn't answer. He just passed Hana the *bokken* and nodded to Jack to draw his swords too.

'But I've never used one of these!' she exclaimed.

'You'd better learn fast then,' he replied.

The Scorpion Gang edged closer. Jack looked around for an escape route, but the stepping stones led only to the shrine and he knew that was a dead end. Returning to the riverbank offered no hope either. They might be able to fight off a few of their attackers, but inevitably they'd be overwhelmed.

Kazuki laughed cruelly at their plight. 'Nowhere to run now, *gaijin!*'

Realizing the futility of putting up resistance, Jack sheathed his swords. If he was killed, he couldn't warn Akiko of the danger she was in.

'What are you doing?' exclaimed Hana.

'Get ready to jump!' he replied, under his breath.

Hana looked over the edge of the waterfall at the seemingly bottomless drop. 'Are you crazy?'

'I've done it before and survived.'

'From *here*?' questioned Ronin, incredulous.

'Not exactly,' Jack admitted. 'Halfway down.'

'But I can't swim!' said Hana, her eyes darting in terror between the approaching mob and the perilous jump.

'You can't wield a sword either,' reminded Jack as Raiden stepped within striking distance. 'NOW JUMP!'

Jack grabbed Hana by the wrist and pulled her over with him. Ronin, shaking his head in disbelief at what he was about to do, leapt after them. Raiden's sword sliced through the air, just missing his back.

They plunged downwards, Hana screaming all the way and Jack silently praying they wouldn't hit the *butai* or crash on to the rocks below. The wind shrieked past their ears, the waterfall thundering around them. Suddenly they were engulfed by spray and a second later hit the water. The roar of the falls became a deep boom. The churning rock pool flipped and rolled them. Then the current snatched Jack, and Hana was ripped from his grasp as they crested the lip of the pool into the river. Just at the point he thought he'd drown, his head popped to the surface and he sucked in air with relief.

A cry alerted him to Hana, who flailed in the waters. She disappeared back under and Jack kicked hard in her direction. Hana bobbed up again, weaker this time. He desperately swam to her rescue, but the river swallowed her again. Diving under, Jack blindly sought the girl who'd once been just a thief to him and was now a friend. His fingers clasped a sodden kimono and he pulled Hana to the surface. She came up spluttering and choking.

The river became calmer, though the current no less strong. Jack let it bear them downstream, holding Hana's head above the water. A moment later, he spotted Ronin swimming towards them. Then he heard a shout.

From the top of the falls, Kazuki stood screaming his revenge.

'You cowardly dog! I'll hunt you down, *gaijin*!'

32

BROKEN

The three fugitives kept up a brisk pace as they trekked south along a forest path and away from Kyoto. They had let the river take them out of the gorge and into the main valley, only dragging themselves from the waters when the current had eased. Ronin now took them on a circuitous route that avoided the main road and any settlements. Although their daring escape had given them a head start, they couldn't risk slowing down or being spotted.

Jack took up the rear, using his ninja skills to ensure their tracks were covered, while Hana maintained a non-stop monologue.

'I can't believe we survived! Did you see Raiden's face as we jumped? He looked more shocked than I was. You were awesome in the duel, Jack. I honestly thought you were beaten. But you tricked Araki! He was livid. Don't you think the three of us make a great team? We got back your swords *and* your pearl! Shame about the gambler losing all your money, but I can always steal some more if you want. And I'm sorry I lost your staff, Jack. But I managed to keep hold of the *bokken*, Ronin! Do you want it back?'

'Keep it,' he grunted, quickening his pace more to escape the incessant chattering of Hana than to stay ahead of Kazuki and his Scorpion Gang.

'Really?' she replied, and slipped it proudly into her *obi*. 'My first sword! Will you teach me, Ronin? I want to be a samurai like you and Jack.'

'You need to be *born* samurai.'

'But Jack's not even Japanese!'

'He was adopted by a samurai. And he's not a thief either!'

'Oh!' replied Hana, a little upset by Ronin's curt reply. She pondered for a moment. 'You could adopt me!'

Ronin stopped in his tracks, his face blanching. He turned to reply, then thought better of it and strode off.

Hana looked at Jack. 'Was that a yes? Or a no?'

Jack shrugged noncommittally, but knowing Ronin he didn't think the samurai was the adopting type. 'We'd better keep moving,' he said.

They powered on, not even stopping for lunch. A couple of times they had to backtrack to avoid other travellers and skirt a village. As dusk settled, they worked their way into a lower valley and found a secluded spot beside a stream.

'We'll camp here for the night,' Ronin declared, clearing the ground for a fire.

Hana went off to collect kindling, while Jack cut some branches from a tree and made a simple clotheshorse so they could dry their damp kimono. Ronin opened the cloth sack that held their food and cursed loudly.

'What's wrong?' asked Jack.

Without replying, Ronin angrily shook the bag's contents on to the earth. A straw container of rice, a small cooking pot, an onion, half a cabbage and a couple of white *daikon* fell out. These were accompanied by an ominous tinkling as several ceramic shards tumbled out too. The impact of landing in the water had smashed Ronin's last bottle of *saké* to smithereens.

Hana returned with the wood and saw the enraged expression on Ronin's face. The samurai snatched up the cabbage, sat upon a log and began to hack at the vegetable.

'Let me do that,' suggested Hana, worried that most of it was going on the ground rather than in the pot. 'Why don't you make the fire?'

Grunting moodily, Ronin shoved the mauled cabbage into Hana's hands and started breaking the branches and throwing them into a pile. Thinking it best to leave Ronin to himself, Jack helped Hana with preparing the food. They heard him curse a few times as he tried to light the tinder and the two of them exchanged concerned looks. But once it caught Ronin settled down and contented himself with prodding the fire with a stick. Although their meal was meagre, the vegetable soup and rice seemed to revive Ronin's spirits a little.

'News will travel fast of Araki's defeat,' he said to Jack, 'and with this Scorpion Gang hunting you, you need to make for Nagasaki and home as fast as you can.'

'I have to go to Nara first.'

Ronin shook his head. 'Not worth the risk.'

'But Nagasaki's the direction Kazuki will expect me to go in.'

'True. However, he'll use the main roads to get ahead of you and block your path. Even I would question your ability to defeat an entire gang single-handedly.'

'I'll have to take that chance. I *must* go to Nara. My father's diary is there. I also want to know what happened to me. Several days of my life are missing. A blank. This Botan will be able to tell me.'

'You've got your pearl, kimono and your swords. Is your father's diary *that* important?'

Jack nodded his head, deciding now was the time to fully trust Ronin and Hana. They had certainly proved their loyalty in the past few days. 'It's much more than a diary,' he replied and began to explain the *rutter*'s true signifiance.

When Jack finished talking, Ronin queried, 'So this logbook is irreplaceable . . . *invaluable*?'

'Yes,' replied Jack. 'But only I can decipher all its content. And I made an oath to my father to keep it safe. It's my *duty* to find it.'

Ronin sighed deeply and threw another log upon the fire. 'I understand a son's duty. You've a responsibility to fulfil your father's dying wish, and I respect that.'

He stabbed at the glowing embers with a stick.

'You can't be allowed to fail your father . . . like I did mine.' Ronin appeared no longer to be aware of Jack or Hana. He began to mutter to himself. 'It was *my* fault I let that monk in. *My* fault I didn't search for weapons. *My* fault I was fooled by a deceitful disguise. *My* fault my father's now . . .'

Ronin trailed off and said no more. He just stared into the fire, the flames reflecting in his eyes, more bloodshot than ever. He sniffed, a tear rolling down his cheek.

'Are you all right?' asked Hana softly.

'Fine,' snapped Ronin, wiping a forearm across his face. 'The smoke's just getting in my eyes, that's all.'

33

HININ

The three of them sat round the fire, an uncomfortable silence hanging over them.

'Nara it is then!' said Hana in an effort to lift the mood. She picked up her *bokken*. 'Botan had better watch out – Hana the samurai's on his trail!'

Ronin ducked just in time as Hana swung the sword through the air.

'Put that down!' he growled, clearly regretting the decision to let her have it in the first place. 'I told you, you're *not* a samurai!'

One look at the scowling Ronin, his hands trembling, convinced Hana to do as she was told. 'You *could* teach me how to use it,' she ventured quietly.

Ronin glared at her.

'So what's the quickest way to Nara?' asked Jack, hoping to divert Ronin's darkening temper with a change of subject.

'Through the Kizu Valley,' replied Ronin.

'Isn't there *another* way?' said Jack, feeling his frustration rise. They were about to retrace their steps yet again!

Ronin shook his head. 'The mountain trails would take too

long and crossing points over the Kizu River are few and far between. We'll just have to take the risk.'

'I've been to Nara before,' Hana revealed. 'It only takes a day to get there.'

'Do you know where the Tōdai-ji Temple is then?' asked Jack, showing her the green silk *omamori*.

Hana grinned. 'You can't miss it. The temple must be the biggest building in the world!'

Noticing that Ronin's hands were still shaking, Jack shifted along the log. 'Come closer to the fire, Ronin.'

'I'm not cold,' he mumbled, trying to control the trembling. 'I'd be fine if only I had some *saké*.'

Hana, frowning, gave Ronin a troubled look. 'Tell me, why do you always need to drink?'

'To forget.'

'You want to forget your . . . father?' ventured Hana.

'That's none of your business!' snapped Ronin.

Hana looked wounded by the return of Ronin's harshness.

Ronin grunted an apology. 'Ironic, isn't it, Jack? You can't remember but want to. I can remember and don't want to!'

With that, Ronin moved away and bedded down against a tree to sleep. Jack saw him shudder and wondered if it was the lack of *saké*, the chilly night or his troubled past that was the cause.

Jack and Hana sat in silence for a while as the night closed in around them. Only the crackle of wood burning and the buzzing of insects broke the stillness. Their faces flickered in the firelight as Jack poked the embers with a stick and sparks flew into the night sky.

'I love how the flames dance,' mumbled Hana dreamily, gazing into its blaze.

Jack stared at the orange glow and lost himself in it too. For a moment, the fire consumed everything in his vision. Just like it had when the *Niten Ichi Ryū* had burnt. He thought he saw a face in the flames – Kazuki laughing – and recalled his rival's threat on Akiko's life.

He grasped his stick, his knuckles going white with fury at himself. How foolish he'd been to let slip that Akiko had survived her injuries.

But then he realized that as long as Kazuki was after *him*, he couldn't be searching for Akiko. The problem would arise when Jack left Japanese shores for England – Kazuki would have free rein to carry out his terrible revenge. The thought of Akiko being hurt was too much to bear. Jack knew a final confrontation between him and Kazuki was inevitable. The stick in his hands snapped in a fit of enraged frustration. He blinked, suddenly aware of his surroundings.

'Can I ask you something?' whispered Hana tentatively.

Jack nodded and threw the broken branch into the fire.

'When you've found this *rutter* in Nara, can I come with you to Nagasaki?'

Jack hesitated, not sure how best to reply.

'I don't think that would be a good idea,' he said. 'It'll be just *too* dangerous now. I'm not even sure you should be coming to Nara with me. I'm wanted by the Shogun *and* hunted by the Scorpion Gang. Besides, once in Nagasaki, I'm leaving Japan for home.'

'But there's nothing for me *here*,' Hana replied dolefully. 'Being with you and Ronin is the first time I've felt I *belonged*.'

Jack felt the crushing loneliness in Hana's heart. 'I understand . . . but might it not be safer to stay with Ronin?'

Hana looked over at the samurai, who'd fallen into a fitful sleep. She shook her head sadly. 'He wouldn't want me around. It was stupid suggesting he adopt me!'

She made to move away from the fire. 'Just forget I asked to join you. No one wants me. I'm a *hinin*.'

'A *hinin*?'

'An outcast. A nobody.'

'You're *not* a nobody,' stressed Jack. 'You're Hana.'

'Am I? I don't even know my real name. I just called myself "Hana" because I heard someone say it and liked it. I was hiding in a bush, when a samurai lady stopped and pointed, saying, "Hana, hana." For a moment, I thought she was pointing at *me*! But she was just showing her daughter the flowers . . .'

Tears welled in Hana's eyes at the memory.

Jack didn't know what to say. He pulled the bedraggled *origami* crane from the sleeve of his kimono and handed it to Hana.

'My good friend Yori gave me this to bring luck upon my journey home. I want you to look after it. To remind you that you're *not* a nobody. You have a friend in me.'

Hana took the crane and smiled. 'Thank you,' she whispered, wiping her eyes. 'That means a great deal. I've never had a true friend before.'

Jack reached over. 'Look, you can pull its tail and make the wings flap.'

Hana giggled and Jack felt grateful that, for once, he'd been able to pass on the joys of friendship. So far it had always been about him trying to fit in, to become accepted by others.

Looking at Hana then at Ronin snoring away, he realized all three of them were outcasts of Japanese society – a masterless samurai, a girl thief and a foreigner. But, bound together by fate, they were no longer outcasts. They were friends.

34

BUDDHA'S NOSE

Jack looked up from beneath Ronin's straw hat and gasped. He'd never seen a building so immense and grand. The Tōdai-ji's main hall dominated the landscape. Broad as a mountain and taller than the highest spire, it made the monks and pilgrims who wandered the temple grounds seem like ants. Constructed entirely of wood, its walls were painted white and the beams varnished a deep russet brown as if built from the armour of a king. Crowning the uppermost roof were two curved horns that glinted of gold in the morning sun.

Jack followed Ronin and Hana down the wide thoroughfare that led to the steps of the temple. On either side were beautifully manicured gardens and throughout the grounds roamed hundreds of deer. Some of the animals were taking food from the hands of monks. Hana caught him staring at this strange sight.

'Deer are seen as heavenly creatures by the people of Nara,' she explained. 'They're believed to protect the city from harm.'

Passing a large stone lantern set into the path, the three of them headed towards a covered wellspring. Jack and Hana washed their mouths and hands, while Ronin took a covert swig from a fresh bottle of rice wine.

'That's all the purification I need,' he said, smacking his lips in satisfaction.

On their way through Nara, they'd passed a *saké* store and Ronin had been able to satisfy his thirst. Fortunately for Jack and Hana, there'd been a shop next door selling *manjū*, so they spent the small amount of money left on three steamed buns and some more dried rice.

Having purified themselves, they climbed the stone steps up to the main hall. Outside its entrance was a large urn, trails of incense smoke wafting from a pincushion of burning sticks. The six great doors, five times the height of a man, were wide open and welcoming. They stepped inside the hall's darkened recesses and once again Jack's breath was taken away.

Seated before them, right palm held out, left hand resting in his lap, was a colossal bronze statue of the Buddha. Framed by an ornate golden backdrop, the effigy towered over the three of them, its gaze fixed upon the horizon. Even Ronin was awed in its presence.

To either side, further within the hall, were two gigantic warrior statues. Carved from wood, one painted yellow, the other red, these fierce guardians were almost as tall as the pillars that held up the Tōdai-ji's roof. Hana wandered off to take a closer look. Beside the entrance was a young priest and Jack approached, head bowed. He pulled the green silk *omamori* out of his kimono.

'Ah! I see you've been here before,' said the priest softly, greeting Jack with a humble bow.

'No, I'm afraid not,' replied Jack. 'I actually found this and believe it belongs to someone from your temple. Perhaps you know the person who lost it?'

The priest smiled serenely and gave a gentle shake of his head. 'We sell many of these amulets,' he explained, pointing to a stall bedecked with green silk *omamori*. 'That one could belong to any of a thousand pilgrims.'

Jack gazed at the rows upon rows of amulets, and despaired. The clue – the single piece of evidence he had from his attack – had come to nothing. He bowed his thanks to the priest and returned to Ronin.

The only lead remaining was the name Botan. 'How are we going to find this samurai now?'

'I'll have to ask around town,' replied Ronin, 'but it *will* draw attention to us.'

'Look at this!' cried Hana.

'Shh! Please don't break the silence,' cautioned the monk beside her.

'My apologies,' replied Hana, and mutely beckoned Jack and Ronin over to a large wooden supporting post towards the rear of the great hall.

The pillar, as broad as an old oak tree, had a hole running straight through its base. As Ronin and Jack approached, Hana expressed her thanks and bowed goodbye to the monk.

'Would you believe it!' she exclaimed. 'This hole is the same size as one of the giant Buddha statue's nostrils. If you can pass through it, the gods will bestow luck upon you and you'll be blessed with enlightenment in your next life.'

'Pah!' dismissed Ronin.

Ignoring his scepticism, Hana knelt down and wriggled through the hole. She popped out the other side a moment later.

'I'm enlightened. Who's next?'

'After you, Ronin,' said Jack.

'I don't believe in the gods,' he muttered. 'And they certainly don't believe in me.'

Jack felt he had nothing to lose. Furthermore, he recalled the Riddling Monk mentioning the Buddha's Nose. This had to be it. Crouching down, he looked through the hole. It was far smaller than he'd imagined. Quickly checking no one was watching, he passed Hana his hat and Ronin his swords before entering the narrow tunnel, arms first. Crawling along, he got about halfway when his shoulders jammed. Jack kicked with his legs, but it was no use.

'I'm stuck!' he whispered as loud as he dared.

Hana's grinning face appeared at the other end. 'Don't worry, I'll pull you through.'

Jack squirmed, his legs waggling on one side, while Hana tugged on his arms from the other. Ronin just smirked at Jack's comical predicament. With much heaving and effort, Jack inched his way through and finally shot out and on to the floor, Hana falling backwards in a fit of smothered giggling.

'That had better be worth it,' panted Jack.

As he got to his feet and put his hat back on, Jack spotted something out of the corner of his eye.

A samurai had entered the main hall and was conversing with the head priest. Accompanied by a small entourage, the man was evidently important – either a high-ranking retainer or a lord. He was dressed formally in a black winged *kataginu* jacket, a pleated *hakama* of black-and-white stripes, stark-white *tabi* socks and, most unusually, his swords had handle wrappings of white silk.

But what had caught Jack's eye was the small rectangular box on the samurai's hip. The *inro* and its *netsuke* were exactly the same design as the one *daimyo* Takatomi had given him.

It couldn't be coincidence. This *had* to be the man they were seeking.

35

SASUMATA

'Are you certain this time?' asked Ronin as the three of them discreetly followed the samurai and his entourage around the temple grounds.

'That's my *inro*,' replied Jack, nodding. 'Do you think he's Botan?'

Ronin shook his head. 'I was under the impression Botan was a low-ranking samurai. This man is of too high a status.'

'So *who* is he?' said Hana.

Ronin approached one of the monks feeding a tame deer to enquire. The monk humbly bowed his head as he answered. 'That is *daimyo* Sanada, Lord of Nara Province.'

Jack felt a cold chill run through him. How had a samurai lord come into possession of his *inro*? This suggested an association between *daimyo* Sanada and the samurai Botan. Could it be that Botan and his gang had been working for *daimyo* Sanada all along? If so, this samurai lord might also have the *rutter*. And if he was aware of its significance the logbook could already be on its way to the Shogun!

Leaving the monk with his deer, the three of them continued to walk down the main thoroughfare, trailing their quarry.

'I think *daimyo* Sanada could be behind my attack,' said Jack.

'The *inro* could be a copy?' Ronin proposed.

Jack shook his head. '*Daimyo* Takatomi had the gift specifically commissioned. It's one of a kind. Myself, Akiko and Yamato were each given different designs.'

'Well, perhaps he bought it from Botan.'

Jack considered this. It was certainly possible. Whatever the truth, a connection between the two was indisputable and it might just lead them to the *rutter*.

'I could steal it back for you,' suggested Hana.

Ronin frowned at her. 'His bodyguards would chop your hands off before you got anywhere near him.'

Her face went pale at the thought and she protectively pulled her hands inside her kimono sleeves.

'We need to meet with him,' said Jack. 'Find out how he acquired my *inro*. And discover the whereabouts of the *rutter*.'

'You can't just walk up to him,' said Ronin. 'We'd need a formal invitation.'

Cautiously, Jack ventured, 'Would your father's name hold any sway?'

A shadow passed across Ronin's face. 'I doubt it. He was well respected but had his enemies. Besides, you wouldn't get away with hiding your face in the presence of a *daimyo*.'

'Why don't we just find out where this lord lives?' said Hana. 'Then we could sneak in at night and search for the *rutter*. Like we did with the pearl.'

Ronin dismissed this suggestion with a wave of his hand. 'A *daimyo*'s mansion is heavily guarded and likely to be booby-trapped. No samurai, let alone a girl thief, could accomplish such a mission. You'd need to be a ninja to get inside undetected!'

Jack tried not to smile at this. His *ninjutsu* stealth training meant *he* could attempt it.

'It's our only option,' he said, much to Ronin's surprise and Hana's delight. 'Let's at least follow him home.'

Daimyo Sanada was already heading out of the Great Southern Gate and Jack and the others quickened their pace to catch up. Passing between the immense pillars that supported the gate's curving roof, Jack spotted two fearsome muscular guardians upon either side of the entrance. These wooden statues, Agyō and Ungyō, the protectors of Buddha, glared down at them. They each held out a hand as if in warning to stop. But the warning came too late for Jack, Ronin and Hana.

As they stepped out of the Tōdai-ji's grounds, the sound of dozens of running feet greeted them. In moments, they were surrounded by a company of *dōshin*. Each man held either a long bamboo staff or a *sasumata* – a pole with a vicious-looking U-shaped prong.

Ronin, Jack and Hana went for their swords, but they were immediately beaten with the staves, blows raining down upon them from every direction. Even if they could have used their weapons, their attackers remained out of reach at the ends of their poles. Driven back against the gate's pillars, the three of them were pinned by the throat and arms with several *sasumata*.

'And they said you were dangerous!' smirked the leading officer, although he still kept a wary distance.

Just as Jack thought the punishing beating was over, his head was clamped between four bamboo poles that formed a box round his skull. Released from the grip of the *sasumata*, Jack tried to struggle free, but the four *dōshin* on each end squeezed the poles together and he was wracked with pain. It was so unbearable he was completely incapacitated. Ronin and Hana were both in the same predicament. Their swords were taken and the three of them were at the mercy of the *dōshin*.

'Come on! Let's not keep his lordship waiting,' shouted the officer, and the *dōshin* marched them into town.

Grimacing in pain, Ronin muttered, 'This is *not* the formal invitation I'd envisaged.'

36

DAIMYO SANADA

'Truly a magnificent work of art!' declared *daimyo* Sanada, drawing the blade of Jack's *katana* and admiring its exquisite *hamon*. In the sunlight, the swirling pattern of waves upon the steel shimmered as if flowing.

Having been escorted into the garden of the *daimyo*'s mansion, Jack, Ronin and Hana were now on their knees, their heads bowed and their hands bound behind their backs. They stared in submission at a chequerboard of black and white paving stones, awaiting their fate. The path along which they'd been dragged was laid out with black and white pebbles. And, sneaking a glance, Jack saw the mansion itself was built of white walls and black pillars. Just like his striped *hakama*, everything in the *daimyo*'s domain appeared to be either black or white.

'Shizu's craftsmanship is beyond compare,' said *daimyo* Sanada, sheathing the blade with the utmost respect. 'Certainly far too good for a *gaijin*!'

He handed the *daishō* to one of his retainers, a bald-headed man with sharp slanting eyebrows and a sour crumpled face. Jack's heart sank. Having risked so much to retrieve them, his precious swords had once again been taken from him.

The *daimyo* paced in front of his three prisoners. 'I didn't expect your capture *so* soon. The warrant for your arrest was only delivered by the *metsuke* this very morning.' He waved the scroll before them. 'Three travellers – a *ronin* with a beard, a *hinin* girl and a hat-wearing *gaijin* samurai carrying red-handled Shizu swords. I suppose it wasn't hard for my officers to spot you. But I'm puzzled why you've come to Nara in the first place?'

Jack saw little reason not to answer the *daimyo*. Despite their dire situation, he still wanted to know the fate of his father's *rutter*.

'I've been trying to reach Nagasaki and leave Japan – as decreed by the Shogun – but I was ambushed on the border of the Iga mountains and had all my belongings stolen. We came here looking for them.'

The *daimyo* sighed in mock sympathy. 'That is such a great shame. And what exactly have you lost?'

'The *inro* on your *obi* to begin with,' said Jack, nodding to the lacquered carrying case. 'One of your samurai stole it from me.'

'That is a very grave accusation. This was a gift from my advisor, Kanesuke-san,' revealed Sanada, indicating the bald-headed retainer. 'Are you calling him a *thief*?'

'Why not ask him where he got it?' challenged Jack.

Kanesuke's face screwed up with barely concealed outrage, but *daimyo* Sanada didn't even glance in his direction. 'Why should I even entertain the suggestion? *You* are the felon here.'

'But that *inro* was a gift to me from *daimyo* Takatomi for saving his life from the ninja Dragon Eye –'

'*Daimyo* Takatomi?' interrupted the lord, his interest suddenly piqued. 'A *most* honourable and astute man. He sits on the Shogun's Council next to me. I do recall he once mentioned this incident in your defence to the Council. *If* it is yours, I need proof first.' He undid the *inro* and held it close to his chest. 'Describe to me the design and I'll believe your claim.'

Jack nodded his assent.

'But if you fail,' added *daimyo* Sanada, his eyes narrowing, 'Kanesuke gets the pleasure of cutting off the *hinin* girl's right hand.'

A guard seized Hana, undid her bonds and forced her to hold out her arm. Kanesuke, borrowing another guard's *wakizashi*, placed the blade's edge upon her wrist. Hana looked to Jack with terrified pleading eyes.

'A *sakura* tree,' blurted Jack, 'in gold and silver.'

The *daimyo* looked unimpressed. 'You could easily have seen that when you were brought in.'

'The blossom is in ivory!'

'I still need *convincing*.'

'But I've told you the design!' Jack insisted as Kanesuke raised his sword and Hana began to scream.

'Then tell me, *gaijin*, how many birds are in the tree?' the *daimyo* demanded, a crafty smile upon his lips.

Jack wracked his brains, trying to remember. His mind had gone blank under the pressure. Hana's scream faded into a pitiful whimper, her face turning deathly pale as Kanesuke adjusted his grip upon the sword, ready to do the deed.

'Wait!' cried Jack as the *daimyo*'s trick dawned on him. 'There are *none*!'

Kanesuke looked to his lord for permission to cut off the hand, but *daimyo* Sanada's smile disintegrated into a scowl. 'Correct.'

Kanesuke, incensed by the disclosure, brought down the sword to chop Hana's hand off anyway.

'NO!' ordered Sanada, glaring at his advisor. 'The *gaijin* won the challenge. And it would appear *he's* telling the truth about this *inro*.'

The man visibly shrank under the severe gaze of his master, returned the sword and shuffled, head bowed, to his former position. Hana clasped her hand to her chest with relief.

The *daimyo* toyed with the *inro* in his hand. 'I'd willingly give this back to you, but you'll have little use for it where you're going.' He passed the carrying case to another of his retainers. 'So, we have your *inro* here and, of course, your swords . . . what about this book called a *rutter*?'

Jack's mouth dropped open in shock. 'You have it?'

The *daimyo* slowly shook his head. 'I was hoping you did. The Shogun has requested its return.'

'Return?' Jack exclaimed. 'But it's mine. It belonged to my father.'

'You lay claim to much, young samurai,' said the *daimyo*. He walked over to a small wooden table, tutting in disappointment. 'It's most unfortuate you no longer have it. I'd have gained great favour with the Shogun for finding this *rutter*.'

Surprisingly, Jack discovered he was relieved to hear that the *rutter* had not been found. The Shogun was the last person he wanted to own it. That meant Botan might still have the logbook, unless he'd traded it . . . or thrown it away . . . or used it for tinder. With a death sentence hanging over his head, Jack realized he might never know.

Daimyo Sanada seemed lost in contemplation for a moment.

He sat down at the table on which a set of black and white stone counters was arranged in a complex pattern across a square grid scored into the table's surface. From a bowl he removed another small white stone and placed it down with a *clack*.

'Have you played the game of Go before?' he suddenly asked.

Jack shook his head.

'How uncivilized your country must be!' remarked *daimyo* Sanada. 'Then it's my duty to introduce you to Go before you die.'

Astounded, Jack couldn't help himself. 'As you intend to kill us, why on earth would I want to play *any* game with you?'

'For your freedom?' suggested *daimyo* Sanada to Jack's utter disbelief. 'In respect of the great service you showed *daimyo* Takatomi, I propose a game for you to win your life back.'

'But I've no idea how to play,' said Jack.

'Oh, the rules are simple,' said the lord, waving away his protest. Sanada looked to Ronin. 'I assume you know the game.'

Ronin, tight-lipped since their arrival, gave a barely perceptible nod.

'Good. Then I'll give you the rest of the morning to teach the *gaijin*.'

'You're too kind,' Ronin muttered.

'But if I beat you,' interjected Jack, 'how can I trust your word?'

'I'm an honourable man who plays by the rules and my word is my bond,' replied the *daimyo*, offering an ingratiating smile.

Jack knew that was probably the best he'd get. 'And what about my friends?'

The *daimyo* considered them for a moment, then threw up his hands. 'Why not? I'm in a generous mood. You'll all be released . . . *if* you win.'

Turning to Kanesuke, *daimyo* Sanada instructed, 'Keep six guards on them at all times. They can use the game board by the tea house. You are responsible for them, but first I need to speak with you *alone*.'

As the *daimyo* and a very repentant Kanesuke headed for the mansion, Ronin leant close to Jack and whispered, 'He's playing a cruel game with us. We don't stand the remotest chance of winning Go against the likes of that man!'

'But he said the rules were easy,' interjected Hana, with a desperate look of hope.

'Go may be simple to learn,' acknowledged Ronin, 'but it takes a *lifetime* to master.'

37

THE RULES

Despite his pessimism, Ronin agreed to teach Jack, since the postponement of their death sentence might give them an opportunity to escape.

While the three of them sat round the board beside the tea house, going over the rules, the six guards stood at a distance. But so far they hadn't taken their eyes off their prisoners or their hands off their swords.

'Think of this board as a piece of land to be fought over,' said Ronin, his fingertip marking out the grid of nineteen by nineteen lines. 'Go is a game of territory and your aim is to control as much of the board as possible and to capture your opponent's pieces by surrounding them.'

Ronin removed a black counter from a smooth, rounded rosewood bowl.

'These stones are your "men",' he said, placing the counter upon one of the grid intersections. 'You can put them on any unoccupied point, known as a "liberty". Once played, the stones are not moved. They can be surrounded and captured during the course of the game by the enemy occupying all of its adjacent "liberties", in which case they're removed from the board as prisoners.'

Taking three white counters from a second bowl, he placed them on the empty points immediately above and to either side of the black stone, leaving the one space below unoccupied.

'A stone's liberties are horizontal and vertical, but not diagonal,' explained Ronin. 'The black counter is now in *atari*, meaning it's about to be captured because it only has one liberty left. Where would White put a stone to take Black as prisoner?'

Ronin handed Jack a white counter. Without hesitation, Jack placed it on the vacant point below the black stone.

'Good,' said Ronin. 'But always handle your stone between your second and middle fingers. It's more elegant and good etiquette.'

Removing Jack's white counter from the board, Ronin replaced it with a black and added several more in an L-shape.

'Stones occupying adjacent horizontal and vertical points create a connected group. Think of these groups as mini-regiments. They share each other's liberties, so are stronger and more resistant to attack. A group can only be captured when *all* its liberties are occupied by enemy stones.'

He surrounded the Black L-unit with white counters.

'This group is now held prisoner –' he removed the black pieces – 'and White has gained all this territory in its attack. Such battles as this will decide who wins the game. At the end, once both players can find no way to take more territory, capture stones or reduce their opponent's area, the liberties inside their own territory are counted along with any prisoners they've taken. The winner is the player with the highest score.'

'That seems easy enough,' said Jack, grasping the concept with little difficulty, since the game didn't appear to be any harder than the Draughts he'd played with his father.

'Don't be fooled!' warned Ronin. 'Capturing stones is only *one* way of gaining territory. Eventual victory has more to do with the deployment of your stones to surround territory. Strategy is everything in this game.'

Ronin began to lay various groups of counters across the board. 'Placing stones close together helps them support each other and avoid capture. See?' He pointed to a connected Black group that appeared surrounded by White but still had two liberties. 'On the other hand, placing stones far apart creates influence across more of the board and helps you gain territory.' He surrounded the board's top right corner with a division of white counters to demonstrate this in action. 'The challenge of Go is in finding a balance between these conflicting interests. You need to be both defensive and offensive, always choosing between tactical urgency and strategic planning.'

'How do you know all this?' asked Hana, who sat cross-legged beside them, enthralled.

'My father and I played every day,' Ronin replied wistfully.

Jack noticed the faintest of smiles appear at the corner of the samurai's mouth, but then it was gone.

'He believed it should be a part of every warrior's training. The game is essentially a martial art. And the best way for you to learn, Jack, is to play the game.'

Ronin slid the bowl of black stones over to him.

'Black goes first. I'll explain more concepts along the way.'

Stone by stone, Ronin and Jack played a mock game. At first Jack placed his stones randomly across the board, but soon found himself under attack from all quarters by White. As the game progressed, Ronin showed Jack how to connect his own stones, cut through his opponent's groups, reduce their area of influence and invade another's territory.

'Life and Death is played out upon the board,' explained Ronin. He pointed to two of Jack's groups. 'Despite having liberties, these are already dead since they can't avoid eventual capture. So don't waste your time playing these groups any more.' He indicated one of his own units formed into a figure of eight. 'This group is alive and can *never* be captured. See the two "eyes" in the middle here and here. You can't place a stone at either point because, with no liberties, your counter would be committing suicide. Formations like this are the key to your survival on the board.'

They played through several matches, each time Jack lasting a little longer and gaining more knowledge of the game. Ronin introduced him to the concept of *sente* – a play that threatened capture and allowed development of other positions – and even when to sacrifice groups in order to carry out a plan in a more important area.

Jack felt as if his head would burst. There was so much to take in. He understood the basic gameplay and tactics, but the larger strategic concepts still eluded him. Go was far more subtle and complex than it appeared.

'You'll have to do a lot better than that!' scolded Ronin. 'Your mistake is to concentrate on single conflicts. You need to see the game as a whole, look for patterns and formations, as if commmanding a battle with many fights occurring simultaneously across the board.'

They started again. Jack was concentrating so hard that he lost all track of time and only realized it was lunch when a servant appeared with a meal of plain rice and water. They ate while they played on.

Taking Ronin's advice, Jack decided to treat Go as a martial art and tried applying his Two Heavens training to the game. Just as he split his attention to wield two swords, he divided his focus between different areas of the board. The game transformed in his mind into a simultaneous duel against four swordsmen, and gradually he began to make gains against Ronin – first he captured an entire group, then he managed to create two 'eyes' and was even beginning to invade Ronin's territory!

'I think you're winning!' exclaimed Hana, delighted. Then she looked at Ronin's grave face. 'Jack *is* winning . . . isn't he?'

Studying the board, Ronin went to reply when Kanesuke skulked into the garden and over to the tea house. He had a devious grin on his wrinkled face.

'Time to play.'

38

A GAME OF GO

A table had been set in the middle of the garden's chequerboard courtyard. The *daimyo*, in an all-white *hakama*, sat to one side, his expression solemn, as befitted a game of Go. Jack faced him, equally serious, trying desperately not to show his pre-match nerves. Despite the *daimyo*'s sombre attitude, it was still just a game for him, but for Jack it was a matter of life and death.

Ronin and Hana knelt at the edge of the courtyard, guarded by the six samurai. Kanesuke, having arranged tea for his master, settled at a respectful distance to the side of the board as official adjudicator.

'I'm looking forward to this game, however short it may prove to be,' *daimyo* Sanada revealed, taking a sip of *sencha*. 'You see, I'm intrigued as to how the foreign mind will strategically tackle Go.'

Jack couldn't believe the man's audacity. He was playing with their lives purely to satisfy his own curiosity.

'As this is your first proper game and I wish to be fair, you can be Black and I'll also give you an advantage of four stones.'

Jack looked to Ronin for an explanation.

'You can place a counter at each of the corners, three points in, before the *daimyo* makes his first move. This gives you influence in all key areas of —'

'Enough!' interceded the *daimyo*, holding up his hand. 'Explanation of the rules allowed, but no further tutoring!'

Jack laid out his four starter stones, remembering to hold each between his second and middle fingers. Nodding with approval at the correct etiquette, the *daimyo* gently placed his first counter in the upper left corner of the board.

'Let battle commence.'

For the first dozen moves, Jack followed Ronin's pre-planned opening strategy. He tried to exert influence over the lower right-hand side of the board, letting the *daimyo* lay claim to the top left. He then began a campaign to exclude White from the bottom half, but the *daimyo* countered – positioning a White stone against his lone Black and reducing its liberties by one. *Daimyo* Sanada attacked again, seizing another liberty, and Jack immediately had to strengthen his own stone by forming a group of two Blacks.

The game continued in this manner, each player loosely making claims to territory in different parts of the board, while occasionally invading with a direct threat to take prisoners.

The *daimyo* sighed contentedly. 'A game of Go is a work of art. The play of black upon white and white upon black has a creative magic, don't you think?' He didn't wait for Jack to answer. 'The flow of spirit and the harmony of the players is like music in the mind.'

His next stone hit the board with a loud *clack* to emphasize his point. The *daimyo* had made an aggressive move, cutting between two of Jack's groups with the aim of further destroying Black's influence in the lower area. The smaller unit was now isolated and Jack knew he had to act decisively to avoid its imminent capture. A similar situation had occurred in one of Ronin's mock games and he'd rallied to their defence, but Ronin had reprimanded him for this. Instead he had to go on the offensive – be the instigator of *sente* – otherwise he'd be forever on the back foot. Jack attacked White hard, aiming to surround one of its upper groups.

'*Kiai!*' said *daimyo* Sanada, surprised at Jack's tactics. 'You have fighting spirit, *gaijin!*'

With White forced to flee the assault, Jack was given the opportunity to stabilize his own threatened group *and* potentially trap three of the *daimyo*'s stones in the process.

Daimyo Sanada studied the board carefully. 'Mmm . . . you've taught him well, Ronin. I'll need to raise my game.'

'Recess,' announced Kanesuke, following a nod from the *daimyo*.

Having one last look at the board, *daimyo* Sanada took a short walk round the garden to contemplate his next move. Although unaware such breaks were allowed, Jack was thankful. His brain was aching from the intense period of concentration. He got up too and stretched his legs, passing as close to Ronin and Hana as he dared.

'I can't believe it!' hissed Ronin. 'You've got him on the run!'

'But he's seizing control of the entire upper board,' replied Jack under his breath.

Ronin shook his head. 'The outcome of the game may well hinge on the fate of those three White stones,' he explained. 'If you can kill them and White gets no compensation in any other area, the *daimyo* will lose. But if they live, White will win the game.'

Jack glanced at the board. The three little White stones represented their three lives and he felt the intense pressure upon him grow. So far he'd been employing Ronin's tactics, but now, as they entered the middle phase of the game, he'd have to rely solely on his own strategies.

The *daimyo* returned from his walk and sat back down, indicating for Jack to join him.

'Good luck!' whispered Hana, barely concealing her anguish.

Taking a deep breath, Jack gave her his most confident-looking smile and returned to the board. *Daimyo* Sanada, a stone in hand, held it tantalizingly over the game.

'Now the battle *really* begins.'

39

CONSTELLATIONS

White opened with an invasion into Black's right-hand territory. Jack tried to block it with his next stone, but a masterful play by *daimyo* Sanada simultaneously threatened the capture of a Black group and the future freedom of the three key White stones.

Jack retaliated, attempting to stop White building a lifeline and saving them. But in spite of his best efforts, he found his defences crumbling under the *daimyo*'s onslaught. He was being attacked from all quarters and his battle strategy began to unravel. Focusing on surrounding the three White stones and killing them, Jack missed *daimyo* Sanada's drive across the upper half of the board. Before he'd even realized it, a group of four Blacks had been surrounded and taken prisoner.

Jack despaired. He'd lost virtually all influence in the upper territory. How could he ever hope to win now?

'Can I call a recess?' he asked.

'By all means. I'm *enjoying* this game immensely,' replied *daimyo* Sanada, taking the opportunity to talk with Kanesuke.

Jack paced the courtyard, slowing as he passed Ronin and Hana.

'Don't worry,' whispered Ronin, with as much conviction as he could muster. 'It's possible to suffer losses in one area, but still fight back and win.'

'How can I?' replied Jack. 'He's surrounding all my groups.'

'You have to see the *patterns* in his strategy! Predict his movements. View the whole board –'

'Time!' called Kanesuke, noticing the exchange.

Returning to his seat, Jack stared bleakly at the board. He couldn't see any 'patterns', only individual conflicts. The configuration of Black and White was almost meaningless on a large scale and there appeared no obvious way to interpret a strategy from it.

'If he takes much longer, we'll be playing by starlight!' remarked Kanesuke sarcastically.

Constellations!

Jack was hit with a flash of inspiration. As a ship's pilot, his father had taught him how to navigate by the stars. At first, there'd been so many constellations he'd been unable to interpret the sky at all. His father, though, had shown him how to *see the small in the large and the large in the small*. Gradually, Jack had learnt to recognize key star clusters and then, all of a sudden, he was able to read the heavens at a single glance and steer a safe course across the featureless ocean.

If he viewed the White stones as stars and his Black as the night sky, he could picture the whole battle in his head. Almost at once patterns started to emerge, and a strategy formed, revealing a glimmer of hope that he could navigate his way to victory.

He now saw that the *daimyo*'s plan was to sacrifice his three White stones and in the process destroy Black's prospective territory at the bottom of the board. Immediately Jack made a play for this area. Two groups formed – White and Black – and there was a race to capture one another. Jack got there first, seizing four prisoners and securing the zone.

The *daimyo*, his nostrils flaring, snatched up a White stone and retaliated with an invasion for the mid-left. But now he could see the game in its entirety Jack's instincts told him to ignore this. Instead he placed a stone in the centre of the board with a loud *clack*.

'*No!*' exclaimed Ronin at such a reckless move. But it was too late. The stone had been placed.

Daimyo Sanada grinned. The *gaijin* had made a fatal error!

Yet Jack's intuition told him that this was the right strategy. He kept deploying stones in seemingly unorthodox positions and the *daimyo*'s initial gloating turned to worried confusion. As the battle intensified, *daimyo* Sanada started to run his fingers noisily through his bowl of counters. Jack, gathering from Ronin's expression that this was inappropriate etiquette, knew he'd thrown the *daimyo* off his game.

Frowning deeply, *daimyo* Sanada hesitated in all his responses. But his mood lightened once he managed to create a group with two 'eyes'. He then positively grinned when he connected this living group to the three White stones.

Shaking his head in despair, Ronin could no longer watch the game. It was clear they were doomed. His eyes darted to the six guards who stood nearby. There was a chance he could overpower one, maybe two of them. But without his swords any escape attempt was sheer suicide.

'That's an illegal move!' declared Kanesuke tersely.

Ronin's attention was brought back to the board and he saw that Jack had put a Black within one of White's 'eyes'.

'With no liberties, you're committing suicide,' explained *daimyo* Sanada with glee.

'But doesn't my stone capture *that* piece?' Jack asked innocently, pointing to the adjacent White trapped against the edge.

Ronin took a second look at the gameplay and gasped. 'A *false* eye!'

Although Jack's stone appeared to be surrounded, he actually had captured one of White's. The *daimyo*, having been distracted by Jack's unconventional strategy, fumed at his error in judgement. Whatever he did now, he could no longer save this group since it was enclosed on all sides by Black. On Jack's next move, the other 'eye' was filled and he imprisoned the false living group – along with the three key White stones. Like an entire constellation of stars dying at once, Jack had surrounded a quadrant and taken it prisoner.

The game entered the final phase . . . with everything to play for.

The battles over stones and fights for territory were bitter, each and every liberty hard won. Jack no longer consciously thought about strategy. He just relied upon his instinctive reading of the board.

Daimyo Sanada pushed into the one remaining gap in Black's wall of defence, but Jack quickly shut him out, preventing further capture. The boundaries between White and Black were now fixed. The *daimyo* recognized there were no more stones left vulnerable to attack and he passed on his next move, handing Jack a White prisoner as required by the rules. Jack passed too, surrendering one of his own Black stones in return.

'Game over,' stated Kanesuke, and the count of unoccupied liberties and prisoners began.

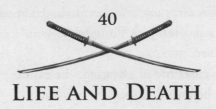

40

LIFE AND DEATH

Jack sensed he might snatch an unthinkable victory. And he could see it in the *daimyo*'s eyes too. After all the conflicts, the balance of Black and White was too close to call.

Stooping in to count, Kanesuke stumbled and fell into the table, scattering the stones everywhere.

'You fool!' exclaimed *daimyo* Sanada, with something that sounded like relief. 'How can we judge the score now?'

Kanesuke bowed his head in shame, but Jack caught the crafty grin on his face.

'Jack won,' stated Ronin.

'There can be no winner!' the *daimyo* snapped. 'The count was incomplete.'

'Black conquered White by two points.'

'You couldn't see from over there.'

'But I did!' snarled Ronin, getting to his feet. Two guards seized him before he'd even taken one step towards their lord.

'The game is forfeit,' declared *daimyo* Sanada. 'Take them away.'

'But that man fell on purpose!' Hana protested as she was dragged across the courtyard. 'You cheated!'

The *daimyo*, stepping into her path, grabbed her by the throat. For a second, Jack thought he would order Hana's immediate execution.

'*No one* accuses me of cheating,' he said in a cold tone, reaching for his sword. 'Especially a *hinin*!'

Hana didn't back down. 'Your word . . . is your bond!' she spluttered.

'I should kill you right now for your insolence. But I *am* a man of honour and respect the *bushido* code,' he said, letting her go. 'Our agreement was *if* the *gaijin* won, I'd set you free. But unfortunately there was no winner.'

'Then play again,' she said, shrugging off the guards.

Daimyo Sanada turned to Jack. 'As entertaining as the game was, I have business to attend to. Another time perhaps. Yet, in fairness, I will give you the chance to win your freedom.'

The *daimyo* asked for Kanesuke's money pouch. Emptying the coins on to the table, he then picked up two Go stones from the ground and put them in the cloth bag.

'Choose a stone,' he said, presenting the money pouch to Jack. 'A white means life. Black is death.'

Jack contemplated the innocuous bag. Once again the fate of his friends lay in his hands. At least, this time, he had an even chance of saving them.

'I'm not having you decide whether I live or die!' Hana snapped, grabbing Jack's hand as he was about to reach in.

'I don't care who does it,' said *daimyo* Sanada impatiently.

'We'll let *janken* decide,' Hana announced, pulling Jack and Ronin aside.

'What's *janken*?' asked Jack, bemused by Hana's sudden intervention.

'Rock, paper, scissors,' she replied, rapidly making a fist, an open palm and a V-shape with two fingers. She lowered her voice to a whisper. 'I saw the *daimyo* put *two* black stones into the bag.'

'You can't accuse him of cheating a second time,' said Jack. 'He'd execute us all on the spot.'

The three of them had a mock game of *janken*, not even paying attention to the result. They were purely playing for time in a desperate hope one of them would think of a plan.

'He never had any intention of letting us go,' spat Ronin, glancing round at the circle of heavily armed guards in preparation for a last-stand fight.

'No more time-wasting,' said *daimyo* Sanada, shaking the bag. 'It's a simple choice. White or Black. Life or Death . . .'

'Let me do it,' said Hana to Ronin and Jack.

'What's the point?' said Jack. 'We *can't* win!'

'Trust me,' she insisted, a mischievous twinkle in her eyes.

Striding over, Hana reached into the bag. A triumphant smirk formed on *daimyo* Sanada's lips in expectation of the result.

Jack and Ronin waited with baited breath. They both knew she couldn't plant a white stone in the bag. The *daimyo* would simply accuse *them* of cheating, since there would be three stones in play. So what was her plan?

With a flurry, Hana drew out her hand and clumsily dropped the stone before anyone saw its colour.

'Oh, no!' she cried as it landed among the other Go counters on the floor. 'Now we don't know which stone I took out.'

'No matter,' said *daimyo* Sanada, his patience worn thin. 'You've lost your chance for freedom.'

He beckoned the guards.

'Wait!' said Hana excitedly. 'We *do* know which colour stone I picked. Just look in the bag.'

Jack and Ronin exchanged glances at Hana's brilliance. She snatched the pouch from the *daimyo*'s hand and emptied the contents into her palm. A black stone tumbled out.

'See, I picked the white!' she exclaimed. 'LIFE!'

Daimyo Sanada fumed at being outsmarted. The guards faltered, unsure whether to proceed or not.

'Your word is your bond,' reminded Hana, smiling sweetly at him.

41

A PARTING OF WAYS

'I can't believe he let us go,' said Jack as they fled the outskirts of Nara and entered the lower slopes of a mountain forest.

A light rain was falling, but even this couldn't dampen their spirits. The *daimyo*, incensed as he was, had remained true to his word, even to the point of returning their swords and handing over the *inro*.

'He won't let us get far,' said Ronin, supping on a fresh bottle of *saké*. Hana had been sly enough to slip a couple of Kanesuke's coins into her kimono sleeve and they'd stopped briefly for supplies. 'But at least we have a *chance* of escape. Thanks to Hana.'

Ronin clamped a hand on her shoulder, squeezing it with affection. 'How did you ever think to outwit the *daimyo* like that?'

Hana lowered her eyes bashfully. 'I've done a few confidence tricks in my time. It just takes one to know one.'

Laughing, Ronin pulled her close. 'I take back what I said about you, Hana. You may be a thief, but you're more courageous and loyal than many samurai I've known.'

Hana beamed at such praise. Seeing them together, almost

like father and daughter, Jack realized they were good for one another – perhaps even *needed* each other. It was certainly the first time Ronin's eyes had been filled with something other than regret.

As they came upon a crossroads, Ronin's expression turned serious once again. 'This is our parting of ways,' he announced.

Hana's jaw dropped, all her joy extinguished in an instant. 'B-b-but why?'

'There's a warrant out for our arrest. As a group, we're too easily spotted.'

Jack knew Ronin's decision made good sense. With the Shogun's samurai, Kazuki and his Scorpion Gang, and now *daimyo* Sanada's men after them, they had little hope of avoiding capture. Individually, at least, Ronin and Hana could blend in and disappear.

'But where would I go?' said Hana, highly distressed at the impending split. 'I *like* being with you both.'

Seeing her in such a state, Jack knew Hana would more than likely wander straight into one of the search parties.

'Couldn't she go with you, Ronin?' Jack suggested tentatively.

'Yes!' Hana exclaimed, seizing the possibility. 'Ronin, you could be my teacher and I could cook for you and . . .'

Ronin shook his head firmly, but couldn't bring himself to look at her. He was clearly finding this as hard as she was.

'I attract trouble,' he said, glancing darkly at his *saké* bottle. 'That's no place for a girl to be.'

Hana grabbed hold of Ronin's sleeve. '*Please*. You won't even notice me.'

'No!' said Ronin, snatching his arm away.

Tears welled in Hana's eyes, the rejection hurting more than the idea of separation.

Jack couldn't risk Hana accompanying him to Nagasaki either. He was even more of a target than Ronin. But he had another idea. And it solved a problem that had been burdening his heart since Kyoto.

'Hana, I need you to go east . . . to Toba.'

'Another quest?' she replied, brightening slightly.

'Yes, an extremely important one,' he urged. 'You must warn Akiko that Kazuki is looking for her and wants revenge.' He handed her the *inro*. 'Show this to Akiko and she'll know you're my friend. She'll look after you.'

'Come with me!' Hana implored.

'I can't. I'd lead the Scorpion Gang right to her,' Jack explained. 'I'll be going in the opposite direction and intend to leave a trail, ensuring that I get spotted so as to draw them away from Toba. Will you do this for me?'

Hana grasped the *inro* in both hands and nodded with determination.

'Thank you,' said Jack, relieved there was now a possibility Akiko would be forewarned.

They shared out their provisions and Jack and Ronin watched Hana stride up the path, waving one last time before she disappeared over the rise.

'She's a brave soul,' said Ronin. 'I'll miss her.'

'Even her talking?' said Jack, surprised to hear such an admission from the samurai.

'Even *that*,' admitted Ronin. He turned to Jack. 'I'm sorry we couldn't find your *rutter*.'

'We tried,' Jack replied, putting on a brave face. 'But I agree, it'd be suicidal to continue our hunt for Botan under the circumstances.'

He knew it was time to face the hard truth. As devastating as it was – the *rutter* was lost. *What you want is sacrificed*, the Riddling Monk had said. *This* must be the sacrifice he was talking about. After all the effort, hardship and risks, Jack had to forgo his last connection to his father, his guarantee of a future and break his promise never to let the logbook fall into the wrong hands.

'Don't you worry, I'll keep an eye out for that rogue . . . and the *rutter*.'

'You've done more than enough,' insisted Jack. 'Please don't risk your life any further.'

'I don't have much of a life left to risk,' said Ronin, holding up his bottle. 'But it was an honour to help you, young samurai.'

He bowed and headed north towards Kyoto.

'Wait!' said Jack. 'I owe you for your services.'

'You owe me *nothing*.'

'But I do,' insisted Jack, running after him. 'It's a matter of honour. We agreed, you could choose one item from whatever we recovered.'

'But I couldn't take your swords.'

'Then . . . have the pearl,' offered Jack, opening up his kimono to pull out the gold hairpin. He hated to sacrifice the black pearl, but Akiko would have wanted him to stand by their agreement. It was the right thing to do.

'How touching!' said a voice thick with sarcasm.

Jack and Ronin spun round. A samurai in a dark brown

kimono grinned at the confused expressions on both Jack and Ronin's faces. Barrel-chested, with arms like knotted ropes, he looked a formidable and experienced warrior. His rugged handsome face was framed by a neatly trimmed goatee and moustache. But his nose was flattened, certainly as a result of being broken in a fight, and a battle scar marked his chin.

'Ronin! I never thought I'd see you again,' said the man, opening his arms in a friendly gesture.

Ronin stared at him, bemused and wary. His hand went to his sword.

'I feel hurt that you don't remember me.'

Ronin squinted and studied the man's features more intently. 'My memory's hazy. Remind me.'

'You were quite drunk at the time. In fact, I'm surprised you haven't climbed all the way into that bottle by now.'

'Who are you?' demanded Ronin.

'Botan, of course.'

Jack and Ronin simultaneously drew their swords, stunned their quarry had found *them*.

'Why would you want to attack an old friend?' said Botan, showing no concern at their hostility.

'I'm no friend of yours,' Ronin replied. 'Where's the *rutter* you stole?'

Botan laughed. 'I was about to ask you that very same question!'

'What do you mean?' said Ronin, frowning.

'Come now, you *must* remember. Kanesuke was most insistent that I find this book called a *rutter*. Now, my friend, please tell me where it is.'

Jack was as perplexed as Ronin by this line of questioning. 'We were seeking you because *you* had it.'

'I wasn't speaking to you, *gaijin*,' snarled Botan. 'You're supposed to be dead.'

He turned back to Ronin, all smiles and pleasantry. 'I must admit I was surprised to discover you were accompanying the *gaijin*. Especially as *you* helped rob him in the first place!'

Both Ronin and Jack's look of acute shock sent Botan into convulsions of deep booming laughter.

'You liar!' said Ronin, but a shadow of doubt passed across his face nonetheless.

Jack caught it and stared at his friend in disbelief. Had Ronin really attacked him before they met at the tea house in Yamashiro? Was their whole friendship based on a deception?

He looked first to Ronin, then to Botan, searching for the truth.

'I can't believe *neither* of you remember,' exclaimed Botan, shaking his head in amusement.

Suddenly the man's laughter was all too recognizable. The scar. The broken nose. And the odour of excess *saké* originating from Ronin became disturbingly familiar too.

Like the clearing of a sea mist, a memory emerged from the recesses of Jack's mind . . .

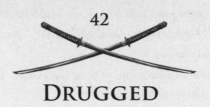

42

DRUGGED

'Allow me to buy you a drink,' slurred the drunken samurai, sitting down uninvited at Jack's table in front of the village inn, set beside the mountain road.

'That's kind of you, but my vows don't allow it.' Jack was disguised in the blue robes of a komusō, a Monk of Emptiness, and wore their trademark wicker basket over his head so as to be unrecognizable as a foreigner. And he wished to keep it that way by avoiding company, especially any samurai.

'I insist.' The drunk waved the innkeeper over. 'A saké for me and for my friend a . . .'

'Sencha,' said Jack, realizing a refusal might draw an angry reaction from the samurai and he didn't wish to attract any more attention. There was a group of three samurai on another table, chatting and joking. One in particular – a muscular man with a scar on his chin and a deep booming laugh – had been glancing over at him since his arrival and Jack didn't fancy his chances if he was forced to fight his way out.

The innkeeper scurried off with their order.

'I'm Ronin by the way . . . and you are?'

'Takeshi,' replied Jack, using his guardian Masamoto's first name.

'Pleased to meet you,' said Ronin, his head lolling in an attempt at a formal bow. He reached out and prodded Jack's hat. 'Why do you wear these funny baskets?'

'It's a sign of our detachment from the world,' Jack explained, steadying the basket with his hand.

'Strange to hide your face like that.'

Their drinks arrived and, much to Jack's relief, Ronin was distracted from further enquiry.

'I'll pour,' Ronin offered, fumbling with the teapot. With an unsteady hand, he decanted a cup and pushed it across the table to Jack.

'Kampai!' said Ronin, knocking back his saké in one.

Jack took a sip. The tea was extremely bitter and of poor quality. Ronin, smacking his lips appreciatively at the rice wine, spotted Jack's shakuhachi on the table.

'I've always wanted to play one of these,' he said, picking up the long bamboo flute that was the other symbol of the komusō monk. He put his lips to it and blew hard. A strangled screeching sound burst out.

'Must be broken,' he said, giving it a cursory inspection before handing it back. 'Anyway, where are you headed?'

'South,' replied Jack, quickly finishing off his tea. The conversation was entering dangerous territory again.

Ronin sucked in air between his teeth. 'Dangerous. Many bandits.'

'Thank you for the drink,' said Jack, picking up his pack and swords, wrapped in a cloth so as not to rouse suspicion.

'Tell you what, Takeshi, I'll be your guide.'

'That won't be necessary.'

'But I insist,' he said, getting unsteadily to his feet. 'Don't want a monk getting into trouble, do we?'

Jack took off at a good pace down the road and entered the mountain forest.

'In a real hurry to pray, aren't you?' remarked Ronin, catching up as they hiked through the countless cedar trees. 'Good thing I know a short cut!'

He dragged the protesting Jack off the main road and along a narrow path that cut through the woods, following the edge of a narrow gorge. They hadn't gone far when Jack began to feel drowsy and a wave of nausea hit him.

Seeing Jack stumble, Ronin said, 'You should rest a while.'

In no fit state to argue, Jack let himself be helped over to a tree and sat down. His limbs felt as heavy as lead and the earth seemed to be rolling beneath him. He closed his eyes against the sickening sensation . . .

43

LIVE TARGET

'*You* drugged me!' shouted Jack, backing away, one sword raised at Botan, the other now at Ronin.

'I did?' replied Ronin. And then the memory slowly dawned upon him as well. '*You* were the *komusō* monk?'

'I thought you were honourable. A man of *bushido*! A samurai!'

'It was the drink!' he implored, shaking his bottle with disgust. 'I was desperate and *needed* work. I was told we were trapping a spy . . . disguised as a *monk*! And I have good reason to hate spying monks.'

Jack ignored his pleas. 'That's why the gambler in Kizu knew your name. You're one of Botan's gang! How can I trust you now, Ronin?'

'I've been helping you since –'

'But I wouldn't be in this mess if it wasn't for *you*!' interrupted Jack.

Ronin lowered his head in shame. 'I made an unforgivable mistake.'

'Is that you or the drink talking? It's no surprise you're a *ronin*. No master would want you in their service!'

'I'm sorry to interrupt this lover's tiff,' smirked Botan. 'There are more pressing matters at hand. Now what did you do with the *rutter*, Ronin?'

Jack glared at Ronin, equally eager to hear the answer.

Ronin regretfully shook his head. 'I . . . I can't remember.'

'You're a useless waste of a samurai, Ronin,' said Botan, throwing up his arms in frustration. 'No wonder you failed your father.'

Anger flared in Ronin's eyes. Brandishing his *katana*, he charged at Botan.

'Put down your swords!' shouted a man emerging from the forest. It was the gambler from Kizu. 'Or else your friend dies!'

Ronin stopped in his tracks when he spotted Hana, a knife held to her throat by the gambler.

'Perfect timing!' said Botan.

Three more men emerged from the forest to surround Jack and Ronin.

'If you harm one hair on her head,' growled Ronin. 'I'll –'

'You're in no position to make threats,' said Botan. 'Do as Shoda says.'

With no alternative, Jack and Ronin laid down their swords. Immediately, they were both seized and forced to their knees.

'This is your last chance, Ronin. Where's that book?'

'I told you I don't remember.'

'Perhaps this will jog your memory,' said Botan. He turned to one of his men. 'Tie the girl to that apple tree over there.'

Once Hana's arms had been bound to the trunk, Botan borrowed Shoda's knife and stood beside her. 'Tell me, or I'll cut this little girl's tongue out.'

He grabbed Hana around the head and forced her jaw open. She struggled and squealed, but Botan was too strong.

'Have mercy!' cried Ronin. 'She's got nothing to do with this.'

Ignoring him, Botan put the blade inside Hana's mouth.

'Stop!' shouted Ronin. 'I think . . . I might remember.'

Botan smirked. 'See, all it took was a little encouragement.'

'It's still a blur,' Ronin admitted, rubbing his forehead. 'I don't even recall the robbery! I just remember waking up next to a gorge . . . a bearded man . . . in red robes . . . sat before me, gibbering away in rhymes . . . I thought I was dreaming or gone mad . . . He had a book in his hands – the *rutter* I presume – and riddled me for it . . . but I got the answer wrong . . .'

'What nonsense!' snorted Botan, raising the knife once more to Hana's terrified face.

'No!' said Jack. 'He must be talking about the Riddling Monk.'

Botan and his henchmen laughed at this. 'He's just a myth. A story told to scare little children.'

'But I've met him,' Jack insisted, desperate to save Hana. 'I can take you to the shrine he prays at.'

Botan released Hana from his grip and walked over to Jack.

'You'd better not be lying, *gaijin*,' he said, waving the knife menacingly before him. 'Otherwise, I'll cut out far more than your tongue.'

'Release Hana first.'

Botan contemplated this. 'No, but you can . . . with these.' He pulled out five *shuriken* from a pouch on his *obi*.

Jack's eyes widened in disbelief at seeing the throwing stars his ninja friend Tenzen had given him.

'I found them in your pack,' explained Botan, noting Jack's expression with curiosity. 'Don't tell me you pretend to be a ninja too!'

Jack didn't reply.

'We'll soon find out. Shoda, put a fallen apple on the girl's head. We're going to have a little game before we leave to find this Riddling Monk.'

Botan held one of the *shuriken* in his right hand and took aim at Hana, who stood petrified, still tied to the tree.

'The problem with a live target is that they often scream –' he threw the star '– and bleed.'

The pointed *shuriken* struck her. She cried out as blood began to flow. The throwing star's razor-sharp edge had clipped her right ear.

Botan passed Jack a ninja star. 'Let's hope, for Hana's sake, you're more accurate than I am. Hit the apple, she goes free. But if you don't . . .'

44

BULLSEYE

Jack hadn't practised with a *shuriken* since leaving the ninja village. He weighed the weapon in his hand, trying to get the feel of it again. The stars were deadly, capable of wounding, incapacitating and even killing their victims.

For a moment, Jack considered using the *shuriken* to attack Botan or one of his gang, but Shoda had his knife again and was close enough to slay Hana before he'd taken two steps. Ronin was still on his knees, morosely staring at his bottle of *saké*, and could no longer be trusted to help.

'I need three attempts,' stated Jack, indicating the other *shuriken* in Botan's hand. 'It's been a while since I threw one of these.'

Botan eyed him suspiciously. 'If that's what it takes.'

Jack lined himself up with Hana. She was a good thirty paces away. He couldn't afford to make even the slightest error of judgement. He'd have to allow for the breeze, while the growing drizzle of rain made the throwing star slippery to hold. Taking a deep breath to calm his nerves, he decided on an over-arm technique and launched the star at Hana. The *shuriken* whistled through the air but was wildly off target.

The point slammed into the trunk beside Hana's right wrist.

'You almost took my hand off!' she exclaimed, much to the amusement of Botan and his gang. 'Have you *ever* done this before?'

'Once or twice,' Jack replied, giving her a sheepish look and taking the next *shuriken* from Botan.

Hana's face went pale as Jack tried an under-arm delivery this time. The spinning star flashed towards her, in direct line with her eyes. She screamed . . . as it lodged itself a hair's breadth to the left of her head.

'You're getting closer,' smirked Botan.

'No more, Jack!' Hana pleaded, staring in horror at the deadly star.

'I think I'm getting the hang of it now,' replied Jack, holding up the third *shuriken*.

He flicked the weapon with a side throw. It spun crisply towards its target, striking the apple dead centre. The fruit exploded, sending chunks flying everywhere. Botan's gang broke into spontaneous applause at the feat, while Hana almost fainted with relief.

'Very impressive,' said Botan, flipping the remaining *shuriken* in his hand. 'But I can do better than that. *Her heart!*'

'I thought you might,' replied Jack, roundhouse-kicking the samurai in the stomach before he could release the star.

As soon as Shoda saw his leader attacked, he drew his knife and went for Hana. Jack snatched the *shuriken* from Botan's hands and launched it at Shoda. The star pierced his leg, hobbling him.

'Run, Hana!' cried Jack. 'I've cut you free!'

Hana glanced down to see the *shuriken* next to her right

hand had sliced into the rope. She yanked hard and it snapped. One of Botan's men rushed to seize her. Hana shook off her bonds, grabbed the *shuriken* beside her head and immediately drove one of the star's spikes into the man's arm. Yelling in pain, he clasped his bleeding wound. She kicked at his knee with all the force she could muster and there was a sharp crack before the man crumpled to the ground.

Meanwhile, Jack dived to evade Botan's sword slicing him in half as the samurai, roaring with rage, recovered and attacked him. Rolling to his feet, Jack ducked as another swipe of the sword almost beheaded him. His *katana* and *wakizashi* lay out of reach on the ground behind the samurai. Without these, he wouldn't survive long.

Ronin had snapped out of his despair as soon as he'd seen Hana set free and now leapt into action. He threw *saké* into the eyes of his captor, then used the man's own swords to finish him off. Snatching up his discarded *katana*, he went to attack Botan but the fifth samurai of the gang stopped him and they became embroiled in a bitter duel.

Unchallenged, Botan advanced on Jack. His sword whirled through the air and Jack retreated before the deadly blade. Driven back against a tree, he had nowhere to go and Botan closed in to seal his fate. But an apple flew out of nowhere and struck the samurai full in the face.

'Bullseye!' cried Hana, punching the air.

Botan staggered backwards and Jack seized the opportunity to run for his swords.

Hana's delight was short-lived as Shoda came lurching towards her, knife in hand. She began to pelt him with apples too. But the gambler batted them away and she ducked behind the tree. Shoda came round the other side, blocking her escape. She screamed and ducked as he slashed for her face.

Ronin, seeing her desperate plight as she ran round and round the tree, redoubled his efforts to defeat his own opponent. He smashed the man's sword aside and mortally wounded him with a devastating slice across the belly. The samurai collapsed, clutching his entrails, as Ronin dashed to Hana's rescue.

The rain now fell in earnest as thunderclouds rolled over the mountains. Jack snatched up his swords and confronted Botan. Despite the samurai's intimidating physique, Jack felt empowered with his Shizu swords in hand and raised both weapons into a Two Heavens guard.

Wiping the apple remains from his face, Botan snarled at Jack, 'That fancy sword work won't save you!'

Botan attacked and their swords clashed like lightning against the darkened sky. The samurai proved brutal. His immense strength was an advantage and Jack felt his arms shudder with every impact. He had to call upon all Masamoto's sword training to defend against the onslaught.

The rain ran into their eyes and the ground became treacherous underfoot as the wet earth turned to mud. Jack attempted an Autumn Leaf strike in the hope of disarming Botan, but the samurai kept hold of his sword and managed to counter with a thrust that sliced across Jack's upper arm. Blood gushed out as the blade dug deep. Jack reeled away, parrying the sword to one side. He glanced at his injury. It was a flesh wound, but deep enough to compromise his left arm's fighting ability.

Botan knew this too and began to focus all his attacks on Jack's weak side. A heavy blow caused Jack to lose grip on his *wakizashi* and he was left to rely solely upon his *katana*. Exhausted and bleeding, Jack was forced into a retreat. Botan kept up the pressure, hammering him with strike after strike. Jack stumbled over one of the dead samurai, slipping in the mud and falling to one knee. Seizing the opportunity, Botan was on top of him in an instant.

'It's time to claim my reward!' he declared, aligning his sword with Jack's neck.

As the blade arced towards him, time stood still for Jack . . . then the steel tip of another blade pierced Botan's chest. Groaning, the samurai clutched at his heart and fell to the ground, dead.

Ronin stood there, thunderous and bloodstained. Shoda lay motionless at the foot of the apple tree. Hana, shaking like a leaf, appeared unharmed. Ronin took a step forward. Jack hurriedly got to his feet and raised his sword. Ronin may have just saved his life, but the samurai was no longer to be trusted.

'What now?' Jack demanded, his temper fired up by the heat of battle. 'Are you going to drug me? Kill me? Steal my swords? Or have you been after the *rutter* all along? You've been leading me round and round. Never getting anywhere! You're not a samurai. You're a drunk and a liar!'

45

MOUNT JUBU

'You're right, Jack,' admitted Ronin, a dark look on his face. 'Though I never lied to you, I have failed you. Like I failed my father. And I failed myself. No master wants a drunkard for a samurai. I don't deserve to bear these swords.'

Ronin drove his *katana* into the earth. It stuck there, quivering with the force of his rage. Picking up his half-empty bottle of *saké*, he strode off into the pouring rain.

Hana ran over to Jack. 'Where's he going?'

'To the nearest inn, probably,' said Jack, tearing a strip of cloth from Botan's kimono to bind his bleeding arm.

'But he didn't say goodbye.' Tears now mixed with the raindrops running down her face. '*Ronin, come back!*'

Ronin kept walking, the bottle pressed to his lips.

'We're better off without him,' replied Jack, taking another swatch of cloth and applying it to Hana's bleeding ear. 'He can't be trusted. He was part of Botan's gang.'

'I don't believe it,' said Hana, turning on Jack. 'Ronin saved my life. He killed Botan saving *yours*!'

'He also drugged me and stole my possessions.'

Hana stared aghast at Jack. 'If that's true, why's he been helping you?'

'Because he couldn't remember robbing me in the first place! But you heard him; he *had* the rutter. And, for all we know, he would have taken everything again and killed me for the Shogun's reward.'

'That's *not* the Ronin I know,' protested Hana, defiantly folding her arms.

Jack went over and wrenched the *shuriken* from the tree. He knew he wasn't making perfect sense. Before Botan appeared, Ronin had just been about to walk away without accepting *any* payment. True, the samurai was flawed – volatile, unpredictable and ruled by the bottle – but he wasn't evil. Jack sensed a deep loyalty and feeling of duty in the man's heart. After everything Ronin had done for him, Jack now regretted the things he'd said in the heat of the moment. But none of it changed the fact that Ronin was responsible for his predicament.

Jack collected the other four *shuriken* and put them in their pouch. Another of his possessions found. Only the *rutter* remained. And if Ronin had been telling the truth, then Jack knew where to look for the person who had it.

'I'm going back to Kizu,' announced Jack. 'Hopefully, I can retrace my steps back to the Shinto shrine where I met the Riddling Monk.'

'I'll come with you,' said Hana.

'No, I need you to warn Akiko. This monk shouldn't be too hard to find, unless he *really* is a myth and I dreamt him.'

'He's no myth,' Hana revealed. 'He lives in the old abandoned temple on Mount Jubu, north-east of Kizu, on the other side of the river. No one's crazy enough to go there. But . . .' She swallowed and seemed to go a little pale. 'But I could guide you in its direction and head to Toba afterwards.'

'Let's go then before anyone else turns up,' said Jack, pulling his damp kimono around him.

He took off down the path before realizing Hana wasn't following him. She still stood beside Ronin's *katana*, her head bowed.

'What are you waiting for?' he asked.

'Ronin will come back for his sword,' she said, wedging the *origami* crane Jack had given her into a gap in the *katana*'s handguard. 'And when he does, I want him to know he still has a friend.'

Hana and Jack passed through Kizu in the dead of night. Once certain no one was patrolling the bridge, they crossed the river and immediately turned north-east off the road and into the thickest part of the forest.

'We have to follow the river valley,' Hana explained.

'How do you know the way?' asked Jack, noting there wasn't even a path.

'I don't,' she admitted. 'But once I was forced to hide out on this mountain and got lost. I saw the Riddling Monk while I was up here and caught a glimpse of his temple at the top. I'd heard the rumours about him and ran away.'

The two of them stumbled on, following animal tracks and sometimes having to cut their own trail through the undergrowth. The route steepened and, in the darkness and rain, the footing became treacherous. Eventually, Jack called a halt when they reached an overhanging rock face.

'We should rest here for the night. Out of the rain,' he suggested.

'You're right,' said a breathless Hana. 'We'll need our strength to climb Mount Jubu in the morning.'

They took shelter from the downpour in a small cave. Jack tried to get a fire lit, but all the wood was too wet. Without any heat, they sat shivering on a rock and had to make do with cold rice and raw vegetables. Jack braved the deluge once more to cut down some leafy bushes to form a makeshift bed. It was damp but better than the hard stone floor.

Lightning flashed across the sky and thunder rolled down the valley, its deep rumble reverberating within the cave. Hana instinctively edged closer to Jack.

'I hope this storm passes soon,' she chattered, her trembling now seeming to be from both cold and fear.

Jack put an arm round her and began rubbing her for warmth. 'You needn't worry,' he said. 'I've sailed through far worse at sea.'

'You don't understand. This is a cursed mountain,' she said, looking up at him with eyes as wide as the moon. 'They say the mountain god of Jubu roars when he's angry.'

Another burst of lightning scorched the sky.

'That's him fighting the river god. If he loses, his sides run with blood, he blocks the rivers and floods the valley below.'

Hana cowered into Jack's embrace as thunder filled their ears.

'Is that why this temple's abandoned?' asked Jack.

'Partly. But it's also haunted by *onryō*.'

'Real *onryō*?'

Hana nodded. 'I heard a *kōshakushi* tell its tale once. Many,

226

many moons ago, at the time of Emperor Temmu, Jubu Temple was a place of dark magic. A monastery of mystic monks. It was said they could move mountain boulders with a single hand; read a man's mind and bend it to their will; they *even* had the power to control the elements.'

She shuddered at this thought. Jack felt her fear, but inside he smiled to himself. Her description reminded him of the ninja and their *kuji-in* magic. He'd witnessed the *shinobi* accomplish just such things using the power of the Ring of Sky. *He* had even been taught some of their dark arts.

'The Emperor declared them evil spirits and sent his army in to destroy the temple,' she explained, her voice thin and hollow. 'A huge battle took place. Of the ten thousand troops that climbed this mountain, only a hundred returned and most of them had been driven mad. Of the thousand monks that supposedly resided at the temple, none of their bodies was ever found. But their spirits *still* haunt the grounds. And anyone who trespasses is subject to their wrath and never seen again.'

'So how has the Riddling Monk survived?' asked Jack.

'He's *one* of those ancient monks. They say, if you can't answer his riddle, he takes your soul.'

She went deathly quiet.

'We should get some sleep,' suggested Jack, unsettled by the story himself but not wishing to show it. He'd been riddled by the monk and had yet to provide an answer.

They lay down upon the leafy bedding, Jack keeping his swords close to hand. Through sheer exhaustion Hana was soon fast asleep. Jack listened to her steady breathing and the sound of the raindrops echoing in the cave. As he hugged himself for warmth, he touched the soft silk of the *omamori* hanging from his *obi*. Unhooking it, he stared at the amulet's little green bag.

How had he come into possession of this?

Again he wondered what had happened after Ronin had drugged him. Had the samurai also been responsible for his injuries? Why had Ronin split from the gang? And how come he'd been left in possession of the *rutter*?

Jack willed himself to remember. The sky flared and the mountain god roared again. Just as he drifted off to sleep, the memory slipped back . . .

46

MUGGING

'Take a look at this fancy inro, Botan,' said a voice.

Jack felt the carrying case tugged from his obi. He floated on the edge of consciousness, too weak to move. The basket upon his head had twisted and all he could see were four pairs of sandalled feet.

'Hey, what's going on?' slurred a voice belonging to Ronin.

'This is no longer your business,' replied a gruff man.

'I thought he was to be interrogated,' said Ronin. 'Not robbed!'

'You've done your job. Now take your saké and go.'

'Botan, when did a monk ever carry swords like these?' questioned a third man.

'Hey, Manzo, he's got a string of money too!' exclaimed the first voice. 'And a bag full of food, clothes and a . . . book?'

'Who is this man?' questioned the gruff voice. 'Shoda, let's see his face.'

The basket was wrenched from Jack's head.

'A gaijin!' exclaimed a gaunt-looking samurai, dressed in a grey threadbare kimono. He stumbled away, basket in hand.

'You're so easily scared, Shoda. He's just a boy!' teased a younger samurai with high eyebrows and a jutting jaw. He was wielding one of Jack's swords. 'You know I could defeat anyone with a weapon like this.'

'I wasn't scared, Manzo. I just didn't expect to see another face as ugly as yours!'

Ronin, quaffing on a large bottle, stared in shock at the unexpected foreigner.

'This isn't just any gaijin,' said Botan. 'Blond hair, blue eyes and samurai swords. He can only be the gaijin samurai those dōshin are seeking. We've struck gold! There's a reward of a whole koban on this boy's head.'

Shoda's eyes widened in greedy delight.

'Tell me, is this gaijin worth more alive or dead?' he asked, his leering face drifting in and out of focus before Jack.

'Not sure,' replied Botan. 'But it's too much effort dragging him to Kizu. Just take his head.'

On hearing this Jack wanted to scream, but could only manage a feeble groan.

'Let me!' volunteered Manzo, hefting Jack's katana in one hand.

'No!' shouted Ronin, drawing his sword and blocking Manzo's blade. 'This is not what was agreed.'

'Plans have changed,' said Botan.

'I won't stand by . . .' Ronin swayed uncontrollably '. . . and let you . . .' He shook his head trying to clear it '. . . murder an innocent boy . . .'

Ronin collapsed to the ground, his bottle rolling into the bushes.

Manzo laughed. 'I can't believe you drugged his saké too.'

Botan stood over the comatose Ronin. 'Remind me never to hire a drunken samurai again.'

'What are you going to do with him?' asked Shoda.

'Nothing. He won't remember any of this by the morning.'

'Good, then we won't have to split the spoils with him either.'

'It'd be unfair to leave him with absolutely nothing,' said Botan, *picking up Jack's* rutter *and dropping it into Ronin's lap. 'At least he'll have something to read when he eventually comes round!'*

Botan gave a deep booming laugh at his sick joke.

'Now kill the gaijin and bag his head.'

Grinning, Manzo swung the blade at Jack. Facing certain death, Jack's survival instinct sent a surge of adrenalin through him. Willing every muscle in his body to move, he rolled out of the way as the blade sliced for his neck, embedding itself in the tree instead.

Struggling to his feet while Manzo tried to pull the sword free, Jack snatched up his shakuhachi *and brought it crashing down on the back of the samurai's head. Manzo dropped to the ground like a stone.*

'Stop him!' snarled Botan.

Shoda rushed in. Jack, too drugged to react to the flurry of punches, was caught full in the face. His lip split and blood flooded his mouth. With a desperate thrust, he drove the end of the shakuhachi *into Shoda's gut, winding him. Having no real control over his body, Jack then did the first thing that came to mind — Demon Horn Fist — a ninja technique of simply driving head first into your opponent. Like a battering ram, Jack struck the wheezing Shoda, knocking him off his feet.*

A moment later, Jack was sent flying by a devastating kick from behind. He landed upon the lip of the gorge and barely had the strength to stop himself rolling over the edge. Losing grip on the flute, he watched it bounce down the slope and drop into the raging river below. Defenceless, he tried to crawl away into the bushes, but Botan was already bearing down on him.

Blows pummelled him into the earth. Every time he tried to rise, Botan hit him again. His vision blurred as he was struck on the head and his left eye swelled. Then Botan kicked him in the stomach before hauling him to his feet.

'I'm going to enjoy killing you,' he said, spitting into Jack's face.

In a last-ditch effort, Jack headbutted Botan. There was a satisfying crunch as his nose broke. Botan roared in agony and let go. Jack's legs, too weak to hold him, gave way and he lurched towards the edge. As he toppled backwards he grabbed for Botan's obi, *but his hand only caught the green silk* omamori *hanging from it. Jack tumbled over and over, his clothes tearing on the thorny bushes and the rocks battering his body, until his head struck . . .*

. . . Jack awoke, the grey light of morning seeping into the cave. It was still raining, but the worst of the storm appeared to have passed.

Rubbing his eyes wearily, he stood up and groaned with pain, his left arm stiff and sore from the sword cut. But at least he now recalled everything. How he'd got his injuries. How he'd acquired the *omamori*. How he'd escaped. And how *he'd* broken Botan's nose!

Most importantly, he knew Ronin hadn't really been part of the gang. He'd been deceived too, and he *had* tried to save Jack's life.

But it was too late to worry about such matters. Ronin had his demons to deal with and Jack had the *rutter* to find.

47

ALL MAD

Leaving Hana to sleep on, Jack performed a healing mantra before changing the bandage on his arm. Then he foraged for some breakfast to supplement their dwindling supplies. When he returned to the cave, he found Hana awake and pacing the floor in an anxious state.

'There you are!' she exclaimed. 'I thought an *onryō* had taken you in the night.'

Jack smiled. 'No chance of that. Remember, I was one myself!'

His joking seemed to calm her and when he produced a sleeve full of berries and nuts, her face positively lit up. They tucked into their breakfast, then looked for a route up the sheer cliff. Halfway along, Jack spotted a face carved into the rock. It was partially hidden by a bush and covered in lichen. With wild hair, three eyes and long sharp teeth, the terrifying image did nothing to allay their fears. But it did indicate a narrow ledge along which they could ascend.

'At least we know we're on the right path,' said Jack, going first.

Clinging to the wall, they sidled up the cliff in painstaking steps. The rock was slippery and Hana's legs trembled all the way. Jack was impressed by her courage – she didn't complain or freeze at any point. Reaching the top, Hana let out a huge sigh of relief.

'That's the easy part over,' she gasped.

Below them, the forest formed an unbroken carpet all the way to the river, which wound like a silver snake down the valley basin. Above, a new forest began, giant cedar trees stretching as far as the eye could see.

'Where's this temple then?' asked Jack.

Hana pointed to the wooded peak of Mount Jubu in the distance. A glimmer of a pagoda spire could be seen jutting out of the canopy.

'No wonder it's abandoned,' said Jack, realizing it would take them all day to reach.

A narrow track wound its way upwards through the forest and they trudged along, the rain dripping heavily from the spreading cedars overhead. Their trek took them through countless swollen streams and they had to negotiate several trees that had fallen during the night's storm and blocked the path. Quickly the forest became claustrophobic. The maze of cedar trees had strangled all life from the ground and what little sunlight there was struggled to break through. Jack was glad when they finally emerged from its disturbing gloom to stand beside an expansive mountain lake.

'Let's stop here for lunch,' he suggested, cupping his hands and drinking from its waters.

Sitting upon a large boulder, they shared half the remaining rice and admired the waterfall cascading over a craggy rock face and into the lake. The point at which the lake flowed into a river was clogged with fallen trees, forming a natural dam. The scene was quite beautiful and for a moment they both forgot about their quest.

As soon as they finished eating, Jack suggested they move on. Once again, the forest swallowed them. By late afternoon, the path they'd been following petered out and Jack was forced to rely on his natural sense of direction to guide them. The trees crowded in on either side of them and the forest grew darker, but his confidence rose when he spied another of the gruesome faces carved into a boulder.

Jack was keeping his eyes peeled for another sign, when Hana grabbed his arm.

'I think there's someone ahead,' she whispered.

Sure enough, a figure sat motionless upon a rock, his back turned to them.

Not daring to breathe, Jack and Hana hid behind a tree and observed the man.

Several long moments passed and nothing happened. Jack waited a little longer before deciding to make an approach. Signing for Hana to stay where she was, Jack stood, his hand ready upon his sword, and walked up to the man. He still didn't turn round. In fact, he didn't move at all. It was then that Jack realized the man was a statue.

The figure was unsettlingly lifelike, almost as if the man had been turned to stone where he sat. But the eyes had been plucked out, his tongue was forked and the mouth was fixed in an eternal scream. The image sent a cold shiver through Jack.

'It's a warning,' said Hana, almost making Jack jump out of his skin. 'An outer demon to the temple.'

A crashing through the undergrowth made them both spin round. But, when they looked, there was no one there. Just an eerie stillness among the trees.

'What was that?' said Hana, her voice no more than a whisper.

'Must have been a falling branch,' replied Jack, keeping a firm hold of his sword. 'Best keep moving.'

The rain now dripped in a sluggish rhythm from the canopy above and the air seemed heavy, almost too dense to breathe. A mist hung among the trees and Jack felt a growing sense of foreboding.

All of sudden, disembodied giggling echoed through the forest and a branch cracked nearby.

'Did you hear that?' gasped Hana, flinching, her eyes round with fear.

'Yes.' Jack nodded and drew his *katana*.

They crept onwards. A clump of ferns twitched, seemingly alive with spirits. But when Jack hacked them down, there was nothing.

Hana's breathing became agitated and rapid as panic overwhelmed her. '*Onryō*. We should get out of here!'

'Stay calm. It was probably just some animal,' said Jack, though he too felt the creeping coldness as the mist wrapped its tendrils around them.

Shadows flitted between the trees. Jack and Hana picked up their pace, fear driving them on. The ground beneath their feet hardened and the mist parted briefly to reveal a hidden pagoda. Lopsided, with green walls, the forest had grown into it, tree roots wrapping themselves around its base.

They had entered Mount Jubu's abandoned temple.

But it didn't feel very abandoned to Jack or Hana.

Maddened laughter assaulted them from behind. Turning, they saw a skeletal man in a tattered robe, his eyes sunken and his cheeks hollow. He stood beneath an ancient *torii* gateway, the entrance through which Jack and Hana must have passed unwittingly. Lurching towards them, one foot dragging behind, one hand outstretched, he croaked, 'Have you the Answer?'

Jack and Hana backed away from the hideous *onryō*. As they passed another decrepit building, a bony hand shot out from a shadowy doorway and grabbed Hana. She screamed and Jack wrenched her from its grip.

'Have *you* the Answer?' beseeched a voice from the building's dark recesses.

Several more voices joined the entreaty. '*Have you the Answer? . . . The Answer? . . . The Answer?*'

More emaciated bodies materialized out of the mist. Upon a flight of crumbling stone steps a man rocked to and fro, mumbling gibberish to himself. Another was slapping his head with his hands and howling like a wolf. Crouched in a corner, a woman was putting pine cones into a bowl, emptying them on to the ground, then repeating the process endlessly.

'They're all mad!' said Hana.

The chorus of '*Have you the Answer?*' grew and the skeletal man advanced on them, others joining his ranks. Jack and Hana found themselves surrounded and backed up against the pagoda.

Then suddenly the chanting ceased and the *onryō* scattered, disappearing into the shadows.

Glancing up, Jack saw a head thrust out of an upper window

of the pagoda. Bald, bug-eyed and bearded, it gawped down at him with wild delight. The head vanished and a moment later reappeared in a window on the floor below. It popped out again on the third, second and first floors, before the Riddling Monk, in bright red robes, burst from the pagoda's doorway and bowed with great ceremony.

Skipping round Jack and Hana, he waved a dead branch and scattered leaves over their heads in a bizarre imitation of a Shinto purification ritual. He stopped before Jack, bringing his face so close that their noses touched.

'Fish to a cat, you came back!'

48

RIDDLE ME THIS!

'I'm here for the *rutter* you riddled from Ronin,' explained Jack, trying his best not to be unsettled by the monk's proximity.

'A riddle he utter –' the monk's eyes rolled towards Hana – 'yet mine is still to answer.'

'He's *already* asked you a riddle!' exclaimed Hana with alarm.

Jack nodded. Hana pulled him away from the monk, whispering urgently, 'But you *have* to answer it. He'll take your soul if you don't.'

'You *really* believe that,' replied Jack, glancing at the monk who was now picking lice from his beard and eating each one with relish.

Hana pointed at the maddened ones hanging in the shadows, eyeing the Riddling Monk with devoted reverence. '*Onryō* or not, they look to have lost their souls to me.'

With a cold dread, Jack realized Hana could be right. The monk he'd taken for a harmless fool may be mad, but he had a powerful grip over the minds of others. Whatever his secret, he was a dangerous individual.

'Let's find the *rutter* and get out of here,' said Jack.

Hana stuck close to Jack as he approached the monk.

'Answer me this first,' he demanded. 'Do you know where my logbook is?'

The Riddling Monk smiled inanely. 'I have many a book. But what it took to take, you must challenge me or . . . your mind will break.'

'Be careful, Jack. It could be a dangerous trick,' said Hana.

'Why take life so seriously?' the monk laughed, dancing a jig around her. 'You can't get out of it alive, believe me!'

'Hana, too much is at stake,' said Jack, under his breath. 'Too many people have sacrificed themselves for this *rutter*. I made a promise to my father. There's no going back –'

'Of course you can't leave, you're in a circle, see!' interjected the monk, pirouetting on the spot. 'Once bound inside, it's riddle you, riddle me, riddle die.'

At that moment, the sun dipped behind the horizon and dusk fell upon the temple. The air chilled and the whole place became as ghostly as a graveyard. Like living corpses, the monk's maddened disciples slunk out of the shadows and encircled Jack and Hana.

'Looks like we don't have a choice,' said Jack, taking Hana's hand.

'Good! Better! Best!' exclaimed the monk, clapping with manic joy. 'The challenge is set, no more bets!'

He dragged them inside the ruined pagoda. Black as the devil's cave, they stumbled over bones, both animal and human, strewn across the main hall. The Riddling Monk disappeared into the darkness and Hana gripped Jack tighter as the sounds of slithering and ragged breathing shuffled around them. A leathery hand touched her face and she cried out. Jack drew Hana to him, shielding her from whatever horrors hid within.

The Riddling Monk clapped twice and several of his disciples lit torches with a guttering candle. The flickering flames revealed hungry, gaunt faces, toothless and terrifying, their cracked lips ceaselessly whispering, '*The Answer? . . . The Answer? . . . The Answer?*'

Spiders, the size of fists, crawled up the walls and cobwebs hung like veils from the rafters. The Riddling Monk was now perched upon a wooden throne, festooned with rotting fruit and long-dead flowers. He wore a crown of thorns and in his hand was a gnarled staff, which he beat upon the floor.

Thunk. Thunk. Thunk.

The whispering ceased and his disciples lay themselves down among the bones. Jack and Hana stood, still and silent, amid the madness.

Like a preacher in his pulpit, the Riddling Monk proclaimed, 'Unless a fool dies, he won't be cured.'

His disciples all cried, '*He* has the Answer!'

'Only a fool thinks he knows everything. It's the wise man who knows he knows nothing.'

'*He* has the Answer!' they praised.

The Riddling Monk stared at Jack and Hana with bulging eyes. 'Are you wise fools or foolishly wise? Let's see you pull the truth from its disguise!'

'*Ask a Riddle! Ask a Riddle! Ask a Riddle!*' chanted his disciples with feverish excitement.

The Riddling Monk held up a hand for silence.

'Riddle me this! What can run but never walks, has a mouth

but never talks, has a head but never weeps, has a bed but never sleeps?'

Jack was taken by surprise. He'd expected the original riddle about God and the Devil. But there'd be no point in arguing with a madman. He'd agreed to the challenge and so decided it was easier to play along with the monk's crazed game. He thought hard over this conundrum. The one the monk had given him the first time they met – *What gets wet as it dries?* – had a logical answer despite its seeming contradiction.

Hana looked anxiously to Jack, whose brow was deeply furrowed. 'Could it be a baby?' she suggested.

'Is that your Answer?' chirped the monk.

'NO!' said Jack quickly. He whispered to Hana, 'It can't be a baby. They weep.'

The answer was on the tip of his tongue. *A bed . . . a head . . . a mouth . . .*

Recalling his nautical lessons with his father, Jack addressed the Riddling Monk. 'The Answer is a river.'

'*Is it? Is it? Is it?*' intoned his disciples.

The Riddling Monk thumped his stick upon the floor. He glared at Jack before suddenly bursting into a crazed grin.

'Co-rr-ect,' he replied, emphasizing each part of the word as if it pained him to say so.

A collective gasp from the disciples filled the pagoda's creaking hall.

'Now I must give an Answer for an Answer. Yes, I know of this *rutter*.'

Jack was taken off-guard by the Riddling Monk's unexpected lucid response. 'Where is it then? Do *you* have it?'

The Riddling Monk laughed wildly, slapping the side of

his throne with glee. 'Two more questions, two more riddles! Once again, you're in the middle.'

Jack had been tricked. The Riddling Monk was playing games with them.

'Riddle me this! What's so fragile when you say its name you break it?'

Jack and Hana again fell into thought. This time the ideas weren't so forthcoming. Not for the first time, Jack wished Yori was with them. A dull headache began to pulse at his temples and Jack saw Hana was rubbing hers too.

'A china cup?' offered Hana, but dismissed it straight away. 'No, no, what other things break? Your leg . . . a wave . . .'

Then Jack thought of Jess and Akiko. 'Your heart! When you say a loved one's name that can break your heart, can't it?'

Hana nodded slowly, but still looked unconvinced.

'Answer me now or forever cower!' taunted the monk.

His disciples began to beat the floor. '*The Answer! The Answer! The Answer!*'

'What else could it be?' said Jack, the rhythmic pulse piling on the pressure and his headache intensifying.

Hana didn't answer. Her eyes were screwed up with pain. Jack felt it too, like a drum inside his head that only the correct Answer could end. He turned to the Riddling Monk. 'The Answer is –'

'No!' cried Hana, putting a hand over his mouth. 'Remember what that monk said to me when I shouted for you in the Tōdai-ji Temple – *Please don't break the silence.*'

Above the cacophony of pounding, Hana cried, 'The Answer is silence!'

The beating stopped and all eyes fell upon the Riddling

Monk. His face seemed to swell, burning bright red with annoyance.

'Co-rr-ect,' he spat.

The disciples wailed. Jack stared at Hana in amazement, now glad more than ever to have her company. The headache began to fade like a receding wave.

The Riddling Monk leapt out of his throne and began to pace the floor, muttering, 'I need a riddle, a riddle of rhyme, a riddle that turns and twists the mind.'

Behind him, Jack heard shuffling and saw the door had been blocked by a group of enraged disciples. A cry of jubilation brought his attention back to the monk, who now danced a jig upon the raised dais of the hall.

'Riddle me this! The one who makes it sells it. The one who buys it doesn't use it. The one who's using it doesn't know he's using it. What is it?'

This riddle proved even harder to fathom than the last. Jack's mind seemed unable to hold thoughts. They kept slipping away like eels, and his headache returned with a vengeance.

Hana fell to her knees. Jack dropped beside her. 'Hana! What's the matter?'

'I . . . I . . . I can't think . . .' she stuttered.

Jack realized whatever strange power the monk had, he was working its magic upon them. Driving them to the brink of madness.

49
THE ANSWER

As the vice-like grip on their souls increased, Jack felt as if he was fighting the monk – not with swords, but with the mind, each riddle an attack and every answer a parry. His mind strained under the stress of battle. It was now almost impossible to think of the Answer. Hana writhed upon the ground in agony, gibbering to herself. The disciples chanted louder, beating the floor with their fists.

'*The Answer! The Answer! The Answer!*'

Jack clamped his hands over his ears, his brain fit to burst. He felt as if he was dying . . . The beating sounded like a hammer . . . *Thwack! Thwack! Thwack!* . . . The cooper's wrinkled toothless face swam before Jack's eyes . . . *Funny, isn't it? How the person who pays for the coffin never wants it and the one who gets it never knows . . .*

'A COFFIN!' screamed Jack. 'THE ANSWER IS A COFFIN!'

Silence descended upon the pagoda.

Then a whispering, no louder than the wind, began. '*Is it? Is it? Is it?*'

The Riddling Monk threw his thorny crown across the room in disgust.

'Co-rr-ect!' he howled. Distraught, he jumped up and down upon his throne like an infuriated monkey. 'Riddle me this! Riddle me this! Riddle me –'

'No more!' said Jack, drawing his sword and pointing it at the monk. His disciples rushed to protect their master. 'We've answered all your riddles. Now answer me.'

The Riddling Monk stopped, neatened his robes and plonked himself back upon his throne. 'No need for violence,' he said, as if *he* was the one hard done by. '*Where is it?* Here. *Do I have it?* Yes!'

'Then hand over the logbook and we'll leave you, unharmed,' said Jack as he helped a trembling Hana to her feet.

The Riddling Monk wagged a bony finger at Jack, the mad glint in his eyes back again. 'No, no, no. You've still your first to go,' he taunted maliciously.

Hana stared at Jack in horror. '*None* of those was your riddle?'

The Riddling Monk's demented cackle echoed around the hall.

'Riddle me *this*, young samurai! What is greater than God, more evil than the Devil? Poor people have it, rich people need it, and if you eat it you'll die. Tell me this and I *shall* give it to you.'

Jack and Hana stared blankly at one another. Their faces were beginning to take on the gaunt strained look of the Riddling Monk's disciples. The web of riddles he'd cast had captured their minds. And each one they escaped only led to a more complex maze. Feeling his mind stretch and rip like a sail in a storm, Jack fought to control his sanity.

Think like Yori! Think like Yori!

He banged his fists against his skull, willing the Answer. 'What is it? What is it?'

'Only . . . the wisest of men . . . could work this out . . .' gasped Hana as she felt herself collapsing under the strain.

'What did you say?' asked Jack.

'Only the wisest –'

'You're right!' he said, grasping Hana by the shoulders with joyous relief. 'And the monk's already given us the Answer.'

She blinked uncomprehendingly at him.

'Only a fool thinks he knows everything. It's the wise man who knows he knows *nothing*,' explained Jack. '*Nothing* is greater than God, *nothing* is more evil than the Devil. Poor people have *nothing*, rich people need *nothing*, and if you eat *nothing* you'll die. The Answer is NOTHING.'

'Co-rr-ect!' fumed the monk.

'*He* has the Answer!' the disciples gasped in awe.

They all began to bow before Jack. But the Riddling Monk made a show of being less impressed. Indifferently inspecting his fingernails, he acted like a child bored with torturing an insect. 'You outfoxed a fox, but is the fox a fox at all?'

'Enough of your riddles, monk!' said Jack.

'As promised, you tell me the answer and . . .' The Riddling Monk rummaged in an old chest beside his throne. 'That is what I give you . . .' He opened his empty hands and crowed with laughter. '. . . NOTHING!'

Jack strode over and held the blade of his *katana* to the Riddling Monk's throat. The disciples didn't intervene this time. The monk swallowed and went pale.

'Here's a simpler riddle for you,' said Jack. 'What one object can save a life?'

With an unsteady hand, the Riddling Monk reached back into the chest and pulled out the familiar black oilskin that contained the *rutter* and Jack's pack, with Sensei Yamada's red silk *omamori* still attached.

'Co-rr-ect,' said Jack, slipping the pack over his shoulder and carefully stowing the logbook.

Backing out slowly, Jack and Hana emerged from the torch-lit confines of the pagoda into the temple courtyard. A pale moon shone, rain clouds skudding across the night sky. The monk's disciples parted to allow Jack and Hana through.

As they passed beneath the *torii* gateway, the Riddling Monk appeared at the pagoda door. Scuttling around his feet was a small furred badger-like creature with sharp teeth . . . a *tanuki*.

With a malicious smile, the Riddling Monk waved Jack and Hana goodbye.

'There are many paths but only one journey,' he cried, 'and the only true journey is the one within.'

He held a bony hand to his chest.

'Find your heart and you'll find your home, young samurai. But be prepared to lose far more than a book before your journey's end.'

50

THE LAKE

Glad to be leaving the malevolent monk behind, they stumbled through the forest, blindly following their old route down the mountain. They passed by the screaming statue and weaved through the labyrinth of cedar trees. The noise of a waterfall grew louder, so Jack knew they were getting close to the lake.

In the darkness it was hard to see more than a few paces ahead, so he used the blind fighting skills Sensei Kano had taught him the year before and navigated by his hearing only. They broke through some undergrowth and Hana cried out, dropping suddenly.

Only by the luck of the gods, Jack caught her arm as she tumbled over the lip of a craggy rock face, the waters of the lake shimmering below.

With an almighty heave, Jack dragged her back to safety.

'It's too dangerous in the dark,' he said, letting Hana recover from the shock. 'We need to find a place to rest until daylight.'

They gingerly skirted the edge of the drop until they rediscovered the main trail down to the lake. Taking shelter beneath a tree, they ate the remains of the cold rice, then bedded down for the night.

Jack was awoken by the sensation of water lapping against his feet. Looking around, he saw the lake had risen during the night and their chosen path was now completely flooded. The sky was overcast, but he guessed it was long past dawn so nudged Hana. Rubbing the sleep from her eyes, she yawned, then saw the lake.

'It's twice the size!' she exclaimed.

They waded round the edge to its outflow. Among the debris and trees that formed the dam, Jack spotted several dead fish caught up in the branches. With great care, he clambered across the creaking structure and managed to retrieve several of them.

Keeping two for breakfast, they stowed the rest in his pack. After a prolonged search, Hana found dry tinder and wood. In the meantime, Jack gutted the fish and plucked some wild herbs to season it. Once the fire was going, the mouthwatering smell of cooking fish filled their nostrils.

While they waited, Jack flicked through the pages of the *rutter*. His father's handwriting and codes brought comfort to him and he could almost hear his father's voice, instructing him in the craft of being a pilot. There was so much knowledge contained within the logbook: knowledge his father had discovered and that could change the fortunes of a nation. Jack was relieved to have it back in his hands, but the nightmare of the Riddling Monk's temple and the crazed looks of his disciples would haunt him forever.

'Do you think Ronin's all right?' Hana asked as she turned the fish on the fire.

'He's tougher than an old boot,' replied Jack, imagining the samurai propped up in some inn, a bottle in his hand. 'I only wish I had the chance to take back what I said. To let him know I no longer blame him.'

'I heard a storyteller once say, "Words are like water. Easy to pour but impossible to recover,"' said Hana. Then, sadly: 'I wish Ronin was with us now. I know he can be grouchy, but I do miss him.'

They both lapsed into silence, lost in their own thoughts.

'The fish is ready,' announced Hana.

They ate, savouring the smoky herbed flavour, and their spirits were lifted slightly.

Breakfast over, Jack stood and observed the dam. 'I think we should cross here.'

Hana eyed the rickety pile of trees and debris mistrustfully. 'But it could collapse at any time.'

'We'll have to take the risk. Unless you fancy swimming!'

Hana shook her head firmly. 'You know I can't.'

She warily followed Jack across. The tangle of branches and broken stems made the going treacherous. Water trickled steadily through the criss-cross of tree trunks. Conscious of the pressure building up behind the makeshift dam, Jack recalled the ninja Grandmaster's teachings . . . *Nothing is softer and more yielding than water, yet not even the strongest may resist it. Water can flow quietly or strike like thunder.*

Jack just prayed it would continue to flow quietly.

'Almost there,' he said, when they were balanced upon the final tree trunk.

Suddenly the tree shifted beneath their feet and a wave of water gushed towards them. Hana screamed. Dropping to all fours, Jack turned to grab her.

But miraculously she managed to cling on and the dam held.

With cautious urgency, they crawled along the remainder of the narrow trunk, knowing that any shift in weight could send the whole lot crashing down the mountainside, a lake full of water following in its wake.

Reaching the opposite shore, they both breathed a sigh of relief. Looking back, Jack now wondered how he'd even dared cross the precarious dam. It was a death trap waiting to happen. The familiar pitter-patter of rain began to send ripples across the surface of the lake and Jack and Hana ducked into the shelter of the cedar forest. Retracing their steps, they headed downslope and out of the valley.

'Still raining!' groaned Hana, pulling her head back from the cave's entrance.

After surviving the dam crossing, they had arrived at the lower cliff around late afternoon. Exhausted, they'd agreed it was best to stay the night, then head off at the break of dawn. But there was no sun to greet them. Rainclouds filled the sky, drowning out the feeble morning light.

'Rain's good,' replied Jack, much to Hana's surprise. 'It means less people on the roads.'

Leaving the shelter of the cave, they headed south-west towards the bridge at Kizu. Hana was soaked to the skin in a matter of moments, but the wide-brimmed straw hat Ronin had lent Jack kept him dry a little longer. Back on the main road, Jack walked with his head bowed, in case they met other travellers. But he needn't have worried. It was too early in the day and the torrential rain had convinced people to remain in their homes.

Emerging from the forest, they came upon the raging torrent that was the Kizu River. On the opposite bank was the town of Kizu itself. The wooden bridge, propped up on its legion of stilts, was completely deserted, its walkway now barely above the waterline. Wasting no time, they stepped on to the bridge and began to hurry across.

'I hope this is the last time I see this place,' said Jack.

'Me too,' said Hana, peering over the bridge's handrail at the fast-flowing waters. Then she turned to Jack. 'But I hope to see you again . . . one day.'

Jack smiled warmly at her. 'My mother used to say, a journey is best measured in friends rather than miles. Nagasaki's still a long way off, but I've travelled further with people like you helping me . . . and Ronin . . . than I ever could have done on my own. I'm forever grateful for that.'

'That's what friends are for, aren't they?'

'And I'm blessed to count you as one.'

Hana bowed her head, embarrassed. 'I'm simply happy you've got back Akiko's pearl, your swords and particularly your father's *rutter*.' She held up the *inro*. 'I'll be sure to return this to you . . . when we next meet. I wouldn't want you thinking that I steal from friends!'

'It's yours,' said Jack. 'A gift.'

'*Really?*' she replied, staring at the exquisitely crafted case in rapture. 'I've never been given such a valuable gift before. Thank you.'

She bowed again.

'*I'm* the one who should be bowing to *you*,' said Jack. 'I'm indebted to you for going on this quest.'

'It's an honour,' Hana replied, attaching the *inro* next to her *bokken*. 'I just pray I can get to Akiko in time.'

'Praying won't help,' said a familiar voice.

51

THE BRIDGE

'I said I'd hunt you down, *gaijin*.'

Kazuki stood behind them, his shaved head glistening with the rain.

Like warrior statues, the Scorpion Gang formed an unbroken line across the entrance to the bridge. Clad in black kimono, their red sun *kamon* upon their chests, the five young samurai – Nobu, Hiroto, Goro, Raiden and Toru – glared at Jack, hands upon their weapons, eagerly awaiting Kazuki's command so they could be unleashed.

Hana tugged on Jack's arm and they began to back away.

'There's no escape this time,' laughed Kazuki, nodding towards the other side of the bridge.

Glancing over his shoulder, Jack saw the Kizu end had been blocked by a garrison of *dōshin*. Armed with iron *jutte* truncheons and vicious *sasumata*, they formed an impenetrable barrier.

One look at the swollen river told Jack that their only other option would be suicidal, especially for a non-swimmer. It was now apparent why there had been no one on the bridge – Jack and Hana had walked straight into a trap.

Jack confronted Kazuki. He'd realized this day would come, but hadn't imagined it would be quite so soon. He also knew there was no hope of survival against such overwhelming odds. But he *had* to defeat his old rival. He couldn't allow Akiko to come to any harm at the hands of his enemy.

'I see the Two Heavens failed you,' smirked Kazuki, pointing to Jack's bandaged left arm.

Jack ignored the jibe. Despite a long session of *kuji-in* healing, his arm was still stiff and he had reservations about its effectiveness in a sword fight.

'Let Hana go,' he demanded. 'She has nothing to do with us.'

Kazuki shook his head, tutting. 'When will you learn that *anyone* who helps you signs their own death warrant?'

Hana took hold of her *bokken*. She briefly struggled to pull it from her *obi*, then unsteadily raised its tip to Kazuki. 'Jack's my friend . . . I'll willingly lay down my life for him.'

Jack was astounded at her courage. Despite being totally untrained, she was prepared to take on an experienced swordsman.

Kazuki burst out laughing. 'Yet again, a girl fights for you, Jack! And a *hinin* at that!'

Incensed, Hana rushed forward and slammed the *bokken* into Kazuki's thigh. 'I'm *not* a nobody!'

Taken by surprise, Kazuki buckled under the blow. Hana went to hit him again. This time Kazuki blocked it with his right forearm. Miraculously, the strike didn't break the bone; instead the wooden sword deflected off to one side. With terrifying speed, Kazuki drew his *katana* with his left hand and sliced for Hana's belly, aiming to cut her in half.

Jack ran to her aid, thrusting his sword between them and halting the lethal attack. The two young samurai glared at each other, their rivalry as fierce as ever.

The pounding of feet across the boardwalk announced the rapid advance of the Scorpion Gang.

'I *will* have my revenge, *gaijin*,' snarled Kazuki.

'No, you won't!' cried Hana, whipping him across the gut with her *bokken*.

Kazuki doubled over. But before she or Jack could finish him, the Scorpion Gang was on them. Driven into retreat, Jack battled to keep them at bay. Although he didn't have the strength in his left arm to wield two swords, his skill with a single *katana* meant he was no easy kill.

Hiroto came in first. 'I'm going to stick you like a pig,' he squealed in his cruel high-pitched tone. 'Just like you did me.'

Jack remembered throwing a knife at the boy in a last-ditch effort to stop Hiroto from hanging him during the attack on the *Niten Ichi Ryū*. The blade had pierced Hiroto's stomach and the boy had let go of the noose. Jack's mercy in allowing Hiroto to live might now be his undoing.

Meanwhile, Hana was confronted by one of Kazuki's hulking cousins, Toru.

'You hurt Kazuki,' he grunted. 'I hurt you.'

Toru didn't use a sword; instead he favoured a *kanabō*, an immense iron-studded club. He swung it at Hana. Squealing, she ducked and was forced to leap out of the way as the club came smashing down a second time. It ploughed into the floor, cracking the wooden deck and sending splinters flying. Hana valiantly tried to block the follow-up blow with her *bokken*, but the force of the strike knocked her to the ground.

Seeing the danger she was in, Jack feigned a wide attack on Hiroto. The boy went to block it and Jack kicked him hard in the stomach, targeting his old injury. Hiroto crumpled, wheezing for breath. As Toru moved to crush Hana with the club, Jack charged at him, his head down in Demon Horn Fist, screaming at the top of his voice, '*KIAAAIIIII!*'

Startled, Toru turned to pummel Jack instead. He raised his club just as Jack collided into him. It was like hitting a brick wall. But the impact was enough to knock Toru off-balance. He staggered against the bridge's handrail. It gave way and, pulled backwards by the weight of his *kanabō*, Toru toppled over the rail into the foaming waters of the Kizu River.

Enraged at their loss, the rest of the Scorpion Gang rushed Jack and Hana as one. Pulling Hana to her feet, Jack fled with her in the opposite direction.

The *dōshin* officer ordered his men to march on to the bridge, *sasumata* primed to meet them.

Trapped in the middle, Jack realized there was *no* escape.

'I won't let them take you,' said Jack, his sword held protectively across her.

'And I won't let them kill you either,' replied Hana, her *bokken* trembling in her hand.

Standing back to back, Jack and Hana faced their fate.

52

HONOUR AND SACRIFICE

'The *gaijin*'s head is mine!' shouted Kazuki, pushing through the ranks.

The Scorpion Gang immediately stepped back to allow the declared duel to take place. Kazuki and Jack had fought many times before, both in training and for real. Their sword skills were well matched and no decisive victor had yet emerged. But that was before Kazuki's right hand had been maimed by Akiko's arrow and Jack's left arm injured by Botan.

As Jack prepared for their final showdown, Hana was seized by a *dōshin*.

'You're the thief who stole my wife's fan!' he snarled.

Swinging her *bokken*, Hana managed to crack the man across the shin, forcing him to let go. Other *dōshin* rushed in, pinning her to the ground with *sasumata*. The officer stepped forward to skewer her with his sword.

Jack leapt to stop him, but Kazuki intervened first.

'Don't kill her yet!' he ordered. 'She has vital information.'

The officer reluctantly resheathed his sword, leaving Hana pinned down by his *dōshin*.

Wielding his *katana* left-handed, Kazuki circled Jack in the pouring rain.

'The Shogun's just doubled the reward for your capture – alive or dead,' Kazuki revealed, his eyes narrowing.

'It's good to know I'm valued,' replied Jack, raising his *katana* into a guard.

'But . . . I'll happily kill you for nothing.'

Like a bolt of lightning, a flash of steel cut through the air. Jack instinctively deflected it, then swung his own sword in a blistering attack for Kazuki's neck. Ducking, Kazuki thrust at Jack's stomach. Jack leapt aside, the sword's razor-sharp edge almost scything through his *obi*. He retaliated with a diagonal cut across the chest at the same time as Kazuki sliced for his body. Their blades clashed and they stared at one another between the cross of steel.

'You can't win, *gaijin*,' snarled Kazuki, pushing hard against Jack's sword.

Jack shoved back. 'I don't intend to beat *everyone*. I only need to defeat *you*.'

Releasing the pressure, Jack let Kazuki come for him. As their blades met again, he executed a Flint-and-Spark strike. The steel of his sword grated against Kazuki's. At the last moment, he deflected it aside and struck for Kazuki's heart. Grimacing with the effort, Kazuki barely evaded the attack, the tip of Jack's sword catching his kimono and ripping his red sun *kamon* from his chest.

'You'll have to do better than that!' Kazuki seethed and retaliated with a flurry of furious blows.

They battled through the downpour, while the Scorpion Gang and the garrison of *dōshin* watched on, transfixed by the life-and-death struggle. Kazuki's skill proved to be equal, if not better, left-handed, and Jack was forced to retreat under his onslaught.

'Behind you!' cried Hana.

Blocking Kazuki's strike to the head, Jack glanced round to see Hiroto with his *katana* aimed for his back. Gritting his teeth against the pain in his left arm, Jack drew his *wakizashi* and deflected Hiroto's blade away at the very last second. With almost blinding speed, Jack brought his *katana* down and thrust it backwards, driving the tip into Hiroto's gut.

Hiroto crumpled to the ground, clutching his stomach. 'Not again,' he wailed.

'I *said* he was mine!' snapped Kazuki, without a shred of pity.

Leaving Hiroto to bleed upon the floor, Kazuki turned on Jack.

'That's enough practice. Time to truly test your Two Heavens!'

Jack raised both his swords. The cut on his left arm had opened up and he could barely keep a grip on his *wakizashi*. In his current state, the Two Heavens was likely to be more of a hindrance than advantage against a samurai of Kazuki's ability. But he had no choice.

All of a sudden, chaos reigned in the ranks of the *dōshin*. Screams and cries of pain scattered the men to one side. A *dōshin* standing over the imprisoned Hana gasped, then spewed up blood. He collapsed to the floor, revealing a wild-eyed, bearded samurai behind.

'Ronin!' cried Jack and Hana simultaneously.

Seeing Hana caught beneath the prongs of several *sasumata*, the samurai's fury boiled and he went to work on her captors. Ronin was like a whirling dervish, his blade slicing through any *dōshin* who failed to run.

'KILL HIM!' screamed Kazuki, when his Scorpion Gang failed to respond to the unforeseen attack.

As soon as she was free, Hana scrambled to her feet, grabbed her *bokken* and rushed to Ronin's side. 'I knew you'd come back!' she exclaimed.

'It's a question of honour,' replied Ronin.

'And sacrifice,' said Jack, taking up position next to him as the Scorpion Gang lined up to attack. 'We're *all* trapped now.'

'I'd rather die on my feet – sword in hand – than live on my knees, clasping a bottle,' explained Ronin, looking Jack in the eye. 'I will right my wrongs. I will *not* fail you.'

'You *haven't* failed me,' said Jack, wishing there was more time to explain.

But Kazuki was on the warpath and Jack was forced to fight. His rival attacked with vengeful fury as his sword struck again and again. But Jack fought with equal passion, his strength renewed now the band of three was together once more.

Goro headed straight for Ronin, while Nobu lumbered after Hana.

The *dōshin* – sent into a wild panic by Ronin's slaughter – were running in all directions. Their officer was shouting at the top of his voice, trying to reinstate order. The bridge, already weakened by the raging torrent, creaked and groaned under the added strain of the fighting.

Although Ronin was an experienced warrior, Goro was young, muscular and fresh to the fight. It took all Ronin's focus to battle the boy and he had to leave Hana to fend for herself.

Nobu chortled at the size of his diminutive opponent. His overwhelming bulk towered over Hana, yet still she didn't back down. Swinging her *bokken*, she struck him in the stomach. But it just bounced off.

'Is that all you can manage?' he snorted, raising his own sword to cut her down.

Hana's resolve crumbled and, fearing for her life, she ran. Nobu stomped after her. Jack could only watch as Hana, in her frantic escape, stumbled and fell. She lay there, completely open to attack. Jack cried out to Hana to get up. But it was too late. Nobu had already caught up.

He stepped forward to deliver the killing blow when there was a sharp *crack*.

Nobu dropped like a stone through the bridge's deck. Only his vast waistline, wedged between the broken planks, saved him from falling into the river below.

Hana flipped to her feet and laughed in his face. '*That's Drunken Fist!*'

Her stumble had been a ruse all along. Playing upon her vulnerability, she'd drawn the heavyweight Nobu on to the wooden plank that Toru had cracked earlier. Jack's spirits were lifted by her cunning and he renewed his efforts to defeat Kazuki. But Hana now faced the man-mountain that was Raiden. And he wouldn't be fooled with the same trick.

The *dōshin* officer had finally managed to rally his men and marched them back to slay the fearsome Ronin. Still battling Goro, Ronin was forced to call upon all his drunken fighting skills. Weaving and dodging, he played one *dōshin* off against another. Every time they attacked him, they ended up injuring a fellow *dōshin*. Ronin grabbed one of the wounded as a shield, but Goro could see the samurai was tiring and hung back, waiting for the moment to strike.

Jack was fading fast too. His experience with the Riddling Monk had taken its toll and his left arm, coated in blood, was incapable of lifting his sword much higher than his waist. Taking the decision to discard the *wakizashi* and use his *katana* two-handed, he sheathed the shorter blade into its *saya*.

'Giving up?' gasped Kazuki, breathing heavily from the exertion of their duel.

'Just giving you a chance!' replied Jack, wiping the rain from his face.

Their *katana* clashed again. And still neither relinquished any ground.

Hana had become trapped against the handrail by Raiden. In an effort to save her, Ronin felled the *dōshin* that were in his way and took his eye off Goro, who leapt forward and stabbed him in the side.

'NO!' cried Jack.

Ronin reeled away, bleeding. The *dōshin* surrounded him and closed in for the kill.

Hana squealed, her legs kicking, as Raidon lifted her off the ground by her hair.

Jack was weakening in the face of Kazuki's unrelenting attack and would need a miracle to defeat him and save his friends.

He knew their slaughter was inevitable . . .

53

WASHED AWAY

A rumbling roar brought the whole fight to a stop.

The bridge trembled beneath their feet as the noise grew louder and louder. Glancing up the valley, a terrifying sight rushed towards the battling samurai. A wall of water, twenty feet high, thundered down the river, swallowing everything in its path.

Many of the *dōshin* could only stare in uncomprehending horror at the vast wave. A few broke ranks and ran for their lives. But Jack realized it was too late for that.

Throwing himself at the nearest bridge pillar, he clung on with all the remaining strength he had. A moment later, the Kizu River swelled and the wave struck. Trees and debris collided with the bridge, ripping away large segments of walkway. A *dōshin* beside the rail was hit in the chest and tossed over the side. Water surged past, dragging other screaming helpless bodies along with it.

Jack felt his arms being wrenched from their sockets as the wave clawed at him. He had endured storms, breakers, tempests and typhoons in his time on-board the *Alexandria*, but the force of this flood seemed worse than all of them combined.

The dam had evidently burst and the lake emptied in a single massive rush into the valley, wreaking untold destruction along the way.

The Ring of Water had come to his rescue.

But if he couldn't hold on it would be his death too.

He spluttered for breath as his grip began to slip from round the pillar. His left arm was simply too weak and the tumultuous wave seemed to have no end.

Then, all of a sudden, it passed. The river subsided. Jack gasped in air and desperately looked around for Ronin and Hana. The bridge was decimated. Some sections were missing entirely; other parts of the walkway swayed dangerously on the few remaining pillars. The supporting stilts that had survived stood like a forest of dead trees in the ferocious current of the river.

The wave had washed away all but a few survivors.

And one of them was Kazuki.

Coughing up water, he spotted Jack and immediately struggled to his feet. Staggering across the skewed walkway, he swung his *katana* for Jack's head. Jack rolled out of the way and scrambled along the edge of the twisted remains of the bridge.

As Kazuki pursued him, Jack jumped to the next section.

'You won't escape!' snarled Kazuki, leaping the gap too.

Jack turned on him, *katana* at the ready. 'Nor will you!' he shot back.

Their swords met and the duel continued. As they fought, a supporting pillar snapped loose and toppled into the river, snatched away in an instant by the current. The whole walkway listed to one side and Jack sprang to another smaller section.

Kazuki dived for an adjacent part just as the walkway collapsed and disappeared beneath the waters.

Yet still they battled.

Jack evaded Kazuki's thrust to the stomach and attempted an Autumn Leaf strike to disarm him. But Kazuki, recognizing the technique, immediately countered, rolling his blade out of danger.

'Pathetic!' snorted Kazuki. 'I was *always* better than you at the Two Heavens.'

His blade slashed across Jack's torso and Jack was forced to leap backwards. His tiny section of walkway wobbled precariously under the sudden shift in weight and an ominous splintering was heard.

Kazuki laughed cruelly as the whole structure keeled over.

In desperation, Jack jumped for one of the supporting stilts. He landed on top of the pole, barely enough room for two feet. Cartwheeling his arms, he recovered his balance – Ronin's plum flower pole training yet again a lifesaver.

'Follow me if you dare!' challenged Jack.

Kazuki couldn't reach Jack from where he stood and his determination to kill his enemy outweighed any concerns for his own safety. Grimacing, he leapt for the opposing bridge stilt. He landed well, but the poles were unstable and swayed sickeningly above the waters.

The two of them now battled to stay upright, fighting each other at the same time.

Jumping between stilts, they slashed and reeled, two warriors at the very edge of their abilities. The rain still came down in stinging sheets. The swords still sliced through the air. Jack knew it was only a matter of time before one of them made a fatal error.

As he went to attack Kazuki, he lost his balance and lurched forward. For that one moment, he was completely defenceless.

Seizing the opportunity, Kazuki jumped to a nearer stilt and brought his sword round to cut off Jack's head.

Jack, however, was in total control. Having drawn his rival in with his apparent vulnerability, he struck. Ducking the blade, he retaliated with a lightning cut at Kazuki's legs. Kazuki was forced to leap into the air. But when he tried to land back upon his stilt, he missed and tumbled into the turbulent waters of the Kizu River.

Jack watched him disappear beneath the surface, then pop back up, gasping for air. Snatching out for anything he could, Kazuki seized on to the last of the stilts as he was washed by. The current pulled at him mercilessly and, with his right hand crippled, Jack knew Kazuki couldn't hold on for long.

54

SECRET BLADE

'HELP ME!' cried Kazuki.

Jack stood there, watching his rival flounder in the river. He held no love for Kazuki and made no attempt to rescue him. In a matter of moments, all Jack's problems with the Scorpion Gang would be over. Akiko would be safe from any reprisals.

'*Please!*' begged Kazuki, his face stretched taut with panic. His right hand slipped and he let out a cry.

But he still managed to cling on with his left.

Jack had witnessed many men drown in the treacherous seas of the Atlantic and Pacific Oceans. It was the worst fear a sailor faced. He recalled the poor unfortunate Sam, who'd been knocked overboard during the tempest that had shipwrecked the *Alexandria* upon Japan's shores. Jack could still hear the sailor's pitiful scream as he was dragged beneath the waves. Drowning was by no means an honourable death.

Jack's indifference to his rival's plight wavered. He was finding it hard to simply stand by and let another human being drown before his eyes. Whatever his feelings were towards Kazuki, the samurai code of *bushido* taught rectitude – the ability to make the right moral decision – and benevolence, the principle of being compassionate towards all. For Jack, that meant *even* his enemies. Coming from a Christian family, his father had read the Bible to him every night and those teachings now returned . . .

Do not be overcome by evil, but overcome evil with good.

Was this an opportunity to change Kazuki for the better? A foreigner had unintentionally killed the boy's mother. Could his prejudice now be reversed if a foreigner rescued *his* life?

A difficult choice faced Jack – Kazuki's life was in his hands. He could let his rival drown . . . or save him.

Kazuki's desperate grip upon the stilt was weakening, his fingers slipping off one by one.

Hoping he wouldn't regret his decision, Jack sheathed his sword and leapt across to the remaining section of walkway above Kazuki's head.

'Take my hand!' he said, lying down and reaching for his enemy.

Kazuki stared in disbelief at the gesture.

'You'll drown otherwise.'

The river surged and Kazuki panicked. He clasped on to Jack's wrist.

But Jack didn't pull him up.

'Hurry . . . *gaijin*!' spluttered Kazuki as river water rushed into his mouth.

'Promise you'll leave Akiko alone.'

Kazuki didn't answer.

'Promise!' demanded Jack.

Another wave rolled over Kazuki's head and he choked.

'Yes! Yes! I'll not harm her,' he shouted, nodding furiously.

'And that you'll let me get to Nagasaki.'

'Whatever you want!'

With an almighty heave, Jack pulled Kazuki out of the river. They stood and faced one another, the cold hard rain falling around them. For a moment, Kazuki glared at Jack. Even having lost his *katana*, he appeared to consider continuing the fight.

But then he bowed his head.

'*Arigatō gozaimasu*,' he mumbled by way of thanks.

Jack smiled with relief. It seemed his act of mercy *had* changed Kazuki.

Then Kazuki clenched his right-gloved hand and a gleaming blade sprang out from his kimono sleeve. Taken completely unawares, Jack had no time to react.

The secret blade drove straight for his heart.

55

HANA

Jack was suddenly knocked aside, Kazuki's blade missing him and sinking deep into his saviour's chest. Blood smeared the walkway as Ronin fought bitterly, hand to hand, with Kazuki. They slammed against the rail. It gave way and they tumbled over the side.

Running to the rail, Jack spotted Ronin and Kazuki flailing in the waters. The current had pulled them apart and Ronin was struggling to keep his head above the surface. Ensuring his pack was secure over his shoulder and knowing the *rutter* was safe within its waterproof oilskin, Jack dived into the river after him.

Fighting for breath in the surge and swell, Jack was tossed like a piece of driftwood in an ocean storm. Catching a glimpse of Ronin through the foamy torrent, Jack swam with all his might. But his weak left arm was slowing him down.

As the rapids and white water swirled around, Jack lost all sight of Ronin. He kept swimming, desperate to save his friend. But he knew the badly wounded Ronin might already have drowned. Kicking hard, he made for the position he'd last seen the samurai. A splintered bridge stilt shot by, almost taking Jack's head off. Then he spied Ronin on his back, feebly splashing to stay afloat.

Jack made a last-ditch effort and reached Ronin just as he went back under. Seizing the samurai's arm, Jack pulled him above the surface and began to swim for the bank. But the drag from his pack, swords and an unconscious Ronin meant he made little headway.

The river inextricably drew them downstream, sapping Jack's strength with every stroke. A wave caught him full in the face and he choked on the waters. Too exhausted to keep going, he felt himself slip below the surface. Jack kicked hard and bobbed up briefly. A section of walkway bumped into them and he clung on to it, a life raft of fading hope.

The riverbank rushed by and Jack kicked desperately in its direction. His legs felt like lead and he was on the point of giving up entirely, when they ran aground. With the last of his strength, Jack dragged the dead weight of Ronin clear of the water and collapsed beside him.

The rain pelted the mud around them and Jack sank his fingers into the earth, not wanting to let go for fear of being pulled back into the raging torrent.

Ronin groaned. Jack forced himself to his knees and examined the samurai.

'You're bleeding badly,' said Jack, pressing a hand to the samurai's ribs to stem the flow.

Ronin gasped in pain and moaned, 'Where's . . . Hana?'

Jack shook his head sadly. 'I haven't seen her since the wave struck.'

'Must look.'

Ronin struggled to sit up.

Through the relentless grey rain, the bridge was no more than a few skeletal stilts, a shipwreck of a crossing. Survivors were few and far between.

'I can't see her,' said Jack, realizing it was beyond hope that a non-swimmer would last long in the raging river.

With trembling fingers, Ronin pulled a tattered paper crane from his kimono.

'Hana . . . my little Hana,' he sobbed.

He tossed the tiny bird upon the waters and they watched it float away.

'We'd best go,' urged Jack, putting an arm round Ronin and helping him to his feet. 'We need to hide and take care of your injuries.'

They stumbled along the bank and towards the forest. Just as they reached the undergrowth there was a shout. They both looked round, fearing the worst.

'JACK! RONIN!' cried Hana above the roar of the river.

She stood upon the opposite bank, jumping up and down, waving her arms madly.

A smile of relief burst on to Ronin's sorrowful face. 'Hana! She's safe!'

But, further down, Jack spotted another figure crawling out – Kazuki.

'RUN!' cried Jack, pointing furiously to the danger.

Hana saw Kazuki rise to his feet and she began to back away. Jack and Ronin watched helplessly, the river dividing them.

Kazuki lurched towards Hana, his gloved hand with its secret blade primed to cut her to shreds.

Then he collapsed in an exhausted heap, the battle and the flood having finally taken their toll.

'GO!' shouted Jack and Ronin as one.

Nodding, Hana waved her farewell. She held up the *inro* to Jack, signalling her plan to head for Toba, before disappearing into the treeline.

56

REDEMPTION

Jack helped Ronin lie down upon the straw *futon* in the back room of a small farmhouse. As they'd fled through the forest, Ronin had collapsed several times. Jack had doubted they'd find somewhere to shelter in time to save him, when they came across a farmstead. Despite his initial reluctance, the farmer's compassion had outweighed his fear and he'd ushered them inside.

In the main room where the hearth was, his wife busied herself boiling water to clean Ronin's wounds. Jack spoke quietly to the farmer and he nodded, returning a moment later with an old chipped bottle.

'Here,' said Jack, offering it to Ronin. 'To help numb the pain.'

'What is it?' he mumbled.

'*Saké.*'

Ronin pushed the bottle away. 'No, I don't need it . . . any more.'

'I *won't* let you die, Ronin,' said Jack, alarmed at his words.

Ronin grunted with laughter before grimacing in pain. 'I've suffered far worse in my time. I'll live. But *you* must go.'

276

Jack shook his head adamantly. 'I can't leave you like this.'

'You must. That Kazuki and his gang *will* come after you. You cannot wait for me to heal. Leave now while you have the chance.'

Jack knew Ronin was speaking sense. There would be other bridges, other crossing points, and Kazuki would *never* give up on his hunt for him. Jack had got Ronin to a safe house. There was little more he could do for his friend. Leaving him was possibly the best thing he *could* do. He'd draw their pursuers away, allowing Ronin to recover in peace.

Ronin gripped his hand. 'I just hope . . . one day . . . you can find it in your heart to forgive me.'

'I *don't* blame you,' said Jack. 'I now remember everything that happened to me that day. You were never one of Botan's gang. They drugged you too. And *you* tried to stop them killing me. I take back all I said. You're a samurai of true *bushido*. If I was a *daimyo*, I'd be proud to have you in my service.'

Opening up the folds of his sodden kimono, Jack pulled out the black pearl upon its pin and offered it to Ronin.

'For saving my life,' said Jack.

Ronin looked thoughtfully at the pearl. 'I know how precious this is to you,' he said, and handed it back. 'I appreciate your respect for our agreement, but you've given me something of far greater value.'

Jack stared at him, bemused.

'My honour and dignity.'

He glanced at the bottle of *saké*. 'I've tried to drown my regret for far too long. I've believed myself unworthy to be a samurai, ever since I failed to protect my father from that murderous spy who infiltrated our castle as a monk.'

Ronin groaned as a wave of pain hit him, but he waved off Jack's help.

'I was ashamed that I'd failed in my principal duty. You see . . . I was the one to blame for letting the assassin in . . . I acted too slowly to save my father from his blade . . . The assassin even got away. That's why I harbour such hatred towards *all* monks – one of them might be my father's murderer.'

Ronin looked at Jack, his eyes bloodshot, not from *saké*, but from tearful grief.

'I've lived with this guilt of failure ever since. But now I can hold my head up high. I fulfilled my duty as a samurai in aiding and protecting you. I've made good my mistake. In time, I hope my father's spirit will forgive me too.'

Spotting a straw hat upon the floor, Ronin reached for it. With great care, he placed it upon Jack's head and pulled down the brim to cover his face.

'Now you're a true *ronin*.'

57

RONIN JACK

Leaving the farmhouse far behind, Jack strode through the driving rain. In front of him stretched a waterlogged road, winding through countless paddy fields towards a mountain range hidden behind a curtain of low clouds. He was heading west for the plains of Osaka, where he would meet the coast and follow it round and down towards Nagasaki.

No one else dared brave the storm, but Jack kept the straw hat dipped across his face just as a precaution. To the casual observer, he appeared no more than a wandering masterless samurai. Anyone who looked closer would be in for a shock.

At least Jack was able to avoid towns and main byways for the next few days. With the little money Ronin had left, they'd been able to purchase some rice and provisions from the farmer. But his supplies wouldn't last long and, with the onset of winter, there would be far less food to scavenge. Jack was gravely concerned how he'd survive the long journey ahead.

But, thanks to Ronin and Hana, he *did* have his swords, Akiko's pearl, Tenzen's *shuriken* stars, Sensei Yamada's *omamori* and, most importantly, his father's *rutter*.

The Riddling Monk's first prophecy came into his head

and Jack now saw a pattern in the monk's mystifying words.

What you find is lost . . . He'd found the gang who'd taken his money, but the gambler had lost it all.

What you give is given back . . . He'd given Ronin the pearl, only for his friend to return it.

What you fight is defeated . . . He'd duelled Araki, Botan, *daimyo* Sanada and overcome them all – though Kazuki was one unfinished fight.

What you want is sacrificed . . . What Jack *really* wanted was the companionship of his friends. He missed his loyal brother-in-arms Yamato, wise Yori, the ever-cheerful Saburo, the spirited Miyuki and, most importantly, his best friend, Akiko. But, once again, he found himself alone upon his journey, his friendships sacrificed through no fault of his own – condemned by the Shogun to a life on the run.

Jack stared at the rain falling upon a nearby paddy field. Rings of water rippled outwards from every raindrop and he heard his father's voice in his head from that first day they'd set sail for the Japans . . .

Individually we are one drop. Together we are an ocean.

Jack realized that as long as he was fortunate enough to meet friends like Ronin and Hana along the way, he had a good chance of making it to Nagasaki alive.

Find your heart and you'll find your home, the Riddling Monk had said.

Striding onward, Jack knew *exactly* where his heart was.

Notes on the Sources

The following quotes are referenced within *Young Samurai: The Ring of Water* (with the page numbers in square brackets) and their sources are acknowledged here:

1. [Page 32] 'What lies behind us and what lies before us are small matters compared to what lies within us.' By Oliver Wendell Holmes (American poet and writer, 1809–94).

2. [Page 33] 'Do not walk in front of me; I may not follow. Do not walk behind me; I may not lead.' By Albert Camus (French novelist, 1913–60).

3. [Page 248] 'There are many paths but only one journey.' By Naomi Judd Holmes (American singer, b. 1946).

4. [Page 248] 'The only journey is the one within.' By Rainer Maria Rilke (poet, 1875–1926).

5. [Page 253] 'A journey is best measured in friends rather than miles.' By Tim Cahill (Australian athlete, b. 1979).

6. [Page 262] 'We . . . would rather die on our feet than live on our knees.' By Franklin D. Roosevelt (US President, 1882–1945).

7. [Page 270] 'Do not be overcome by evil, but overcome
    evil with good.' The Bible, Romans 12:21.
8. [Page 280] 'Individually, we are one drop. Together, we
    are an ocean.' By Ryunosuke Satoro (Japanese poet, dates
    of birth/death unknown).

RIDDLE ME THIS . . .

A Young Samurai challenge!

Can you solve the following brainteasers by the Riddling Monk? Or will you go mad trying to think of the answer?

Riddle 1
Which is heavier: a tonne of gold or a tonne of feathers?

Riddle 2
Where's the bottom at the top?

Riddle 3
If a grasshopper halves the distance to a wall on every jump, how many jumps will he need to reach the wall if he starts from ten feet away?

Riddle 4
Jin is standing behind Kuzo, but Kuzo is standing behind Jin. How can that be?

Riddle 5

I have no voice yet I speak to you.
I tell of all things in the world that people do.
I have leaves, but I am not a tree.
I have pages, but I am not a bride.
I have a spine and hinges, but I am not a man or a door.
I have told you all, I cannot tell you more.
What am I?

Riddle 6

No legs have I to dance,
No lungs have I to breathe,
No life have I to live or die
And yet I do all three.
What am I?

Riddle 7

You are in a room with two doors – one leads further into the
dungeon, one leads to freedom. There are two guards in the
room, one at each door. One always tells the truth. One always
lies. What one question can you ask one of the guards that
will help you pick the door to freedom?

Answers can be found on the Young Samurai website
www.youngsamurai.com

THE GAME OF GO

History

Go is one of the oldest board games in the world. It is believed to have originated in China more than 3,000 years ago. Legend says the Chinese Emperor Yao had his counsellor Shu design the game for his unruly son, Danzhu, to teach him discipline, concentration and balance.

Go was introduced to Japan between the fifth and seventh centuries AD and soon gained popularity at the Imperial court. By the thirteenth century, the game had spread to the general population, and in 1612 the Shogun was awarding stipends (a fixed salary) to the four strongest Go players. From this, four great Go schools were founded – Honinbo, Hayashi, Inoue and Yasui.

Over the next 250 years, the intense rivalry between these schools raised the standard of play significantly and a ranking system was established, classifying players into nine *dans* (grades) of which the highest was *Meijin* (master).

The game remains popular to this day with some 50 million Go players in the Far East alone.

Five Go Legends and Facts

1. Go has been compared to playing four Chess games at the same time on the same board!

2. A full set of Go stones (*goishi*) typically contains 181 black stones and 180 white ones, since a 19x19 board has 361 liberty points. As Black goes first, that player gets an extra stone. Traditionally, the stones are made of clamshell (white) and slate (black).

3. Legend says the future of Tibet was once decided over a Go board when the Buddhist ruler refused to go into battle; instead he challenged the aggressor to a game of Go!

4. Go Seigen, who was born in China in 1914 but primarily played in Japan, is considered to be the best player in modern Go – and perhaps of all time.

5. The Atom Bomb Game is a celebrated Go match that was in progress when the first atomic bomb dropped on Hiroshima, Japan, on 6 August 1945. The immense explosion stopped the game, damaged the building and injured some spectators, but amazingly play was resumed after a lunch break! White won by five points.

Learn how to play the game of Go!

For further information on the game and how to play, visit *www.youngsamurai.com* or contact the British Go Association via their website *www.britgo.org*

JAPANESE GLOSSARY

Bushido

Bushido, meaning the 'Way of the Warrior', is a Japanese code of conduct similar to the concept of chivalry. Samurai warriors were meant to adhere to the seven moral principles in their martial arts training and in their day-to-day lives.

Virtue 1: *Gi* – Rectitude
Gi is the ability to make the right decision with moral confidence and to be fair and equal towards all people no matter what colour, race, gender or age.

Virtue 2: *Yu* – Courage
Yu is the ability to handle any situation with valour and confidence.

仁

Virtue 3: *Jin* – Benevolence

Jin is a combination of compassion and generosity. This virtue works together with *Gi* and discourages samurai from using their skills arrogantly or for domination.

礼

Virtue 4: *Rei* – Respect

Rei is a matter of courtesy and proper behaviour towards others. This virtue means to have respect for all.

真

Virtue 5: *Makoto* – Honesty

Makota is about being honest to oneself as much as to others. It means acting in ways that are morally right and always doing things to the best of your ability.

名誉

Virtue 6: *Meiyo* – Honour

Meiyo is sought with a positive attitude in mind, but will only follow with correct behaviour. Success is an honourable goal to strive for.

忠義

Virtue 7: *Chungi* – Loyalty

Chungi is the foundation of all the virtues; without dedication and loyalty to the task at hand and to one another, one cannot hope to achieve the desired outcome.

A Short Guide to Pronouncing Japanese Words

Vowels are pronounced in the following way:
'a' as the 'a' in 'at'
'e' as the 'e' in 'bet'
'i' as the 'i' in 'police'
'o' as the 'o' in 'dot'
'u' as the 'u' in 'put'
'ai' as in 'eye'
'ii' as in 'week'
'ō' as in 'go'
'ū' as in 'blue'

Consonants are pronounced in the same way as English:
'g' is hard as in 'get'
'j' is soft as in 'jelly'
'ch' as in 'church'
'z' as in 'zoo'
'ts' as in 'itself'

Each syllable is pronounced separately:
A-ki-ko
Ya-ma-to
Ma-sa-mo-to
Ka-zu-ki

arigatō gozaimasu	thank you very much
bitasen	copper coin
bō	wooden fighting staff
bōjutsu	the Art of the Bō

bokken	wooden sword
bushido	the Way of the Warrior – the samurai code
Butokuden	Hall of the Virtues of War
Butsuden	Buddha Hall
Chō-no-ma	Hall of Butterflies
daikon	long, large white radish
daimyo	feudal lord
daishō	pair of swords, *wakizashi* and *katana*, that are the traditional weapons of the samurai
dōshin	Edo-period police officers of samurai origin (low rank)
futon	Japanese bed: flat mattress placed directly on *tatami* flooring, and folded away during the day
gaijin	foreigner, outsider (derogatory term)
geta	traditional Japanese sandal with an elevated wooden base
hachimaki	headbands, sometimes reinforced with metal strips
hakama	traditional Japanese trousers
hamon	artistic pattern created on a samurai sword blade during tempering process
hanami	cherry-blossom viewing party
haori	a hip- or thigh-length kimono-like jacket, which adds formality to an outfit
hashi	chopsticks

Hō-oh-no-ma	Hall of the Phoenix
inro	a little case for holding small objects
janken	Japanese name for the hand game of Rock, Paper, Scissors
jutte (or *jitte*)	an iron truncheon or rod with a short pointed hook
kami	spirits within objects in the Shinto faith
kamon	family crest
kanabō	large oak club encased in iron or with studs
kanji	the Chinese characters used in the Japanese writing system
kataginu	a winged, sleeveless jacket of the samurai
katana	long sword
kenjutsu	the Art of the Sword
kesagiri	diagonal cut, or 'Monk's Robe' cut
kiai	a shout; also used in Go to describe a player's fighting spirit in the face of adversity
kimono	traditional Japanese clothing
kissaki	tip of sword
koan	a Buddhist question designed to stimulate intuition
koban	Japanese oval gold coin
komusō	Monk of Emptiness
kōshakushi	traditional oral Japanese storyteller
kuji-in	nine syllable seals – a specialized form of Buddhist and ninja meditation

manjū	Japanese steamed bun made from flour, rice powder and buckwheat with a sweet or savoury filling
metsuke	technique of 'looking at a faraway mountain'
mon	family crest
musha shugyō	warrior pilgrimage
nagare	flow or roll
netsuke	toggle for helping attach *inro* cases to the *obi* belt
ninja	Japanese assassin
ninjutsu	the Art of Stealth
ninniku	the philosophy of the ninja, 'cultivating a pure and compassionate heart'
Niten Ichi Ryū	the 'One School of Two Heavens'
obi	belt
ofuda	a talisman issued by a Shinto shrine, made of paper, wood or metal, inscribed with the name of a *kami* and used for protection in the home
okonomiyaki	grilled or fried savoury pancake
omamori	a Buddhist amulet to grant protection
onryō	vengeful ghost
origami	the art of folding paper
ronin	masterless samurai
sageo	cotton or silk cord attached to the *saya* of a samurai sword
saké	rice wine
sakura	cherry-blossom tree

samurai	Japanese warrior
sasumata	a pole with a U-shaped prong used to trap the neck and limbs to immobilize an opponent
saya	scabbard
Senbazuru	One Thousand Origami Cranes
sencha	green tea
sensei	teacher
sente	term in Go for holding the initiative of the game
Sha	ninja hand sign, interpreted as healing for *ninjutsu* purposes
shakuhachi	Japanese bamboo flute
shinobi	another name for ninja, literally 'stealer in'
shinobi aruki	stealth, or silent, walking
Shinto	the indigenous spirituality of Japan and the Japanese people
Shishi-no-ma	Hall of Lions
Shogun	the military dictator of Japan
shoji	Japanese sliding door
shuriken	metal throwing stars
soba	buckwheat noodles
tabi	traditional Japanese socks
taijutsu	the Art of the Body (hand-to-hand combat)
tanuki	Japanese raccoon dog
tantō	knife
Taryu-Jiai	inter-school martial arts competition

tatami	floor matting
torii	a distinctive Japanese gate made of two uprights and two crossbars denoting the separation between common space and sacred space, found at the entrance to Shinto shrines
ukemi	break falls
uki-ashi	floating feet technique
umeboshi	pickled dried plum
umeshu	plum wine
wagashi	traditional Japanese confectionary often served with tea
wakizashi	side-arm short sword
yamabushi	Lit. 'one who hides in the mountains'; Buddhist hermits who live in the mountains
yukata	summer kimono
Zai	ninja hand sign for sky or elements control
zazen	seated meditation
zori	straw sandals

Japanese names usually consist of a family name (surname) followed by a given name, unlike in the Western world where the given name comes before the surname. In feudal Japan, names reflected a person's social status and spiritual beliefs. Also, when addressing someone, *san* is added to that person's surname (or given names in less formal situations) as a sign of courtesy, in the same way that we use Mr or Mrs in English, and for higher-status people *sama* is used. In Japan, *sensei* is usually added after a person's name if they are a teacher, although in the Young Samurai books a traditional English order has been retained. Boys and girls are usually addressed using *kun* and *chan*, respectively.

ACKNOWLEDGEMENTS

For an author to reach his fifth title in a book series is quite an achievement and I couldn't have done it without the support of all my fans, friends, family and the fantastic team behind me.

Like the Five Rings, the stability of Earth has been provided by my gorgeous wife Sarah, my mum and my dad, Sue and Simon, Steve and Sam (the best bro and sis-in-law I could wish for!) and all my wonderful friends, in particular Karen and Rob Rose, Geoff and Lucy Roy, Matt Bould, Charlie Wallace, Russell and Jackie Holdaway, Nick and Zelia O'Donnell, Laura Colussi et al. . . . thank you for your unwavering belief and patience in me.

The adaptability and strength of the Ring of Water is found in Charlie Viney, my ever dependable agent and firm friend; at Puffin, Shannon Park, an editor whom I admire greatly and am so lucky to work with; Wendy Tse and Helen Gray, my hardworking copy-editors; Tessa Girvan, Franca Bernatavicius and Nicki Kennedy, my overseas agents at ILA; and Trevor at Authors Abroad.

The energy and passion of the Ring of Fire shows both in

the efforts of the fantastic Puffin PR and marketing team (Lisa Hayden, Vanessa Godden, Jayde Lynch, Tania Vian-Smith, Kirsten Grant et al.) and, above all, Francesca Dow, the *daimyo* of Puffin Books), as well as the growing legion of dedicated fans and readers around the world – thank you for continuing to spread the word.

The freedom of the Ring of Wind is seen in the understanding and patient tuition of Sensei David Ansell of the *Shin Ichi Do* dojo (*www.shinichido.org*) and Sensei Peter Brown at the *Shinobi Kai* dojo (*www.shinobi-kai.net*), and also in the constant movement of booksellers, both independent and major, and school librarians who are always working hard to shift copies of the series and promote it to new readers – I truly appreciate your support.

Finally, the creative force of the Ring of Sky that helps me write these books – thank you, but could you make it a little easier next time! I have deadlines to keep, you know!

You can keep in touch with me and the progress of the Young Samurai series on my Facebook page, or via the website at *www.youngsamurai.com*

Arigatō gozaimasu!

CAN'T WAIT FOR THE NEXT JACK FLETCHER BLOCKBUSTER?

YOUNG SAMURAI

THE RING OF FIRE

Here's a **sneak preview** . . .

1

FROZEN

Japan, winter 1614

Jack's limbs were frozen solid. He was so cold he could no longer even shiver. Only sheer willpower kept him putting one foot in front of the other as he battled through the blizzard.

He seriously regretted his decision to take the mountain route. He may have evaded the Shogun's samurai, but he'd barely made it over Funasaka Pass alive. During the night the weather had turned harsh, battering him into submission and forcing him down the mountainside.

The icy gusts cut through his silk kimono straight to the bone like knives. Jack clasped his body for warmth, head down to the wind, his thin straw hat offering poor protection against the stinging snow. Upon his hip rattled the two red-handled samurai swords his best friend, Akiko, had given him. Slung across his back was the pack that contained her black pearl, five *shuriken* stars and, most importantly, his father's *rutter* – the priceless navigational logbook he'd fought tooth and claw to keep safe. Yet, however precious these items were to him, they were now like lead weights round his neck.

Cold, tired and hungry, Jack felt the last of his strength ebbing away.

Glancing up to get his bearings, there was nothing to see. The landscape was shrouded in a thick blanket of white, the sky swallowed up by endless grey clouds. Behind him, his lone track of footprints was already disappearing beneath a new veil of snow.

At least I'm off the mountain, he thought, taking in the vast featureless expanse of the Okayama Plain. *Perhaps I should rest awhile. Let the snow cover my body. No one would find me, not even Kazuki –*

Jack shook himself. He couldn't allow such self-defeating thoughts to overwhelm him. Fighting his exhaustion, he focused on the burning hope in his heart – of returning home to his sister, Jess.

Since leaving his friends – the samurai Ronin and the girl thief Hana – he'd been making good progress with his escape to Nagasaki, the southern port where he hoped to find a ship bound for England. Miraculously he'd passed unscathed through the outskirts of Osaka. He'd then followed the coastal road, avoiding all the samurai checkpoints, to reach the castle town of Himeji. Here Jack made his first mistake. Having run dry of supplies, he risked buying some rice in a market with the last of his coin. But the Shogun's samurai were everywhere – on the lookout for foreigners, in particular a *gaijin* samurai. Although he'd tried to keep his face hidden, Jack was spotted and forced to flee. For the next three days, troops of samurai were hard on his trail. He only managed to lose them when, using his ninja stealth skills, he broke from the coastal road and headed deep into the mountains.

But that decision now looked to be the end of him.

Praying for shelter, Jack stumbled on blindly through the snowstorm. Twice he fell to the ground and got back up again. On the third time, his body simply gave in – the lack of food, sleep and warmth finally taking its toll.

The snow quickly began to settle upon his frozen form.

As the ground consumed him, Jack heard the faint voice of his friend Yori in his head . . . *Seven times down, eight times up!*

The mantra that had been his saving two years before in the *Taryu-Jiai* interschool martial arts contest repeated itself, growing louder and louder.

Seven times down, eight times UP! Seven times down, EIGHT TIMES UP! SEVEN TIMES DOWN, EIGHT TIMES UP!

The lesson of never giving up was burned so deep into his soul that Jack overruled his body's failure. Summoning up a burst of energy, he dragged himself to his feet, snow tumbling from his shoulders. In his determination to rise, he thought he saw the flickering orange flame of an oil lamp in the distance. Staggering towards the light, more lanterns came into view until an entire town materialized out of the storm.

Although Jack avoided civilization whenever he could, desperation now drove him forward. In a final burst, he fell into the shelter of the nearest building, huddling from the bitter wind in the corner of its veranda.

Once he'd recovered slightly, Jack took in his new surroundings.

Lights spilled on to the main street in welcoming arcs and the warm glow of fires beckoned the weary traveller inside the numerous inns and eating establishments lining the road.

The noise of laughter and drunken singing greeted Jack's ears as small groups of samurai, *geisha*, merchants and townsfolk hurried between the wooden slatted premises in search of entertainment and refuge from the storm.

Slumped where he was, Jack realized he was in full view of these people and would soon draw attention to himself. Gathering his wits, he pulled his straw hat further over his face and entered the town, acting like any other samurai.

The smell of cooked rice, soy sauce and steamed fish assaulted his senses. To his right, a *shoji* door was partially open. Three samurai warriors sat round a roaring hearth fire, knocking back *saké* and scooping generous portions of steamed rice into their mouths. Jack couldn't remember the last time he'd eaten a proper meal. For the past week, he'd been forced to forage. But winter was a meagre time. Early on he'd managed to kill a squirrel with his *shuriken*, otherwise in the mountains he'd found nothing, the snow having driven all animals to ground.

As one of the samurai closed the *shoji*, blocking his view, Jack knew food had to be his priority. But with no money to his name, he'd have to beg, barter or steal in order to survive.

All of sudden he collided with something solid, the impact almost bowling him over.

'Watch it!' snarled a burly samurai accompanied by a white-faced *geisha* girl, who began to giggle incessantly.

'*Sumimasen*,' said Jack, apologizing in Japanese and bowing respectfully. The last thing he wanted was trouble.

But he needn't have worried. The samurai was drunk and more intent on reaching the next inn to care any further about Jack.

Up ahead, a *shoji* flew open and three men were ejected from the hostelry. A roar of laughter followed as they landed face-first in the snow.

'And don't come back!' shouted the innkeeper, wiping his hands of them before slamming the door shut.

The three men picked themselves up and despondently dusted themselves down. Dressed in threadbare smocks and trousers, they looked like beggars or impoverished farmers. Whoever they were, it was clear to Jack that this town had no sympathy for vagrants.

While Jack considered the few options he had left, the three men headed towards him. Although they didn't look like fighters, they outnumbered him and, given his weakened condition, posed a threat. As they drew closer, Jack's hand instinctively went to his swords. His fingers could barely grip the handle of his *katana* and Jack wondered if he'd even have the strength to fight them off.

'Go on!' said the apparent leader of the group, a sour-faced man with hollow cheeks and thin weathered lips. He shoved the youngest forward.

Jack stood his ground.

The young man, a nervous individual with a missing front tooth and jug-like ears, asked, 'Are you a … *ronin*?'

Jack simply nodded that he was a masterless samurai and made to walk on. But the young man stepped into his path. Jack tensed in readiness as his challenger summoned up the courage to make his next move.

Taking a deep breath, the young man blurted, 'Do you want a job?'

YOUNG SAMURAI

BLACK-BELT NINJAS & BLOCKBUSTER ACTION

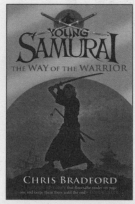

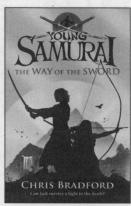

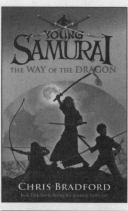

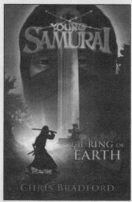

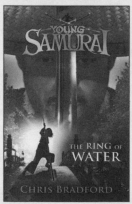

ARE YOU THE NEXT JACK FLETCHER?

THE

YOUNG SAMURAI

CHALLENGE

STEEL YOUR NERVES
FLEX YOUR MUSCLES
GET READY TO SHOW US YOUR
MARTIAL ARTS MOVES . . .

Visit **www.youngsamuari.com** and upload a short film of you in action to **WIN** adrenalin-pumping prizes!

HAVE **YOU** GOT WHAT IT TAKES?

Closing date: 30.6.11. Terms and conditions apply.

And if you don't practise martial arts?
Don't worry, there are prizes for the funniest entries too!